SPECIAL MESSAGE TO READERS

THE ULVERSCROFT FOUNDATION

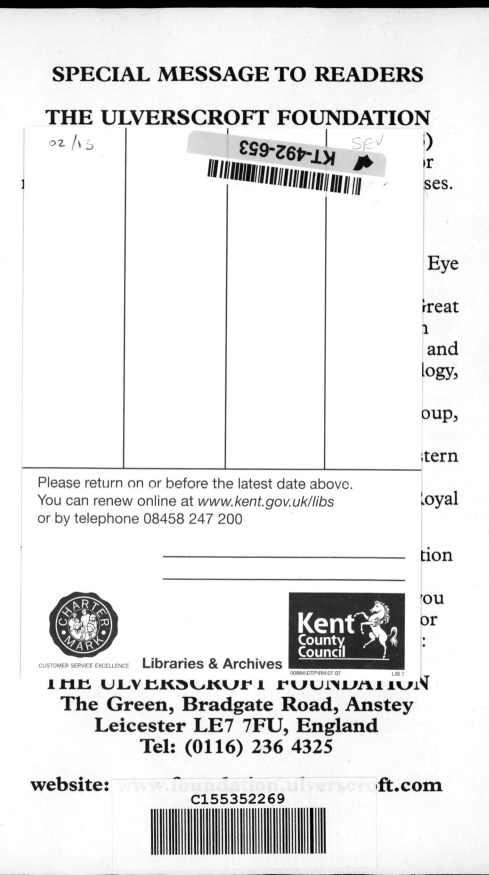

THE ULVERSCROFT FOUNDATION
The Green, Bradgate Road, Anstey
Leicester LE7 7FU, England
Tel: (0116) 236 4325

website: www.foundation.ulverscroft.com

NIGHT CRAWLER

It is Easter 1996, and a young junkie has been murdered. A man is arrested and charged. Marcie Craig, local DJ and good friend of the prime suspect, knows he didn't do it and sets out to find out who did. But this course of action proves to be a tough one, not only on her but also her group of friends. Along the way one is murdered and Marcie herself is beaten up. Then another friend is questioned and Marcie's own life is in danger . . .

DIANE PARKIN

NIGHT CRAWLER

Complete and Unabridged

ULVERSCROFT
Leicester

First published in Great Britain in 2010

First Large Print Edition
published 2013

The moral right of the author has been asserted

This novel is entirely a work of fiction. The names, characters and incidents portrayed are the work of the author's imagination. Any resemblance to actual persons living or dead is entirely coincidental.

British Library CIP Data

Parkin, Diane.
  Night crawler.
  1. Birmingham (England)- -Fiction.
  2. Detective and mystery stories. 3. Large type books.
  I. Title
  823.9'2–dc23

  ISBN 978–1–4448–1429–3

Published by
F. A. Thorpe (Publishing)
Anstey, Leicestershire

Set by Words & Graphics Ltd.
Anstey, Leicestershire
Printed and bound in Great Britain by
T. J. International Ltd., Padstow, Cornwall

This book is printed on acid-free paper

Acknowledgements

The author wishes to acknowledge the invaluable assistance of the following people: Detective Sergeant Russ Cotton, West Midlands Police; Andrea Stephen, Heartlands Hospital Trust; Colin Wall, Birmingham Rock DJ; long suffering members of Solihull Writers' Workshop and Birmingham Writers — specifically David Williams and Mary Hill.

1

APRIL 1996

My name's Marcie Craig. I'm thirty-two years old and the only female rock DJ in Birmingham. I've been on the circuit for around thirteen years. I can be hired for a hundred quid a night, or one-fifty if I use my own gear. I prefer to use house equipment if I can because I ride a Harley Davidson. Not easy with amps and CD players and things. The CDs are mine, I leave them on site and pray the place doesn't get done over. I do get the Jeep out every now and then, when I need to. Generally when I do a private gig.

The Cellar is my regular pitch. It's a poky, sleazy pub at the bottom of a double flight of stone steps. Overhead is one of the biggest small markets in central Birmingham. There's a poorly lit underground car park at the back of the pub — the ideal place to commit a murder . . . Up until then, Easter had been approaching in the same old boring way with not a lot going on. Then came Good Friday and, to borrow a phrase from a great man and massage it slightly, everything went fucking crazy . . .

I always start my show bang on half seven. The punters get a bit panicky if they think you're not turning out. It doesn't matter that you might be ill or on holiday or anything. If I'm not there at half-past seven they start to leave. I like to use the same spiel and play a familiar track, just so they know it's me. Mac, who does Mondays and Thursdays, always starts off with *The Muppets*. Dave, who's here Tuesdays and Sundays, likes *Green Onions*. Me, I prefer a bit of an anthem, some good old fashioned rock and roll.

'Hi there. This is Marcie Craig welcoming you to The Cellar — the hottest little rock spot in Brum. Here's Diamond Head with *Am I Evil?*'

It does get a little loud down here. Scratch that. It gets *very* loud down here, but that's the way they like it. It's also very dark, and they like that too — 'they' being the punters. You walk down the stairs into this disgusting black hole and, if you breathe in too deeply, you get high on the alcohol and drugs fumes. Pendle, the gaffer, doesn't really like drugs on his premises, but he's so pissed half the time he doesn't even notice.

Before the place was all done out recently, you would stick to the carpet. It was so full up with beer and ash, dirt and phlegm. There were other things too but I'd prefer not to

2

mention them. It was filthy. Now you just stick to the dirty tiles instead: heaven. In those days the 'wallpaper' consisted of hundreds of bill posters advertising forthcoming bands. One of Pendle's many protégés had painted a huge mural on the ceiling. Feng Shui she'd called it. Looked like a tart giving a dragon a blow-job to me, but I could have just been looking at it from the wrong angle. Now the walls are painted orange (over anaglypta), and the ceiling is painted matt black. There's the occasional framed disc, or here and there a star photo, placed between the fruit machines.

There's only one room down here. In one of Pendle's more lucid moments he christened it the lounge. It's long and thin with a bar running almost the whole length of the back wall. The brewery have stuck us poor DJs in a tiny cage at one end of the counter. It sounds claustrophobic I know, but the bars give it a sort of airy feel. It keeps the pissheads from falling all over us and damaging the gear, so it isn't so bad. When there's a punch up, or any other sign of trouble, I just duck out the way behind the counter. In the old days we used to end up in the thick of things.

Opposite me, next to the main entrance, there's a step up to this quaint mezzanine with another step down again to the toilets leading off. It's a good job the gallery has those steps, though, as the blokes' loos are always flooding. And it isn't nice. The kitchen is on my left and the fire escape to my right, leading to that delightful little car park I mentioned earlier. That's where I park my bike.

Good Friday had been just like any other Friday, with the usual crowd turning out. I played some Terrorvision, a bit of Motörhead, Lynyrd Skynyrd, Manic Street Preachers, and so on. Woodstock, one of the regulars and a very good mate of mine, had this new friend with him. Woody's gay, something else the gaffer hates. But no-one tells him Woodstock's gay — else he wouldn't still be allowed in — and, again, I doubt he's even noticed.

Woody's a great character. He spends half the time hanging around the ladies loos, the inside, having a good old gossip with the women. He's broken a few hearts too, I can tell you. Everybody likes him, even the Hell's Angels — but I don't think he's broken any of *their* hearts . . . yet.

He's twenty-eight with beautiful smooth olive-coloured skin. Long shiny black hair — in good condition. A hint of a moustache, and big, sad brown eyes. *Sigh*. Such a waste.

4

He always wears an old army combat jacket that hangs from his slim frame, with faded baggy jeans, an old concert tee shirt, and well-worn Doc Martens. I suppose he's about my height, five feet seven inches.

Woodstock was clearly smitten with this new boyfriend of his, and who could blame him? The guy was a good four inches taller, with spiky bleached blond hair and a gold stud in his nose. He was wiry, like Woodstock, but he didn't carry it so well. His clothes were a bit tatty, but that doesn't mean much. Most of the people who come in seem to dress down. He was wearing a black vest that showed off his bulging biceps, and thread-bare jeans. He didn't look very old, but those muscles looked slightly out of proportion to the rest of his body.

I expected Woody to come over for a chat and, despite being as obviously busy as he was, he didn't let me down.

'Hi there Woody. How's things?'

'Oh, you know,' he replied. I didn't, but never mind. 'Will you play a record for Gavin?'

'Is that your new friend?' I tossed my head in the direction he'd just come from.

'Yeah,' he said, turning around and grinning across the room. Gavin flashed a startling smile back.

'Phwoar. He's gorgeous, Woody.'

'Yeah, I know.' He turned back to face me. 'He likes Thin Lizzy.'

I thought that can't be bad — particularly as I like them too. 'Okay. I'll see what I can do.'

'Cheers,' he said, giving me a double thumbs-up and a grin. 'See ya.'

'Sure,' I said as he swaggered off. Does anyone remember the Hoffmeister bear? That's another thing about these people. They strut along, swinging from side to side, just like the bear, or maybe Del Boy out of *Only Fools and Horses*. The women do it too. I've even caught myself doing it once or twice as well. It's very sad.

I looked across at Woody and Gavin in the corner chatting. What a pair of crackers. Nobody would guess from looking at them what they were. Again I found myself thinking what a waste, though obviously they wouldn't agree with me.

I played *The Legend of the Black Rose* by Thin Lizzy for Gavin, it being an old favourite of mine, and followed it with *Emerald*, to which the aforementioned Gavin duly freaked out — a proper little head banger. I do like to make people happy.

After that I don't recall seeing Woody or Gavin for a while, but then the place gets so packed that it's easy enough to lose someone. Many a time I've been asked if I'd seen so-and-so, only to be asked the same question by the person they were looking for about five minutes later.

Eventually the punters get really pissed off at having to wait more than twenty minutes before getting served. It doesn't surprise me when half of them disappear at around half-past nine. Some go to pubs where they know they'll get served, while most go on to Barney's.

Barnaby III used to be a trendy disco-theque, when discos were all the rage that is. Then the Picariello brothers bought the place, Tony and Nico. They discovered that while all the trendies were prepared to queue outside for ages before getting in, they didn't actually spend much money once inside. Now rockers, on the other hand, will pay to get in *and* spend a fortune drinking the place dry once they are in. A much more lucrative situation.

So, the Picariellos kicked all the trendies out and opened up three floors of rock music: heavy metal, traditional rock 'n' roll and grunge — or whatever the latest fashion is. If they weren't loaded before they must be now, but these days they own half the night clubs in the Midlands anyway.

If the punters get to Barney's before ten o'clock, they can get in for half the normal price. Hence the mass exodus from The Cellar at nine-thirtyish. Thank God there are still some people who'd far rather go home at eleven o'clock than head bang until dawn. Otherwise The Cellar would be dead come ten o'clock, and I'd be an hour short on my wages. I do two nights at Barney's myself, Thursdays and Sundays, so maybe I shouldn't really complain. At around twenty-to-eleven I caught sight of Woody and attracted his attention.

'Where's Gavin?' I asked, when he came over.

Woodstock shrugged his shoulders. 'Dunno.'

'What do you mean you don't know?'

'I went to the bar and got us a drink, but by the time they served me, he'd gone.'

'Gone?'

'Yeah. Looks like he's fed up of me already.'

I tried to think what I'd say if this were a boy-girl thing. 'Have you checked the loos?'

'Yeah. Both lots.'

Oh dear, I thought. You see a lot of this sort of thing in my job. I would have carried on with the conversation once I'd changed the record, but just then the place was invaded with Hell's Angels . . . and they weren't ours . . .

2

I shouldn't really call them 'Hell's Angels' because they're not strictly part of *that* particular gang. The bikers we have are more like 'outlaws'. We have three motorcycle clubs here: The Lucifer Beasts (ours); The Cycle Witches (anybody's); and The Death Riders (no-one's).

The Beasts are really cool. They wander about the place looking dead thuggish while at the same time raising loads of money for kiddies' charities. The president, Roach, is my hero and my oldest and best mate. He's a pussycat and I fancy him like mad. If he wasn't such a big kid himself playing big boys' games on motorbikes and in gangs, then we might just, you know . . .

The Cycle Witches are the women's chapter, and they really are anybody's — and don't care who knows it. A bunch of old, well-used bikes riding around on, er, a bunch of old, well-used bikes. 'Stone Age' Sal is their president and we hate each other's guts. She has these mean-looking metal teeth and hair like the two cavemen in the *Wacky Races* — you know, the ones that keep beating each other up with the clubs.

The Death Riders are a violent lot led by Angus, a hot-tempered red-head. They only ever show up to cause trouble and prove how intimidating they can be, usually flying their colours (beautifully embroidered denim jackets with the sleeves cut off, worn over their leathers or tee shirts), and tonight was no exception.

About eleven or twelve of them barged in, forced their way to the bar, and stood like a wall with their backs, and colours, facing everybody.

Roach (my hero) was drinking quietly in a corner, with no colours and no henchmen. The Riders took over. Time, I thought, to duck behind my nice, safe counter, coward that I am. Now, where was that obscure CD I couldn't find?

One young guy must have been prospecting for The Riders as he seemed intent on causing the most trouble. He stormed down the bar and helped himself to someone else's fags. Then he was nicking someone else's matches. From my relatively guarded spot I was able to peer through the bars. The kid looked about seventeen, only just old enough to phutt around on a tiny 125cc, let alone some of the beasts these people usually ride about on.

He was another red-head — it must be some sort of pre-requisite to get into The Riders — but his hair was still the bright orange of adolescence, frizzy and sticking out all over the place. He had tons of massive freckles all over his face, hands and arms. I can't vouch for the rest of him, thankfully. And his cheeks were bright red, as though he'd been running and was out of puff. He was only about five feet four, and no arse to fill his jeans. A beautifully drawn Black Widow spider crawled up his upper arm. The tattoo still looked fresh and must have cost him a fortune, the size of it. It was probably still very painful too.

The next thing the prospect did was 'accidentally' spill one person's beer. Oops. Then he was off swigging ale out of other people's glasses. He did all this while Angus and his chums stood back and watched on with interest.

A prospect is someone who dearly wants to belong to a motorcycle club or chapter. Before he is initiated, however, or whatever it is they do to each other, he (or she) has to prove to the others what a complete bastard he can be, and demonstrate how tough he is.

Until this point it appeared that Roach hadn't seen The Riders, as he had his back to the rest of us. Someone must have pointed them out to him or said something to him, though, as he twisted in his seat. He looked across his shoulder at the alien bikers, but shrugged and turned away again. Did I say he was my hero? Scratch that. He obviously thought they were causing no harm and were better left to it. Besides, he was outnumbered.

Little Mister Prospect continued with his rampage and, on the whole, was left to get on with it. Then he caught sight of me lurking behind my cage.

'And what have we got here then?' he said. 'Not scared of old Ginger are you, girlie?'

Ginger? Now there's an original name. 'No I'm not scared,' I protested, pulling myself up to my far superior height. 'I was getting a CD.'

Now, don't get me wrong. I wasn't in the least bit frightened of this little shit. After all, I have my nice strong *reinforced* cage to protect me. But I didn't really want to look him in the eye in case he thought I was staring at him. Trying not to make eye contact, I looked down at the CD in my hand instead, not really seeing who it was by.

'Do you want me to play you a record or something?' I asked, glancing down at him quickly, then at the clock, and then back at the CD again. 'Only we're almost out of time.' His sharp green eyes also settled on the

CD and the mocking, arrogant expression on his face changed to something much blacker

'You cheeky little bitch . . .'

I checked the name of the band and nearly died. Oh dear, it was The Bangles. Not exactly your every day rock thug's favourite group. For some reason my heart stopped a beat.

Laughing nervously, I tossed the CD over my shoulder. 'Er . . . I didn't mean *this* one . . . you look more like a Therapy? fan, or Sepultura. Name one and it's yours — '

He leaned back and eyed me up and down. 'You'll do.'

What? In his dreams. 'Ha, ha. Good one. Pity this chick's not available.' I put on a Black Sabbath single instead. 'Now, what is it you want?'

'I said you,' he hissed through clenched teeth. 'You deaf or summat?' Ginger wasn't laughing.

I took in the beady eyes, the crazy hair, the massive gaps between chipped and crooked teeth — they looked drug damaged if ever I'd seen it before. He had a body odour problem too. He was only a kid though. I could handle him.

Giving him what I hoped was one of my sexiest smiles, I leaned against the bars of my cage — seductively, of course — and indicated with an index finger that he come closer. He started to dribble and leant his face on his side of the cage, a stupid, inane grin spreading across it. (His face, not the cage.) I missed my vocation. I should have been a lap dancer.

'Listen honey,' I whispered hoarsely, yet loud enough to be heard over the sound system. He was almost panting. 'Why don't you run along home, like a good little boy, and wash that silly tattoo off your arm before Mommy sees it?'

As soon as he realised what I was saying, his face changed again. 'Fucking bitch,' he bellowed. He shoved a freckled fist around the side of the cage and made a grab for my hair, roaring like an animal. He'd make a good Rider. I was too quick for him though and soon bounced out of his reach.

'Come back when you're big enough,' I jibed. This time he leaped up across the counter, his short fat legs stretched out behind him. He reached over and managed to snatch a handful of my hair.

'Ow,' I cried as blood rushed through my veins. He was really hurting me.

'I'll smash your fuckin' head in,' he said, in his best growl.

Where were all of my super heroes now? With adrenaline pumping I had to think fast,

14

especially as the record was ending. I remembered the tattoo and pinched the soft, pink flesh around the drawing between my fingernails, and twisted sharply. As he squealed with the pain I was able to move away from him again. If the cavalry didn't arrive now, I was in deep shit.

Help did arrive just then, but to my surprise it wasn't Roach.

'Are you all right?' asked Angus.

'Yeah, no thanks to you.' I rubbed my head where Ginger had pulled my hair. 'Just get this monkey of yours out of my sight.'

'He ain't one of mine. He just blew it.' Angus turned to Ginger. 'Get outta here, arsehole.' I'd go as far as saying he might have snarled at the boy.

'But Angus . . . ?' whined Ginger.

'You made a mistake picking on the lady. Now get out of this place before you feel the toe of my boot up your arse.'

Wow. 'Lady' eh? Maybe the thug has a soul after all. All the same, he brought his mob in to cause trouble, and that's exactly what they did. Just as the Sabbath record finally finished, Roach put in an appearance.

'What's going on here?' he asked.

'Nothing, now. No thanks to you.' I put another record on quick. 'Angus and his cronies were just leaving.' I glared at the

15

president of the opposition.

Angus glowered back at me for a second. But he gathered Ginger up by the scruff of his neck, who was still simpering nearby, and stalked off. The rest of his gang followed them out, just as the gaffer came in with one of the doormen in tow.

Pendle looked notedly at his watch and then nodded at me, before moving behind the bar and helping himself to a large Jack Daniels.

'It's last orders at the bar, folks,' I announced at the end of the record. Then I played the last two songs for the night: AC/DC's *Back in Black* followed by *Can't Smile Without You* by Barry Manilow. I like to finish on a high note, and if they go out singing then I know the punters have had a good time. Hopefully they'll notice this too and come back for more another night.

★   ★   ★

On a good night it generally takes the guys about an hour to clear up, pack away and have a quick drink — Coke for me of course, as I'm on the bike. I suppose it was well after midnight by the time I left. Like I mentioned, the Harley was in the car park at the back.

The fire door wouldn't budge. I knew it

wasn't locked as Pendle had already had the Fire Service crawling all over him with the pub being underground. There are plenty of this type in Birmingham, something the Irish terrorists found particularly useful during the 1970s. But a locked fire exit contravenes safety regulations and Pendle wouldn't risk his licence — not for something like that anyway.

Vernon, the doorman who'd not long come in with Pendle, gave me a hand.

'What's up?' he asked.

'I don't know. But I can't seem to get this door open.'

'Here, let me have a go.'

It still took the two of us to get the thing free. We pushed and shoved until the door gave. As it opened outwards something fell to the floor. We looked down to see someone lying in a crumpled heap in the dim light.

'Probably stoned,' grumbled Vernon. He crouched down and rolled whoever it was over to reveal a bloody mess for a face.

I clamped a hand across my mouth.

'What is it?' asked Vernon. 'Do you know him or something?'

'Oh my God . . . Yes. I think so. His name's Gavin.'

3

I looked down at the slumped figure of Gavin on the floor. There was blood everywhere. On his face, on the walls, all over Vernon's hands and frilly-fronted white shirt. Now my eyes were becoming accustomed to the poor light, it was getting clear what had gone on out here. In truth, the amount of blood would normally make identification more difficult, but I was pretty certain it was Gavin, despite having only seen him for the first time that evening. I recognised the spiky, bleached blond hair and the black vest.

There was a nasty hole in the side of his head. I shuddered and the adrenaline started soaring. I could feel my nose turning up at the ghastly sight, and felt what could only be bile rising up in my throat. Vernon was busy feeling around for a pulse. Then he gave up, placing his ear to the boy's heart instead.

'Is he all right?' I asked, rather stupidly. Anyone could see he wasn't 'all right' at all. At first I'd been rooted to the spot with shock, but now I didn't know what to do for the best — stay and help, or go and call for an ambulance. Instead, I found myself shuffling around in silly little circles, flexing and unflexing my fingers and shaking my wrists out. Once I realised what I was doing, I tried standing still again.

'He probably is stoned,' said Vernon, still feeling for a heart beat. 'There's a needle over there.' From his viewpoint, hovering over Gavin's chest, he'd seen the needle where it would otherwise have remained hidden. I followed his glance and reached out to pick the hypodermic up.

'Leave it,' he bellowed. I snatched my hand back again. 'You don't know what you might catch from one of those things.'

I caught a fleeting image of Gavin and Woodstock shooting up together, but shook it away again. It didn't bear thinking about. Not Woodstock.

'I'll go and call an ambulance then, shall I?' I said finally, wondering why I hadn't done that in the first place.

Vernon gave up listening for a heartbeat and started massaging Gavin's heart instead. As he did so, he looked up at me still standing there. 'Well go on then.'

'Is he all right?' I repeated. Clearly I was useless in an emergency.

'I don't know, Marcie,' he replied, labouring under the exertion of pounding Gavin's chest. 'I don't think so. It looks as though he's still bleeding, which I think must be good. But I'm not sure. You really ought to go and call for that ambulance.'

What on earth was the matter with me? I heard what he was saying, but couldn't seem to move. You always think you can deal with an emergency, but I'm ashamed to say I must have seemed quite childish.

'You'd better call the police too,' he added.

'Why? Do you think someone tried to kill him?'

'I don't think he gave himself that knock on the head. But if you don't fetch that fucking ambulance soon, there will be no 'tried' about it.'

'Yeah . . . right.' That did it. This time I did move.

I ran back inside the pub to the phone just inside the kitchen. As I dialled nine, nine, nine I could see into the bar and noticed there were still a few 'guests', and they were still drinking.

When the emergency operator finally put me through to the ambulance service, I gave them the barest of details, but agreed with the lady at the other end that there might be suspicious circumstances. She told me the ambulance, and the police, would be there in a few minutes. After I'd finished, the gaffer stumbled past me as he went, once more, behind the bar.

'Whassup Marce?' he slurred. No wonder he was so pissed, he would have been at the hard stuff all night, wherever he'd been tonight that is, before coming back.

'There's been an accident.'

'Oh. Right.' He knocked back what looked like a quadruple Jack Daniels, and poured himself another from the optics. Why he just didn't pour himself a pint of the bourbon I will never know. It was nice to see him so concerned at any rate.

'The police are on their way,' I nudged.

'So what?'

'It's after hours.'

'S'all right. These are my friends.' He flung his arms in a circle, and flung half of his drink all over the place too. No problem, he just helped himself to some more. I almost got the bottle down from the optic for him, to save him time, but I didn't know how to do it. What was that I suggested earlier? Pendle wouldn't risk his licence? Silly me. It depends on how drunk he is, obviously.

The gnawing, sickly feeling in my gut wouldn't go away, but out of courtesy, and because I could see that Pendle obviously wasn't going to warn them, I did mention to his 'friends' that the police were coming. Those who cared drank up and left; those who didn't simply smiled and said 'thanks'.

21

I made my way back to the car park and Vernon, who had now been joined by the other doorman, Tommy, and one of the bar staff. I dreaded what I might find. Tommy was using a clean bar towel to mop up some of the blood from Gavin's face, while Peter, the barman, was pressing another against the hole in the boy's temple in an attempt to stop some of the bleeding. I noticed that none of the other women had come out to watch.

Close up and in his unconscious state Gavin looked to be only about fifteen — a baby. Again I found myself thinking of Woodstock. I wondered if he knew how old Gavin was. Indeed, I wondered if he needed to know. I had no idea how far their relationship had progressed, but I could see that Gavin was well under the age of consent.

Then I remembered that Woody had lost Gavin earlier. Had they had a row? I shuddered at the thought. He hadn't mentioned a row. Even if they had argued, Woody couldn't have done something like this . . . could he? Someone had though. But who? Why?

Vernon stopped the heart massage and looked worn out. He had placed his own jacket over Gavin to keep him warm, and was once more feeling with his fingers for that pulse.

'Yes,' he announced finally, with relief. 'I've found it.'

We all relaxed. 'So he's still alive?' I asked, somewhat unnecessarily.

'Only just. His pulse is very weak. If that ambulance doesn't get here soon . . . ' He left the sentence unfinished and sat back on his heels. The hard, concrete floor must have been killing his knees. Vernon was a stocky bloke, but the drama had taken its toll and he was looking tired and gaunt.

I've always been a bit scared of death. Well, not *death* exactly, but dead people themselves. I'm one of those poor, sad souls who can have nightmares after watching the slightest horror movie, even the comedies and cartoons. I hate graveyards, even in daylight, and I dread walking into any zombies that might be wandering around. At night I make sure my neck is well covered with the quilt so any vampires flying about won't get tempted to take a bite — even in the middle of summer. I never read any horror books if I can help it and I live in fear of some mad axe man coming to kill me. Anything with a face on in my bedroom? Forget it. Okay, okay, I'm afraid of the dark too. But we can't all be perfect.

Now I was glad that I hadn't seen my first ever dead person. Under the circumstances, I

23

think I coped quite well. Then something horrible dawned on me. What if the nutter, whoever had done this terrible thing to Gavin, was still out there? Was he lurking in the shadows in the car park? Lying in wait for his next victim? My bike was out there. How was I going to get home?

'Is that the ambulance?' asked Vernon, still kneeling beside Gavin.

I could hear an engine in the background too. I stepped out into the car park, picking my way around Gavin and the pool of blood that had formed, but hanging onto Tommy's shoulder for safety, to see better. 'No. It looks like a police car.'

Sure enough the Zulu drove into view, blue light flashing but no siren. Two uniformed police officers stepped out, one male and one female. The bloke seemed to lurk in the darkness, making a show of 'examining the scene'.

'It's okay,' I said to the policewoman. 'We don't need you any more. He's alive.'

She stifled a snigger, but said, 'It doesn't quite work like that, love.'

'Where's the bloody ambulance?' asked Vernon.

'Don't worry, sir,' she said. 'It's on its way. We'll take over here now.'

Vernon stood up and allowed the officer to

examine Gavin and his immediate surroundings. Shortly another engine sounded in the blackness and another blue light sliced through the dark. It was the ambulance. At last. Two paramedics in green boiler suits climbed down. Everyone moved out of the way to let them pass.

No sooner had one of them started treating Gavin than he looked up and said in a grave tone, 'I'm sorry. He can't come with us.'

'What do you mean?' I asked. 'Why not? He's not well.'

He gathered together his stuff and made to leave. 'He's not alive, duck. We're not supposed to carry bodies. He's the coroner's property now — '

I clutched the ambulance man by his sleeve. He wasn't going anywhere. I had a queasy feeling I might be needing him. That nice, secure sensation that had accompanied the fact that Gavin was still alive came tumbling down around me.

'He can't be dead. Vernon's been looking after him. There was a pulse. He's bleeding. He can't be dead.'

'I'm really sorry, duck. Your friend obviously did his best. But I'm afraid you were a little too late. He's been dead for quite a while. Any pulse would have been wishful thinking.'

'But the blood . . . ?'

'Common with an injury such as this.' He peered down at me. All I could see was a faceless silhouette in the dark car park. Vernon had been keeping a dead person warm. 'Do you want some fresher air, duck?'

Did I need air? I'd stopped myself from being sick loads of times before. But there's a difference between feeling sick because you've had far too much to drink, and feeling sick at seeing your first ever corpse.

'What about Gavin?'

He looked down at the body. 'You've done all you can here. The police will look after him now. Come on.'

As realisation dawned, all of my good intentions not to throw up went down the gutter, along with half the contents of my stomach. Already the police were on the radio for assistance, and I heard someone complain about contaminated evidence. Was that all Gavin was to them now? Evidence?

The ambulance man dragged me through the pub and up into the clean night air. I suppose there must have been some outside air in that underground car park, but it didn't smell very sweet. I did manage not to puke again, and for that I was grateful. I hate throwing up at the best of times, let alone in public — and this wasn't the first time.

It appeared that the police were now dealing with a murder case. They needed everyone who was still at the pub to go with them to the station. I didn't mind that so much. Steelhouse Lane nick was only around the corner, and I'd be able to come back and collect my bike.

The paramedic, satisfied I wasn't going to be ill any more and that I didn't need treating for shock, went back down the steps with me and rejoined his colleague, who was waiting patiently behind the driver's wheel of the ambulance. Already a bus load of coppers seemed to be at the scene and us 'witnesses' were told that our transport would soon be here.

'Why do we all have to go?' I asked a familiar looking constable as the ambulance pulled away. I think he'd been one of the first to arrive in the Zulu.

'Routine. It looks like we've got a murderer to find. You'll be asked some questions and, hopefully, allowed to go.'

'Hopefully?'

'Like I said. Routine.'

He was wearing a copper's helmet (excuse the expression), but I could see that the dark hair beneath it was quite long for a policeman. He was clean-shaven though, and about ten feet tall . . . well, maybe about six and a half. He had quick, darting brown eyes that looked anywhere but at me. He's embarrassed, I thought.

'Don't I know you?' I asked eventually.

'You should do Marcie. I've been a regular in this pub for about five years.'

'But you're a copper.'

'I know,' he grinned sheepishly, finally looking me in the eye. 'But don't tell anyone, will you?'

While we waited for our transport, which turned out to be two top of the range police wagons, the police started taking names and addresses from those present. There were the two barmaids, Rachel and Norma, Peter the head barman (Basil, the other barman, must have already gone off home), Tommy and Vernon the doormen, and me and Pendle.

They kept on asking if we could remember who had been in that night. In a city centre pub like this one that would normally be quite a difficult question. But rock music has a faithful following so, between the seven of us, we probably covered most of the regulars.

Pendle's guests, or what remained of them, were also questioned. But they can't have been that much help. They didn't know anybody, apart from the gaffer, and didn't arrive until well after eleven o'clock. I doubt that any of us could have remembered any strangers who might have shown up, apart from Gavin of course. Oh, and the Death Riders.

Several people, men and women, in white boiler suits and with plastic bags, brushes and cameras, arrived at the scene. They traipsed around a bit in their little white booties, trying to preserve things and take samples until the two vans arrived. Then us civilians were ushered inside the vehicles and were ferried to the police station.

The seats were hard and the journey much longer than I expected, and very bumpy. By the morning I'd be saddle-sore. I found myself sitting next to the policeman I had recognised, and I racked my brains trying to remember his name.

'It's Reefer, isn't it?'

'Don't crack on you know me,' he hissed.

I gave him an indignant 'sor-ree'.

The rest of the trip passed in relative silence with none of us quite knowing how we'd come to be there. It seemed ages before we arrived.

4

'This isn't Steelhouse Lane Police Station,' I exclaimed as we all finally piled out the back of the wagon. We might have been in the rear yard behind a cop shop, but I still didn't recognise the surrounding scenery. Shit. Where the hell were we?

'Ten out often for observation,' said Reefer dryly.

'So where are we?' We had been off-loaded in the car park, but now we were being led around the front. Well that was something. At least we weren't being man-handled through the back door. It was dark and dank. Inadequate streetlights made some inroads against the night sky, but even they were switching off, one by one. I caught a whiff of old potato skins and noticed we were passing the bins — overdue for a collection by the look (and smell) of them. I stuck close to Reefer.

'Welcome to Acocks Green,' he said at last.

I looked around. He wasn't lying. I could just about make out the Great Western Pub on the corner, silent and dark at this time of night. There were no cars or buses along the

30

usually busy road. Just us fugitives.

'How come?' I asked, trying to take my mind off the horror of everything else so far this evening. When in doubt, make inane conversation.

'Steelhouse Lane's full.'

'So what about Digbeth?' We traipsed along the path in front of the building.

'All of the city stations are full.'

'Full of what?' We climbed up the stone steps and packed into the tiny reception, which smelled of floor polish . . . and something else . . .

'Blacks.'

'What, like black *people*?'

'Yup.' Reefer nodded.

'That's a bit racist isn't it?' What *was* that smell? I felt my nostrils twitch and tried to look around the room without appearing completely disinterested in what he was saying.

'No.' He had a quick word with the desk sergeant, who apparently was expecting us.

'So why are all the city nicks filled with blacks?'

He returned his full attention to me, which felt somewhat comforting. 'You've heard of all this drug warfare between the blacks, haven't you?'

'No.' It meant nothing to me.

'God, Marcie. What planet have you been living on? Don't you read the papers?'

'No.'

'Watch the local news?' he ventured.

'Uh-uh.'

'You *do* live in Birmingham, don't you?'

'Yes. Well no. Oh sort of,' I replied. 'I live on the outskirts.' Actually, I live in the next county, but that's beside the point.

He took a deep breath, ran a hand through his hair, and then put both hands in his pockets. 'There have been these gangs, right?' I nodded. 'Well, they've been shooting each other in this big drugs war that's been going on.'

'What? With guns?'

Reefer coughed a little laugh of disbelief. How to prove what a bimbo you are in one easy lesson. I felt my cheeks flush, but he smiled kindly. 'Actually, with pea shooters,' he grinned. Then he added, 'Yes. With guns.'

Wow! In Birmingham too. I could hardly believe it. I always thought I lived in a nice, pleasant, friendly part of the world — or on the outskirts at least. But in one evening, and one dead body — probably murdered — later, my naïve dreams were shattered. I wanted to go home and, with frustration, I felt my bottom lip start to tremble. I just *couldn't* start blarting now.

'Hey,' said Reefer, his face full of concern. He gave me a quick all-lads-together type of hug, and I felt better. I wanted him to hug me some more, it made me feel safe. But at least I was in control again now.

'Look,' he said finally, seeing I'd pulled myself together. 'I'm going to go and file my report. If you take a seat, someone will be out to have a chat with you shortly.'

He disappeared through a door at the back of the room leaving me feeling quite lonely, and I looked around for a seat. I was a bit stiff after that bumpy ride in the van, and suddenly quite tired. A nice sit down would do me good.

About fifteen of us had been squeezed into this tiny space. I hardly recognised half of them. Who were all of these people? Was one of them really a killer? What was I doing with them in this smelly police station?

Aside from a leaflet shelf, which took up much of the limited wall area and literally dripped literature, there were two rows of four metal chairs, all welded to each other and sunk into the concrete floor — as if anyone would want to nick them. One set was all taken by a single drunk, who hadn't been one of ours, but who was snoring loudly.

Urine. That's what I could smell. This chap, whoever he was, had pissed himself and just been left there to dry. Maybe I didn't need that seat after all.

A secondary-glazed window had been propped open to let in the cold night air. I leaned against the rack of leaflets, helping myself to one that was about to float down onto the pisshead. I turned my collar up against the draught, and read all about how to set up my very own neighbourhood watch scheme.

*　*　*

'Miss Craig,' called a male, Scottish baritone over the din.

'That's me,' I cried back. Over the sea of bodies I could just about see someone beckoning me from an open door on the other side of the room next to the desk. I forced my way through the throng and found myself in an even tinier room.

'Sit down, please.' He indicated one of two plastic grey chairs on one side of a battered, wooden table, and sat down in another on the other side. The quicker I got this over and done with, the quicker I could go home. I tried to tell myself to behave and just answer the policeman's questions. Easier said than done.

'I'm Detective Sergeant MacGregor,' he

said gently. 'I understand it was you who discovered the body?' He flashed his ID at me, although there really was no need. Who else would know their way around this police station and have a key to this door?

'Along with Vernon, the bouncer. Yes.' I flashed a smile at him.

He avoided my eyes and made a note in his little black book. With his head down I noticed the creeping bald spot he was trying to hide beneath wispy, blond hair.

'Tell me, Miss Craig. Did you see the deceased at all in the pub this evening . . . before he died?'

'Yes. I played a record for him.'

'Ah, so you knew him then?'

'No. I've never seen him before tonight.'

'Yet you played a record for him?'

'I'm a DJ. I play records for people.'

'Why? Did he ask you to?'

'No. His friend asked me to.'

'So you know the friend then?'

'Yes. He's a regular.'

'What's his name?'

'Woodstock . . . er . . . Mark. Mark Palmer.'

'But you didn't know the deceased?'

'No. It was Gavin's first visit to the pub.'

'Gavin?'

'Yes. The . . . er . . . deceased.'

35

'Ah.' He made some more notes, then his hazel eyes observed me for a good few minutes. I could hear his brain creaking from the effort. I shuffled nervously in my seat. 'Hmm.'

'Can I go?' I asked, finally.

'No. I'm afraid not.'

'Why? Am I under arrest? Aren't you supposed to read me my rights or something?'

'Have you ever been under arrest, Miss Craig?'

'No.'

'So why should you be under arrest now?'

'I . . . er . . . I don't know.' What the hell was he playing at? If he was trying to intimidate me he was doing a bloody good job.

'Do you have something to hide, Miss Craig?'

'No.'

He watched me again. 'Hmm.'

I'd had enough. 'Look, if you have finished with me, I really do need to go home now. My poor animals will think that I've deserted them. That is, unless I am going to be arrested. I'd really appreciate it if you could hurry up and make up your mind. Then I'd like to call my mom, so I can get her to pop over. I trust I am allowed to make one phone call?'

'No Miss Craig. You are not under arrest yet.'

'Yet? Does that mean that I might be? Am I a suspect? Should I be asking to call a solicitor instead of my mom?'

'Only if you think you need one. Everyone in that room is a suspect, Miss Craig. Anyone who may have used the car park. The fact of the matter is, Miss Craig, that you were the first person to see him dead. You may have also been the last person to see him alive.'

'But he was still alive when we found him,' I'd forgotten what the ambulance man had said about him being dead for a while. 'And Vernon was with me. I couldn't even open the door because Gavin was leaning against the other side.'

'Yes, I'm sure that what you say is quite possible. But look at it from our point of view. The whole sequence of events could easily have been contrived, conveniently arranged to shift all blame.'

'I didn't move from my spot all night.'

'Not even to visit the ladies?'

'No way! Have you seen the loos in that place? Ask any of the others. They'll all tell you what I'm saying is true. The furthest I went was to the kitchen to make a cup of tea — and that's on the other side of the bar to the car park.'

'And if they do confirm your story, then you may go. But until then — '

'Do you really think that I did it?' How could he?

He looked at me again before answering. 'No, Miss Craig, I don't. But it isn't up to me. If you bear with me for a minute, I'll just go and have a wee word with the boss.'

Phew. That was a relief.

There was a second door in this room. I presumed it led through to the offices. MacGregor stood up and left through this door, leaving me alone for a very long minute. I felt like I was there for hours, but according to my watch it was only a few minutes.

I gazed about the spartan room to see if I was being observed by a TV camera or something. I wasn't. This had to be the least decorated room on the planet. Plain glossed walls and a plain vinyl floor. There wasn't even a curtain or a blind up at the window; just opaque glass and more secondary glazing. If I'd had a pen on me I would have probably doodled on the table. 'MacGregor is a dick head', or something to that effect. It was probably just as well that I didn't, I suppose, as I would be in trouble then. If this was the visitors' room, I wondered what the cells must be like.

MacGregor returned and smiled warmly at me. What a transformation. So he was human after all. I was glad I didn't have that pen . . . He didn't sit down.

'Well, Miss Craig. You're in luck. Some of the others have backed up your story.' Oh good. 'And the boss has agreed that once you've given us your witness statement, you may go.' Gee thanks. 'We may want to speak with you again though.'

'Sure. Thanks. Whatever.'

He summoned another officer and they both sat down while I went over everything again and the second officer made notes. What a job. I wondered if they ever got writer's cramp. I told them about the whole evening, from the seven-thirty start, right through to calling for the police. Once the statement was completed, they let me go.

'How am I supposed to get home?' I asked.

'Don't you have any transport?' asked MacGregor.

'No . . . yes. Your officers gave me a lift, remember? My bike is in a police restriction zone.' The Scot raised an eyebrow. 'It's in the car park at the back of the pub.'

'Oh. Right. Whereabouts do you live?'

'Out in the sticks. Near Meriden.'

'No buses?'

I looked at my watch. 'No buses.'

'Right. I'll get one of our officers to run you home.'

'Thanks.' He made to leave the room. 'What about my bike?'

'We can't run that home for you too,' he joked. Then he coughed, remembering his fellow officer. 'Um, as soon as the restriction is lifted, you can collect it.'

'And when will that be?'

'As soon as possible. I'm sorry, but I can't be more specific at this stage.' He changed his mind about leaving me to find my own way and escorted me back into the now virtually empty waiting room. 'If you take a seat, someone will come for you.'

'Thanks.' I sat.

'Goodnight Miss Craig.'

'Yeah. 'Night.'

Well, he didn't seem so bad after all. Quite a nice chap really. When Reefer showed up to take me home, my spirits lifted further. A familiar, friendly face makes all the difference.

'Come on then, Marcie. Let's get you home.'

We retraced our steps out through the front door and walked around the outside to the back. Obviously no back doors at Acocks Green nick after all. He let me in one of those police cars with an orange spot on the roof and three big, black numbers. It smelled new too, though I didn't notice the registration. I gave him my address and he pulled away. Over the constant rattle of the radio, we managed some snippets of conversation.

'So,' I continued. 'Don't they like you to socialise with us folk from the gutter?' I started to fiddle with the sun visor and look around at all the gadgety things.

'Not really. They think a dive like The Cellar is no place for a copper. They reckon that so many shady deals go on that we'd clearly be involved. A bent cop is a bad cop, and there's no room on the force for either.' He thought for a second, then added, 'Allegedly.'

'I didn't see you in tonight.'

'No. I'm on duty.' He glanced down at his uniform and I immediately felt a bit silly.

'Of course.' I adjusted the seat lever so I was in a more upright position. That's what comes of riding a bike, I suppose. I can't understand why people travelling in cars need to lie down. I've even seen some bikers doing it too, though, so maybe it's me.

'Anyway,' he was saying. 'One of you lot would have positively identified me if I had been there on this particular night. Then I'd have been well in the shit first thing Monday morning.'

'What's the matter with them? Aren't you supposed to have any life outside the force?'

'It's not that. They prefer us to mix with our fellow officers.' He pulled a face at the windscreen, and checked the mirrors. He was a good driver. 'It's the drugs and violence that *always* go with places like that.' His sarcastic tone was not wasted on me. 'It's my duty as a police officer to grass on my mates. But I like my job and I like my mates. Best not to tell them about each other, eh?' He glanced across the car and winked at me. Phwoar!

'Don't worry,' I said, pulling myself together. 'Your secret's safe with me.' And I winked back.

'Thanks.' He glanced around outside the car. 'Now, where is it you live?'

I too peered out into the dark to see where we were. 'We're almost there now. It's the next turning.' If any of the neighbours caught me being dropped off in a police car there would be all sorts of gossip by midday. 'Will my bike be okay?'

'It'll have a police escort until they've finished,' he said — sincerely, of course.

'What are they looking for?'

'Clues. Samples. A weapon.'

'Will they let me know when I can collect it?'

'Yes. But let them know if you're going

42

anywhere. They might release it sooner than you think. They don't like to hold things longer than they have to. That's because they are responsible for it, you see, and they don't like that either.'

'I hope they do finish with it soon.' I was missing old Harley already.

Reefer dropped me off outside the park and I resisted a sudden urge to kiss him goodnight. I wanted him to give me another cuddle. It would have been the most natural thing in the world, had it been a habit. I must have been really tired.

He watched me walk safely up the drive. Once at my front door, I waved him off and he drove away into the night.

I did a quick take around the neighbourhood, but all was quiet. Even the curtains at Ivy's caravan were still. Ivy Dennis was the site's champion curtain twitcher, but at four o'clock in the morning, as a quick glance at my watch indicated, even Ivy was in bed. If the rest of the neighbours had any sense, they'd already, or still, be in bed too.

That was where I should be . . .

5

It's at quiet times like these that I really appreciate where I live — I don't get to see this hour of the morning very often. I paused before letting myself in to take it all in.

I live on a caravan site, not actually *in* Meriden, but not far away. It's about fifteen miles out of Birmingham city centre, almost in Coventry. The park used to be a gypsy camp, but is now one of the nicer sites around here. My own caravan — or 'mobile home' as Mother insists on calling it — is a single unit with two double bedrooms, one bathroom, a kitchen-come-dining room and a roomy lounge with dining nook. It's not that big overall, but it suits me. Most of the other homes are double units and very luxurious. But they have mainly families in them. Too big for me. I couldn't afford one when I moved in anyway.

Having escaped what would have been an early marriage at the age of eighteen, I now live alone. The wedding was more for our respective parents' sakes than our own. Pulling out was one of the most selfish things I've ever done. But I don't regret it. We probably would have ended up hating each other's guts and it would have all finished with a divorce. I've never met anyone I'd care to share my life with since.

I have a marine aquarium with seahorses, shrimps and anemones and things, two white mice called Thomas and Jeremy, and a big fat white cat called Sylvester. They're happy and so am I. I like it this way.

Something else I adore, aside from my bike, is my caravan, which is cosy and homely. It's also very tidy, courtesy of my mother. If it was up to me I'd probably live in a tip.

Mom arranged for a woman to come in and 'do' for me. It's a pity she didn't arrange to pay her wages for me too, but I suppose you can't have everything. Jackie lives on the same site and 'does' for me three times a week. Monday, Wednesday and Friday.

There's a small lock-up that goes with the van, which the manager calls and charges as a garage. Blooming cheek. I keep the bike in there. My Jeep stays on a tarmac pad outside my van — partly because it doesn't fit in the 'garage' very well (I wouldn't be able to get out of it for a start, unless I use the boot, which is really useful), but mainly because I value the Harley more.

Gypsies Gate (where I live) consists of a

massive green circled by an asphalt track, and surrounded by the mobile homes. The drive runs right the way round and back out again through the way in. There are about forty units in all (I live in number 12), and each unit has its own bit of garden. Visitors park on the way in, or on the way out, depending on which way they're going at the time. The car park lies in the shadow of an old Dutch barn. I don't think the farmland has been used as such for years, but there are people who don't live at the site who store their touring caravans and boats in the barn when they're not using them.

There are probably about half a dozen of these caravan sites in the area, though mostly they're very crowded and solely for the retired. The owners pack as many caravans in as they can with no room for games or activities. I own my own van outright, though it's possible to rent them. I choose to pay the higher ground rent at Gypsies Gate, if only to enjoy the spaciousness of the park. I'm not claustrophobic, but I guess I'd come close to it at the other sites.

We're not allowed to keep dogs in case the residents exercise them on the green. I like dogs and wouldn't mind following mine around with a shovel and a plastic bag. I suppose, though, that there is always the danger of those who go out to work all day leaving the poor animals to run loose around the park, so maybe the rule has its good side. I make do, instead, with the cat, the mice and the fish.

I breathed in the clean, fresh air and opened the door. One of the mice was using the wheel when I let myself in. If I hadn't have been so tired, the noise would have irritated me. As I moved about the place on auto-pilot, I pulled off my boots and shrugged out of my leather. I'm not a tidy person by nature and my clothes tend to stay where they fall until I need them again, or when someone comes to call. The doorbell will ring and I'll be dashing around shoving junk into cupboards before I let them in. Then I can never find anything when I need it. These are the times that I'm grateful to Jackie, as she puts everything back in the right place on the days that she's here.

By the time I fell into bed the weak spring sun was already showing signs of rising. As soon as my head touched the pillow I was gone. However, no sooner had I surrendered to complete oblivion than the alarm clock started to screech. I didn't even remember setting the damned thing. The clock is a rather naff motorbike that someone gave me for my birthday once. The alarm is set for about half past eight in the morning, which means I'd had about four hours kip. It didn't even seem like five minutes.

I flicked the alarm off, rolled over, and went back to sleep . . .

But the bells kept on ringing in my ears and I couldn't get them to stop.

I hurled the clock across the room and the batteries fell out. Still the ringing didn't shut up. In the end I had to wake up properly, and I discovered that the ringing wasn't the alarm clock after all. I had been certain I hadn't set it. It was the phone.

I padded into the kitchen to pick the phone up.

'Yeah?' At least, that's what I think I grunted into the mouthpiece.

'Marcella?' asked a clipped female voice. I don't really like being called 'Marcella'. It's not very heavy is it?

'Yeah.'

'This is your mother calling.'

Shit. I knew I recognised the voice. I told myself to wake up. 'Yeah.'

'Marcella. Did you forget your sister's wedding or did you just decide not to turn up?'

'Shit.' I'd forgotten.

'I beg your pardon, madam,' continued Mom. 'You're not too big to have your mouth

48

washed out with soap you know, my lady.'

I didn't realise I'd said it out aloud. 'Yes. Sorry. No. I was just on my way.' I checked the kitchen clock. Twenty five to eleven. Double shit. I should have set the alarm clock after all. Penny, my kid sister, was getting married at eleven o'clock.

'You've got ten minutes to get here or the car goes without you.' *Click!*

She hung up on me. There was no way I'd get to the house in ten minutes. I'd have to make my way straight to the church, which was much nearer. Sod the bloody car.

Mom had been planning this wedding for ages — since she'd started mine, actually, and that was fourteen years ago.

I'd always been a bit of a let down to both of my parents — Dad wanted me to go to university — and jilting everybody at the altar on my wedding day didn't help matters. I think my dad was secretly relieved, though — no-one is good enough for his little girl — but I don't think Mom's ever forgiven me for that one, nor forgotten. It probably took her ages to face the neighbours again. Thank God for my little sister, that's all I can say — and thank God she didn't insist on me being her bridesmaid.

'I don't think they do bridesmaid dresses in black,' she'd said, calmly and truthfully.

'Well I ain't wearing one of them frilly, flowery things,' I'd argued.

'It's not frilly or flowery.'

'So what is it then?'

'It's lemon satin.'

'Yuk.'

'Marcie!'

'I don't mind purple . . . or mauve even . . . but lemon?'

'Lilac?'

'No.'

'Well I'm not having a purple bridesmaid.'

I tried to reason with her. 'Look, you don't really want me to be your bridesmaid, do you?'

'I've only got one sister, Marce.'

'Yeah, but what about your friends?'

'What about them? Which ones?'

'Sarah and Kate.' These were Penny's ancient friends from the beginning of time. I don't know any of my mates from school — apart from Roach — but my sister still knows millions. 'Didn't you all promise each other when you were kids that you'd all be each other's bridesmaids?'

'Yes, but — '

'And wouldn't they both look lovely in lemon satin?'

'Well, yes. But — '

'Well then.'

Penny mulled it over, but I noticed that some other bright idea had just occurred to her.

'Go on,' I prompted.

'Okay.' She took a deep breath and I wondered what was coming. 'So you really, really don't want to be my bridesmaid?'

'Not really, no.'

'I'll let you off then.'

'Get on with it.'

'All right then. You can do the disco instead.'

Was that all? 'Yes,' I said, without any hesitation.

'You've got plenty of time to tell Ken Pendle that you can't do The Cellar.' She hadn't seemed to notice yet that I'd agreed with her.

'Or I could swap with someone.'

'But there'll be none of that heavy metal rubbish.'

I was mortally offended. I don't play that much heavy metal, and the rest is nothing like rubbish.

'I do have a shit box too, you know.' This was the term I used to affectionately refer to my 'weddings and other stuff' material. It contains the real shit too, though. Pinky and Perky, Middle of the Road, Matchbox. You know what I mean. Actually, these are some

51

of my favourite records, but don't tell anyone. My street cred will go way down.

'So you'll do it?' The penny (excuse the pun) had dropped.

'Sure. I just said so, didn't I?'

'And you'll not charge?'

''Course not. You're my sister aren't you?'

'Thanks Marce.'

She gave me one of those sloppy, sisterly hugs and had skipped off to tell Sarah and Kate the good news. Lemon satin it was. Sooner them than me.

In the event it looked as though I would have been out of a job for the night anyway, with the murder. Although, I had managed to swap with one of the others, so my wages weren't affected. The pub would be staying closed as long as the car park was.

I had a quick shower and towel dried my hair. I always did prefer the wet look, and both me and Penny have naturally curly dark brown hair. It would be dry by the time we got on to the photographs bit, so that should appease Mother. Of course, I didn't have anything suitable to wear, so we had to go out one of the days and buy me something special — a nice velvet mini dress so I didn't object. I needed a decent going out outfit anyway. Oh yes, *and* it was purple.

Five second makeup is one of my fine arts.

A bit of lippy and some mascara. So I was ready in no time. I caught sight of myself in the full-length mirror in the hall. Not bad, even though I do say so myself. I couldn't have done any better if I'd tried.

Remembering Reefer's advice of the previous evening, I wasted further valuable minutes calling the police station to let them know where I was off to. The wedding was going to take out the whole of the rest of the day, and I really needed them to tell me when I could collect my bike. I locked up, fired up the Jeep and arrived at the church just behind the bride's car.

'You look lovely,' I said to Penny as we both climbed out of our cars. And she did too.

'You look all right yourself,' she grinned through her veil. 'You going to escort me down the aisle after all?'

'Er . . . I'll go on in, shall I? Mom'll be convinced I'm not coming. Good luck, anyway.' I gave both Penny and my dad a quick peck on the cheek each and left them to re-arrange themselves for the pictures. Penny's two friends waited patiently at the main door, looking resplendent in lemon satin in the morning sunshine. It was good of the sun to pop out.

As I waltzed into the church the whole congregation turned, a look of expectation on each of their faces. As they saw me, however, their expressions dropped in disappointment, and most of them turned to face the front once more. I tottered down the aisle on my high heels, waving and grinning at those guests I recognised. Mom, however, gave me a frosty greeting.

'Oh. So you made it then?'

'Looks like it.' I squeezed past her into the front pew. She wasn't moving for any man. The rest of our extended family sat in the pews behind, though I have to confess, I didn't recognise half of them.

'How gracious,' she hissed.

'Penny's outside now with Dad,' I said. I leant forward and waved across at Richard, who looked as nervous as every groom should. He managed a strained grin back.

'She looks beautiful,' I whispered to Mom, who promptly burst into tears, and the Wedding March began.

★   ★   ★

The wedding went as weddings do, totally boringly. Everyone remembered their lines and no-one fainted. As usual, the photographer went on for ages. Rain threatened, but the sun persisted — at least until we were well-covered. By about a quarter to one we were ready to move on to the reception.

The church is in a park called Elmdon, and the do afterwards was at a hotel nearby. Mom and Dad had certainly organised a good show. But, like I say, they'd been practising for years.

At the hotel there were more photographs, but eventually the meal got underway and the speeches got out of the way. At five o'clock, staff at the hotel started moving furniture, which cued me, along with a load of others who didn't live very far away, to take a well-earned break.

Gypsies Gate is virtually just around the corner — well, okay then, it's a bit along the road too — so I nipped home to get changed, feed the animals and collect my gear.

The purple dress was all very nice, and contrasted well with the bridesmaids, surprisingly. But come this evening I needed to look like a DJ and not the bride's big sister.

Tom and Jerry both performed well for their tea. Not a trick I've taught them, by the way, but something they always do. They often go for a good old joint spin in their little wheel. I assume they're expressing their undying gratitude. Before feeding Sly I changed my clothes. He's a lovely cat, but he's got this annoying habit of circling your ankles when you're trying to serve up his food (haven't they all?). I didn't want him snagging my tights or leaving long white hairs all over me.

There was even time for me to grab a quick cup of tea. After the mammoth five-course meal we'd had that afternoon, I was otherwise stuffed. But I do like a nice cup of tea.

My DJ gear is stored in the lockup down by the visitors' car park, so I drove down there to collect it. Most of my rock collection stays at The Cellar, but I leave the weddings and other stuff back at home. When I do Barney's I use their music. With the bike out of the way it was easy to get to my kit. The deck, amps, speakers and leads fit in a storage area behind the back seats in the Jeep, while the CD boxes, which are a lot smaller than the albums and singles boxes of the old days, balance anywhere I can fit them.

As I locked the back door of the Jeep I felt a heavy hand placed on my shoulder and I jumped out of my skin, dropping the keys onto the floor. I turned around to see DS MacGregor and someone else I didn't know.

'Hello Miss Craig,' said the Scot.

'All right.' I bent down to retrieve my keys. 'My bike ready then?'

He avoided the question. 'This is Detective Constable Anderson.' He indicated the younger man who was with him, who flicked open his ID while I unfolded myself again.

'Oh yeah?'

'We wondered if you'd mind accompanying us to the station?'

6

Shit. I was really going to be in for it now from Mother.

'What's going on?' I asked.

'It's about the incident at The Cellar last night,' said Anderson. He was quite a few years younger than MacGregor, without the paunch hanging over his trousers, and with a somewhat thicker thatch of hair — jet black. He was just as tall, and just as mean-looking, with big bushy eyebrows that met in the middle.

'But I gave you my statement last night,' I reminded them.

'Yes, we do know that,' continued Anderson. 'We just need some more information from you. That's all.'

I checked my watch. It was a quarter past six. The evening do wasn't kicking off until half past seven, but I like a good hour to set up. This wasn't looking good.

'You don't understand,' I argued. 'It's my sister's wedding today and I'm supposed to be doing the disco. Besides, if I don't get there soon . . . ' I thought of my mom and left the sentence unfinished.

'It shouldn't take long,' said Anderson.

'But I'm still not a suspect though?'

'No.'

'And I'm not under arrest, or anything?'

'No.'

'So can't it wait?'

The two men sighed and exchanged looks. MacGregor was the first to speak. 'Where is this reception?'

'The Royal Oak Hotel. It's just down the road.'

Anderson checked his watch. 'What time do you need to be there?'

'Half past six. Please, please let me go. I'll come along afterwards.'

MacGregor raised a sandy eyebrow and exchanged another look with his subordinate. 'This is highly irregular,' he said, but thought to himself for a minute or two anyway.

I wished he'd hurry up, but tried the emotional blackmail trick. 'Wouldn't you prefer it if *your* daughter's wedding went ahead as scheduled, without any last minute problems?' And anyway, I'd hate to be in his shoes if Mom ever found out.

'Hmm.'

'At least when you arrest people at the church you let them get married first.' Ha! I'd seen all the films.

'It isn't usual,' said MacGregor finally. He

mused again, but then came to a decision. 'Okay. But DC Anderson will have to go with you — '

'Sarge!' whined Anderson.

MacGregor patted him on the back. 'You'll enjoy yourself — just keep off the pop.'

'Do I have to?'

'No. But it will be taken into account for any future career moves. And besides, I'm telling you to.'

'Sir,' agreed a resigned Anderson. He passed the car keys to MacGregor, who winked at me, then drove himself back to wherever it was he'd come from — or wherever it was he was going to. He'd taken a shine to me and that was going to be very useful.

Me and Anderson made friends, I think. I was grateful he was a detective and in plain clothes, which suited a wedding a bit more than a policeman's uniform. Imagine my mother if I walked in with a copper? Actually, she'd probably be quite proud for a change. Anderson made a good roadie at any rate, and the party kicked off as planned.

Unfortunately Mother couldn't let anything drop, and she just had to have a go at me about being late to the church before — about fourteen years too late — and turning up at the Royal Oak looking like a tramp.

'I couldn't help it, Mom. I was helping the police until the early hours.'

'I don't know how you could do it to me, to your sister, to your father.' She waved her frilly hanky up and down. 'And to think we bought you that lovely dress.'

Lovely dress? She'd hated it when we bought it. Said it looked too tarty — especially for a wedding. I sighed.

'Mom, I wore the dress all day. I'm working now. Okay?'

She wasn't really listening to me but was more concerned with playing the emotional mother bit. I left her to her ramblings but caught my dad's eye and he came over.

My dad's all right really, and being the eldest, I suppose I'm his favourite. When I was supposed to be getting married, he just went along with things. Although he lost quite a bit of money when it was all cancelled, I really do think that he was relieved, after the initial shock wore off. He'd been a great ally ever since. I needed him right now and he came to the rescue.

'You all right, Marcie love?'

Then Mother interrupted with one of her usual retorts. 'I don't know why I bothered to give either of my daughters pretty names.

What's wrong with Marcella? And Penelope? If I wanted them called something short, I would have called them Jane and Ann.'

Dad and me exchanged tired smiles. 'Yeah, Dad, thanks,' I said, in answer to his original question. 'It's going okay isn't it?' He nodded his agreement as he rubbed his hands together and beamed around the room. His hazel eyes settled briefly on DC Anderson, flickered disinterestedly, and met mine again. Great. He was letting me know he didn't approve of this one either. 'Can you get Mom a stiff drink or something?' I whispered. 'She's starting to depress everyone.'

He nodded. 'I think she's had enough already though,' he admitted quietly. 'Come on Doreen, love.' Mom wailed softly, for a change, but allowed herself to be led away to the bar. A double gin should just about do the trick.

Apart from assuming that Anderson must be my latest flame, and approving of the well-dressed young man ('Not like your usual friends, is he?'), she left me alone after that . . . thank God.

* * *

Back at Acocks Green nick, much later that evening, I was once more seated in that

62

marvellous room of the previous night. They hadn't decorated it since then, nor made it more homely with a nice plant or picture. It was still stark.

'Am I going to be arrested?' I asked finally, after Anderson presented me with a tin of pop from a machine somewhere upstairs. MacGregor sat quietly in the corner.

'Hardly,' replied Anderson. 'We would have dragged you in earlier if that was the case.'

'And I'm definitely not a suspect?'

'Is there any reason why you should be?'

'No.'

'Well then. Stop worrying.' He took a swig from his own drink — piping hot coffee — and I tried to get excited about my ice cold Coke. This room was bloody freezing at this time of night. Steam drifted upwards from MacGregor's cup too, and from all of our breath. I must have still looked worried — it was probably the temperature (or lack of it) — because Anderson continued in a kinder tone. 'Look, this is a murder enquiry. We want you to give us some more information. That's all.'

'Like what?'

'Like, who else was there?'

'But I told you all that already last night,' I directed at MacGregor. Talk about belt and braces.

He was right though. All they did want was some more info. He kept asking me, over and over again, to put names to as many people as possible. The other witnesses that had also been questioned the night before would also be asked to be more specific if they could. Then the police would contact everyone named so far, and start the whole rigmarole all over again with them, hoping for a snowball type of effect. Well, that's the impression they gave me anyway.

In the end I had an idea. 'When will the pub be back open for business?' I asked.

'We're not sure yet,' replied Anderson. 'Why?'

'Most of the regulars come in on the same night, or nights, of the week. Apart from a few stalwarts who come in every night and every lunchtime they can, as far as I can tell. We get the same crowd every Friday. Then we get another on Saturdays, and yet another on Wednesdays. Those are the three nights I do,' I explained, and waited for him to speak. He didn't, so I carried on. 'Obviously, if I recognise someone on Wednesday, I'll make a note. But it's impossible to know everyone's names.'

'So what do you suggest?' asked MacGregor, finally.

'If you're no further forward by Friday,

come along to The Cellar and I'll point everyone out to you.'

Anderson and MacGregor looked at each other. They were getting pretty good at that little party piece. Then Anderson replied, all businesslike again. 'In our experience it's unlikely the murderer will return to the scene of the crime.'

I shrugged my shoulders. 'It's the best I can do. It looked like an accident to me, though. The murderer may not even know he's dead.'

I looked from DC Anderson to DS MacGregor, who both looked at each other, *again*. Then MacGregor nodded. 'Okay. It might be worth a go.'

Great. I assumed that meant I could leave. Nobody told me I could, but nobody stopped me either. On my way out I checked the clock. Just gone half past twelve. After a spot of mental arithmetic I reasoned I could still get back into town in time for a couple of hours at Barney's. A bit of a bus man's holiday for me, but I wasn't ready for home yet.

* * *

As I was already in the Birmingham suburb of Acocks Green it didn't take me long to get into town, even in the Jeep. Barney's was humming. Deep Purple's *Speed King* was grooving over the PA system. I satisfied myself with a half pint of cider, sweet and on draught, downed in one, before switching to lemon and lime. It's a real pain not living on a direct bus route.

I don't know why but I was really surprised to see Woodstock mooching about the place. Then I realised that he probably hadn't heard about Gavin yet. He couldn't have popped into The Cellar at lunchtime, or this evening, because it would have still been closed. I decided to go and have a chat with him anyway. The toilet was calling to me but I told myself it could wait.

'Hi Woody. How you doing?'

'Oh, you know.' He shrugged his shoulders.

'Not used to seeing you out on a Saturday.' He wasn't one of the Saturday crowd — well, not in The Cellar in any case.

'Nah.' Talkative, wasn't he?

'Have you been to The Cellar?' I asked, finally, between sips of pop.

'Place was shut, wasn't it?'

'Was it?' Was this a good time to feign ignorance?

'Yeah.'

'Why?'

'Dunno.'

So, he didn't know then. Should I tell him or not? I supposed if it were the other way around I'd like it if he told me something like that. We were old friends, after all. I took a deep breath while he took a swig of his beer.

'You haven't heard the news then?' I asked, tentatively.

'What news?' He wiped a frothy moustache from his own hint of one with the sleeve of his jacket, and turned those big brown eyes to mine.

'It's Gavin,' I said.

Suddenly he was interested. 'What? He came back?' He looked wildly around the dark club as if Gavin were about to spring from the shadows. 'Where is he?'

I felt very sad. He was breaking my heart. I held onto his hand and rubbed the soft skin with my thumb. 'Oh Woody, I'm really sorry.' How the hell was I supposed to break it to him? I moved my arm around his back and placed it gently on his shoulder. 'Gavin never left The Cellar last night.'

'Well where was he then? Where did he go?'

'I found him in the car park. Me and Vernon did.'

'Found him? In the car park? But that's where I left him.'

At that particular moment in time I didn't realise the full implication of his words. Idiot.

I could have warned him.

'He's gone, Woody.' Have you ever felt like a shit? 'Gavin's dead, Woody.'

He looked at me for a second or two before shrugging out of my embrace. He coughed a sort of laugh. Then he was laughing properly in complete disbelief. 'That is a sick joke, Marcie.'

I let my arm fall back down to my side. 'I'm not joking, Woody. I wish I was.'

He stopped laughing just as Ian Gillan started (over the speakers, of course). My bladder was bursting now. Deep Purple turned into UFO and, as I'm not a great fan of theirs, I decided that this was as good a time as any to nip to the loo. If nothing else, it might give Woody time to pull himself together.

'I'm just off for a squirt, Woody. Wait for me.'

He didn't answer. But by the time I came back, he was gone.

7

I don't know why Woodstock disappeared, or where he went. I guessed my bombshell must have been quite a shock for him. He probably went off somewhere to let it all sink in. I was really sorry for him and felt awful for being the one to tell him. Because I was driving I couldn't even get pissed, which is just as well. I was depressed enough and the alcohol would have simply brought on floods of tears. Silly cow. Then I *would* have looked daft.

Nothing much else happened that night immediately after Woody left. Nothing of great consequence anyway. I just mooched around, touring the three floors and chatting to anyone I recognised — as well as a few I didn't. Being a DJ I do know quite a few people, but can't always put a name to many of them. They all think I should remember them, so I pretend that I do. I'm pretty good at putting partners to faces though — then they go and change them so I don't get too cocky.

Barney's isn't a place I generally socialise in. I work here two nights a week and, personally, I prefer The Cellar, even though I do three nights there. There isn't so much of an atmosphere in the club as there is in the pub. The beer isn't so nice either. Some dare to say that the Picariellos water it down, but I don't think I'd make such a suggestion. The brothers are notorious gangsters, even in this day and age, and I value my life too much.

Most of the people who come here are generally stoned — or they come to get stoned. I'm not into drugs myself — honest. Maybe that's why I don't feel at home here.

Also, many of the punters aren't even regulars. They tend to travel in to Birmingham from places like Nottingham, Coventry and Walsall, and probably visit clubs in other surrounding areas too. About four times a year our crowd hire a coach and return the visit. Rock City is always a favourite. There are the regulars who come here at half past nine of course, from The Cellar and other pubs in the city, and those are the ones I get to know.

After I'd been there for about an hour, one such old friend of mine dropped by.

'Hi Daisy,' I said. 'How's tricks?'

She threw back her bleached head (hmm, blonde this evening, then) and laughed like a drain. 'Oh you are funny, Marcie.'

Daisy is about forty-four — no-one is sure

precisely how old she is — and she's been on the game for as long as I've known her, which feels like forever. The thing is, she loves it, or that's the impression she gives, and everyone loves her. The Tart with a Heart is what people call her. Not very original, but perfectly apt. She truly does have a heart of gold. I don't think I've ever heard a wrong word said about her — or by her. She'd give you the coat off her own back if she thought you needed it more than she did, even if you didn't have quite the same penchant for fake leopard skin that she did — or tiger, or snake (yeurgh!). I couldn't tell you the real colour of her hair. She must change it as often as she does her knickers.

Her orange painted talons matched her orange painted lips, which in turn matched her orange painted face (I have no idea how I notice such things). Daisy really does look good for her age I found myself thinking, whatever it may be. She likes to keep herself trim by working out at the city gym — and all of that sex, no doubt.

I like Daisy. She's a nice lady, despite her trade. There's no malice about her and she'll always listen to a good sob story — or even a bad one. David Coverdale was wailing something by Whitesnake over the speakers while I had a chat with her.

'Have you heard the news?' I asked.

'What's that?' She took a swig from her lager.

'Woodstock's latest boyfriend was found dead in The Cellar last night.'

Daisy still managed to light a cigarette, despite my revelation. 'In the lounge?'

'No. Out back, actually, in the car park.'

'What did he die of? An overdose?'

I was taken aback. 'Was he a junkie then?'

'You sound surprised.' She exhaled a cloud of smoke.

I remembered the hypodermic needle Vernon had warned me not to touch. 'I didn't know him that well. Did you?'

Daisy shrugged. 'I'd only met him a couple of times. I don't think Woody's been going out with him that long.'

'Anyway,' I continued, 'Pendle doesn't like them in the place, junkies that is. Nor gays. He won't let them in usually.'

'He can't ban someone just because he *suspects* they're a junkie,' said Daisy. 'He has to be certain . . . doesn't he?' I nodded in agreement, taking a drink from my lemon and lime, and Daisy carried on. 'He probably didn't even notice Gavin anyway, the state he was in . . . '

'Who?'

'Pendle.'

'Why?'

'Well, he was pissed again, wasn't he?'

I frowned and searched my memory. 'I don't remember seeing you.'

'When?'

'Last night.'

'Where?'

'In The Cellar.'

'I wasn't in The Cellar.'

'But you saw him, though?'

'Who?'

'Pendle. Last night?'

Daisy dragged heavily on her fag, and took another swig. 'Er . . . He was pissed though, wasn't he?' She knocked back the rest of her lager and waved at one of the girls behind the bar for another. The girl checked the wall clock but poured her one anyway. The bar at Barney's shuts at two o'clock.

'When is Pendle not pissed?' I said finally, once Daisy was settled again.

'Exactly,' she replied, quickly. Too quickly. 'That's what I meant. It's the state he's in most of the time. So how did he die then?' she changed tack.

'It looked like someone bashed his brains in to me.'

The fag dropped from Daisy's sticky mouth. 'You mean someone *did* it to him?'

I nodded and finished off my glass of pop.

She gazed in the general direction of The Cellar.

'Out there? In the car park?'

'Yep.'

'Ugh! It gives you the creeps, doesn't it?'

'Tell me about it,' I pulled a face.

'And you *saw* him?' she asked in disbelief.

'It was me who found him . . . with Vernon.' I filled her in on the details, adding a bit of flourish here and there to give it more drama. 'And I have to go and collect my bike from there once they lift the police restriction. I'll be parking it upstairs outside the door from now on, like everyone else does.'

'I don't blame you. I don't think I'll be taking any more of my clients out there for a bit either — '

'Daisy! That's a dreadful thing to say.'

'What?'

'You don't . . . you know . . . in the car park . . . do you?'

'Why not? Everyone else does.'

'Like who?'

'Anyone who gets the urge. You wanna go out there half an hour before last orders. There are loads of 'em at it. They shag, smoke dope, shoot up, pee — '

'Ugh!'

'Oh don't be such a prude, Marcie Craig.

It doesn't suit you.' She took another drink from her new lager and I remembered, again, the vision of that hypodermic needle. Was that what Gavin went out there for? 'How's Woody taken it anyway?' she asked.

'Hard to tell.' I shrugged my shoulders and wished I still had a drink. I told her about our earlier conversation. 'He thought he'd been stood up when Gavin disappeared . . . and all the while he was lying out there in a pool of blood.

'He was still alive, you know, when we found him.' I didn't care what the ambulance man had said. 'If we'd only got to him sooner we might have been able to save him. He might still be alive.'

'It's best not to think about it,' said Daisy, patting my arm. 'There's nothing you can do now. The poor sod. And poor Woodstock.'

'Yeah. Poor Woody.'

'I'll see if I can track him down. See if I can comfort him.'

'Daisy,' I looked at my watch. 'It's almost half past two.'

'So?'

'You'll never find him.'

'Don't you worry about that. You're not the only one who knows where he lives at any one time,' she winked and I raised an eyebrow. 'A shoulder to cry on, that's all,' she said. 'You

75

never know. It might make him feel better.'

'I doubt that, Daisy,' I said, just as she was getting ready to leave. Then, from out of nowhere something occurred to me. 'Daisy?'

'Hmm?'

'Were you out there last night? In the car park?' She looked at me quizzically. 'With a punter?'

Her expression changed quickly. 'Sorry, Marcie. I've gotta go. See you around.' She took one last swig from her glass before dashing off.

'Yeah. Bye then.' I watched her disappear into the dark, my unanswered question left hanging in mid air, and I looked longingly at the remains of her drink. Lucky for me I don't really like lager, otherwise I might have finished it off for her. I think lager tastes like sick, without the lumps, and I'd had enough of that the night before. Anyway, the glass had sticky orange marks on it where her mouth had been. That was enough for me to remember I was driving.

Oh well, my last drinking partner was gone for the night, and so was my drink, I could hear my bed calling to me and, looking around, felt relieved that I didn't have to stay and clean up this place. It had been a long day, and Woodstock was the only person I'd seen on that Saturday night who had also been at The Cellar the night before.

'On your way now,' said one of the barmaids as she collected the glasses. She was either new or just didn't do the same nights here I did. 'Haven't you lot got beds to go to?'

'Yeah,' I smiled. 'G'night.'

I found my Jeep, where I'd parked it, and crawled on home to bed.

★ ★ ★

The following Friday The Cellar was back open for business. The police had done everything they needed to and, as far as I could gather, hadn't found the murder weapon. DS MacGregor and DC Anderson showed up as promised. I prayed that PC Reefer might have the good fortune to stay away this evening. When he did turn up, however, luckily for him he was on duty.

As far as I knew, everyone who had been fingered, and the other staff too, were prepared to help the police with their enquiries.

And, so I believe, most were prepared to donate a handful of their hair as a non-intimate sample too, as a process of elimination. The police tell me a single hair can tell them a hell of a lot.

I'd had a spot of good news too myself. Tonight I'd be allowed to collect my bike. It was Reefer, in uniform, who came to give me the go ahead, just before closing time. Apparently I could have collected it on Sunday, only no-one remembered to tell me. They clearly had far more important things on their minds.

There was no way on earth that I was going to go into that car park on my own, so Reefer came with me. I unlocked the heavy chain I keep on my bike, which is sheathed in black rubber tubing, to disguise it against prying police eyes when I wear it across my body.

'You do realise that's an offensive weapon, don't you?' said Reefer.

'It's the only insurance I have against thieves.'

He raised an eyebrow and then frowned. 'I hope not.'

'Well, all right then, yes the bike is insured. But that won't stop anyone nicking it, will it?'

'All the same . . . '

I grinned up at him as I locked the chain around me. 'Are you talking to me now with your policeman's hat on or what?'

He had the decency to blush, straighten his helmet, and grin back. 'Yeah, I suppose I am.

Still, at least I've advised you now.'

I climbed onto my bike and revved up. Amazing. A week in the cold, damp car park and it still fired up first time. What a beauty. Shit, that felt good.

'I'll bear it in mind,' I said finally, squeezing my head into the crash helmet — black, full-faced with my name in gold letters across the front so people know who they're talking to. After a week strapped to my bike in the same car park, the helmet hadn't fared so well. It was damp inside. I'd probably catch a cold now.

'You take care, Marcie,' said Reefer, touchingly.

'Yeah. You too. And thanks for the escort. Will I be seeing you around?'

'Sure.'

I burned off out of the car park and thoroughly enjoyed my ride home. There was still a nip in the air, but there's nothing quite like speeding along the road with a powerful piece of machinery between your legs. Okay, so I wasn't actually speeding. But it was at about this moment that I remembered my Jeep. Shit. It was still in town.

Well, I couldn't leave it there. After six o'clock in the evening all the parking meters in town are free. First thing in the morning, though, my Jeep would be illegally parked. There was nothing else for it. I had to go home, lock up the bike, and get a taxi back into Birmingham. So much for crashing into bed.

By the time I got back home after that little lot it was well after four. I crept into bed and as soon as my head touched down on the pillow, I was gone, blissfully unaware that the police had found their prime suspect.

★ ★ ★

On Saturday morning I was awakened by yet another early morning phone call. What had I forgotten now? This really was becoming quite an irritating little habit.

'Marcie? Is that you?'

'Nmph,' I grunted into the receiver.

'It's me, Woodstock.'

I checked the clock. 'Woody, it's five o'clock in the morning.'

'I know. Sorry. I'm at the police station.'

'Yeah?' So what?

'I'm really sorry, Marcie, but I didn't have anyone else to call.'

'Go on . . . '

'Marcie, they're charging me with Gavin's murder.'

I got to the police station as soon as I

could. But they wouldn't let me anywhere near Woodstock.

DC Anderson said: 'I'm afraid he won't be allowed any visitors until he's appeared before the magistrates.' He had taken me into my usual room.

'And when's that likely to be?' I asked.

'Monday morning.' He said that as though I should know.

'In town?'

'In town.'

'And will I be able to see him then?' I asked, mentally rescheduling my entire day. It wasn't difficult. I generally stay in bed until noon on a Monday — usually alone.

'Only if they grant him bail.'

'And is that likely to happen?'

Anderson pulled a face. 'Probably not.'

'Why not? He's never been in trouble before.'

'It's a very serious offence.' He had the patience of a saint, bothering to explain routine procedure to anyone who cared to ask ... well, me in any case. 'We will strongly recommend that he be kept on remand until the court case.'

'So when will that be?'

'Who knows?' he shrugged. 'It could take months.'

My heart dropped. 'And where will he go until then?'

81

'He'll stay in our cells tonight and tomorrow, but he'll probably go to The Green until the trial.'

I shuddered and started to feel sick — you know that sense of dread that you get? Winson Green isn't one of the nicer places in Birmingham, particularly as it's a prison. I hated the thought of Woodstock alone in that place . . . only he wouldn't be on his own, would he? And that's what really worried me.

I swallowed, and said: 'He didn't do it, you know.'

'Yeah. They all say that.'

'He *didn't*,' I insisted.

Anderson paused.

'You sound pretty certain.'

'I'd like to know on what grounds you're keeping him here.'

'Are you his solicitor now?'

'He doesn't want a solicitor.' He'd told me that much on the phone.

'He needs one.'

'But surely that just supports the fact that he didn't do it?'

'Most of them try that one. But even the innocent should get legal representation.'

'But Woodstock *is* innocent,' I argued.

'You know who killed Gavin?' Anderson was talking about him as if they'd known each other.

'No.'

'Well, we have someone who *knows* it was your friend — '

'Who?' I interrupted. 'It's a lie. Woody didn't do it. How do they *know* it was him?'

'Because they saw him, Miss Craig.'

'Oh, for God's sake, call me Marcie. You are *so* patronising when you say that.' When I saw a flush start to appear above his collar, I apologised to take the edge out of my voice. He was starting to tire of my endless questions, I could tell. 'Who saw him?' I said quickly. 'Who saw him do it?' I knew it was a lie.

'I'm afraid I can't tell you that. Confidentiality.'

'Bollocks.'

'I'll pretend I didn't hear that.' He resumed his aloof manner and clammed up. Damn. 'I'm sorry, but there's nothing more I can tell you at this stage.'

'But — '

'No, Miss Craig — ' I shot him a look. '*Marcie*,' he corrected. No. He definitely wasn't comfortable with it. 'I've already told you more than I should. If you want to see your friend, I suggest you go along to court first thing Monday morning.'

He went to the door and held it open for me. As I walked through I realised that maybe I shouldn't have sworn at him.

'Look. I'm sorry — '

'Good morning, Miss Craig.' He closed the door behind me.

Bastard.

★ ★ ★

Give him his due, everything DC Anderson had told me turned out to be spot on. I went along to the Law Courts and waited a couple of hours while several obviously guilty defendants were given bail by some miserable old bat on the bench. One or two others who were clearly innocent — or at least not as bad as the others — were kept in custody.

Okay, they probably got a few of them right, but I didn't believe for one minute that every decision she made, even following consultation with her two stooges, was the right one. How could she justify fining someone for their fourth offence of drunk driving while banned when another bloke with too many points on his suspended licence was sent down for taking his sick and elderly father to hospital? It just didn't seem right and just to me at all.

These people certainly took their time as well. There were three of them up on that bench, lording it over the rest of us. The foul-tempered-looking, dried up old trout — who was probably only about 55 and possibly quite sweet . . . in another life, and two remarkably grey men. All wore suits and the three of them nodded their heads together as if in a deep discussion, when they couldn't possibly have managed more than a few words to each other.

Every half hour or so, or when a case conveniently ended, the magistrates took a ten minute break. All of us lot in the public gallery at the back had to keep standing up and sitting back down again. This 'audience' changed every time a defendant disappeared back down the steps. These frequent breaks gave me the opportunity to study the room if nothing else. I'd never been in court before and was quite staggered by such opulence and grandeur.

Dark timber panelling lined the walls from floor to ceiling — a very high ceiling, which was ornately carved from a sand-coloured stone. Six lots of six lights illuminated the otherwise dreary interior. We had hard wooden benches to sit on while everyone on the other side of the barrier had nice comfy upholstery. It was quite draughty too — particularly as the door kept on opening and closing. A huge coat of arms looked down on proceedings and a steady flow of defendants.

Woodstock was the last one I bothered hanging around for. He was accompanied by two uniformed officers as he came up the steps. I didn't know either of them. They went to sit on a bench in front of him and kept pulling faces at him to behave himself. Poor Woody. He *was* behaving himself. He appealed to me with those big, sad eyes, but there was nothing I could do for him. At least he didn't look gaunt and unwashed. They must have looked after him at Acocks Green Station. He'd already been advised to keep facing front by one of the monkeys sent in to guard him. I didn't want to get him into any more trouble, so I concentrated my own gaze on a massive wart on the end of the old bat's nose.

As Anderson had predicted, Woodstock was remanded in custody. He had to appear every four weeks before the trial came up. Every four weeks? How long was this trial going to be coming up for?

Before they took him back down the steps, I was at the rail.

'Marcie,' he said, smiling weakly. 'Thanks for coming.'

'Send me a visiting order,' was all I could manage before the two escorting police officers pulled him roughly away.

There was nothing more I could do until the visiting order came.

By the end of that week it had arrived.

On Friday morning I was finally allowed to see Woodstock.

'They're treating you all right?' I asked, trying not to pay too much attention to my surroundings. It was cold and sparse, and they'd sat us at a little table.

'Oh yeah,' he grinned. 'They've given me a phone card and everything.'

'Really?' Honestly, sometimes, little things.

'Really. The prisoners hate us lot who're on remand. We get far more privileges than they do, you see.'

'But doesn't that make them aggressive?'

'They can't touch us. We're quite safe.' Pity I wasn't as convinced as he was.

'So how are you anyway?' I asked.

'I'm fine, actually.' And actually, he looked fine too. 'Three square meals a day. Laundry done for me. And we get recreation time as well.'

'Great,' I said. Palatial, I thought. 'So what have they got on you?' I had to get to the point at some stage, otherwise it would be time for me to leave and I would have got nothing from him.

He shuffled, uncomfortable. 'Someone claims they saw me.'

'But they're lying. They must have something else to go on?'

He fidgeted nervously now on the hard-backed chair. 'Well, actually they have.'

'What?'

'Forensic evidence.'

'Oh yeah?' I didn't believe him . . . them.

'Yeah.'

'What kind of forensic?'

'I'd rather not say.' He fidgeted again. He obviously wasn't going to be very forthcoming, so I tried a different tack.

'Is there something you'd like to tell me?'

'I didn't kill Gavin.'

He didn't need to look me right in the eyes when he said that. I knew he couldn't have killed Gavin.

'I'm not saying you did.'

'So will you help me?'

'What can I do? What do you want me to do?'

Poor Woodstock. Maybe he didn't look so fine after all on closer inspection, now he'd dropped his guard. His hair had lost its sheen, his eyes were hollow, the colour flat, and his lovely olive complexion looked pale and washed out, as though he hadn't seen any sun for a while. He probably wasn't sleeping properly and Gavin's death must have been an awful shock to him. He would still be grieving — given half the chance.

'You have to find Gavin's killer,' he said.

'Why?'

'Because it wasn't me.'

'I'm not a detective.'

'No. But those who are aren't interested.'

'That's not fair. They've worked hard on this case.' I thought of all the lenience they'd shown me, but then I hadn't been banged up.

'Gavin was gay. He was also a junkie and a tramp. No fixed abode, you know? He doesn't have any family mourning him. They don't have the time or the resources to spend on this case. They need a result and I'm it.'

'That's a strong accusation, Woody. And, besides, with no family to pressurise them, they don't have to wind it up so fast. Even if they did, why you?'

'Because they've got someone who said I did it.'

'Surely it's just their word against yours?'

'They can place me at the scene too.'

'How?'

Woodstock looked away. 'Er . . . we'd had sex.'

'In the car park?' He avoided looking at me. 'You and Gavin?' My God. They were all at it. Then something dawned on me. 'Woody, how old was Gavin?'

Woodstock glanced at me, coughed, and

looked away again. 'He was fifteen,' he muttered quickly.

'I think you'd better tell me all about it, don't you?'

I sat back and listened.

9

Woodstock — in his own words

I only ever pretended to be gay, you know, Marce. It was something I started when I was younger, because I'd noticed that girls — attractive girls — always wanted to be The One to change me. It was great. Any young lad's dream. Women threw themselves at me because, obviously, I hadn't found the Right Woman. Someone who would convince me that I was straight and that she was my soul mate.

It just kind of stuck. I had my pick of women and not a single one would breathe a word that she'd slept with me. After all, it was a lot to admit that you'd probably given a bloke the time of his life, fulfilled his greatest fantasies, yet still he preferred men.

I've turned down my fair share too. Stone Age Sal for a start. She is one ugly fucker, and those crazy metal teeth do nothing to help matters. Imagine getting a blow-job off that? Quite frankly, I'd sooner have a wank.

Getting into the ladies' toilets was clever. It was always a good crack. Have you *seen* what some women get up to in the loos once they've had a few? And I mean *outside* the toilet cubicles. It's like having my very own private peep show and it doesn't cost me a penny. I could be standing there, or leaning against a radiator, with this huge, great hard-on and no-one would be any the wiser. Talk about Paradise. And if anyone new ever came in who didn't already know me, one of the other girls would always introduce me: 'Oh, this is Woody. Don't mind him. He's gay.' And the whole cycle would start again with this new bird trying to convince me that she was The One.

It was one of these birds, Julie, who introduced me to Gavin. She knew him through a friend of a friend, and thought he would be my perfect mate. I didn't realise this at the time. Somehow she had decided that it was her mission in life to fix me up with someone — anyone. As I didn't, or couldn't, fancy her, and as she had failed to convince me I was straight, then the least she could do was find me another, ideal partner.

I didn't know she was hoping to set me up with Gavin until it actually happened. I think she must have mentioned his name in passing: Oh-I-know-someone-else-who's-gay. But she dragged me along to the Pink Flamingo — that's a gay club at the back of

Hurst Street. It's been there for years. I'd been to the Flamingo before. Sometimes I'll go along for a quiet drink, if I feel the need to reinforce my cover. Sometimes I'll go if I'm having trouble shaking off a particularly clingy bird. But this was the first time I'd ever been with someone else.

It turned out that this Julie was a closet lesbian after all, just waiting for Mister Perfect Bloke to come along and prove that he's The One and that she's straight. She'd been denying her true sexuality all along.

Julie introduced me to Gavin and then left us to it. I was a bit embarrassed at first. She had made it so obvious that she was matchmaking. And, of course, I wasn't really interested. In fact, if he'd made a pass at me that night I probably would've punched his lights out. But he turned out to be quite interesting and we arranged to meet up again, just for a drink.

This was only about a month or six weeks ago. But I found out more about Gavin in those few short weeks than I've ever learned about anyone else in my whole life.

He was only fifteen, going on forty-five. He'd had a terrible life. He was physically abused by his dad and then sexually abused by his alcoholic mom after his dad ran off with a friend of Gavin's sister. His mom

93

made him have sex with his sister too. I didn't know them but I found myself getting fucking mad at these two cunts for what they'd done to their kids, and to Gavin in particular.

His sister's in a mental hospital now. Gavin was put into care when his mom died of liver cirrhosis. He was even abused at the care home too, though.

Gavin was too fucking good looking for his own good and had the body of a twenty year old man. No wonder they couldn't keep their filthy hands off him.

He got away from the care home in the end and was living in a bedsit in Moseley — not far from my current place in Kings Heath as it happened — making his way as a rent boy and by collecting glasses and emptying ashtrays at the Pink Flamingo.

We were getting on really great and I was horrified to find that I was actually becoming attracted to him. I became angry with all of the people who had spoiled him, damaged him. I was jealous of other guys, old boyfriends, clients of his. And I started to act jealous too.

He'd already sussed me out as far as the gay cover story went. They say that homosexuals can generally tell who's straight and who isn't. But he also suspected that I was developing some sort of crush on him, and that I was fighting my own feelings. He was really quite, I dunno, nice about it all I suppose, very understanding. As though he'd seen it happen before.

And that huge, great stonker I was getting with the birds in the ladies' loos, I was now getting with Gavin. He was beautiful. He was exciting. He was sexy. And he was young. It was all quite . . . scary.

In the end I admitted it, told him how I was feeling, about the confusion, how scared I was. And it turned out he fancied me too. He had this fantasy about being The One, about convincing me I wasn't straight. It was like payback time, I suppose.

Then, on that night we came into The Cellar — as 'partners' for the first time — he said that if I truly cared for him then it was time to choose. Decision time. Was I gay? Straight? Or was I bi? And to prove it, to prove that he was The One, I had to go with him to the car park.

I was so nervous. Excited too. And the whole situation got me going again. I was really turned on by it all. I needed a few drinks, though — a bit of courage. But the time had come for me to come clean. I'd been ranting on that I was gay for half my life. It was easy to slip in to character. Gavin convinced me to at least give it a go, to find out if it was true.

So, after we pretty much made sure that everyone knew we were an item, and once I'd downed a few pints, we went outside — well, underground — to the car park. That's where I usually ended up with most of the women, which is why Ken Pendle never barred me from his pub for being gay. He'd always known it was a lie.

Me and Gavin, we had a bit of a snog — something I'd already tried with him once or twice — and then he started to arrange himself across the bonnet of someone's car, on his back. The way a bird would. That was the shocker. I didn't know you could do it that way . . . well, not with a bloke at any rate. He'd already kicked off his jeans.

That put me off a bit. For as long as I thought we would do it doggie-style I could have got away with it. I could have at least imagined he was a bird if I didn't like it. But this way? This way I had to look at his face and know it was him, know it was a bloke.

I couldn't back out, though. I've called one or two women a few choice names for changing their minds at the last minute. I know how frustrating and painful that can be. I had to see it through. I started to fumble in my pocket for a three-pack, but Gavin stopped me.

He said: 'If you use one of them it'll be just like doing it with a punter.' He always used protection with his clients and was adamant about using his own needles too. 'With you it should be different.'

I wanted to get it all over and done with so I didn't argue. I knew he would be clean. And I was still so turned on. It was distasteful but erotic. It wasn't right, for me, but it was dangerous. What if someone saw us? That just made it all the more exciting. And I did find him incredibly attractive — and I'd had a good few to drink. So I just got it out of the way. He didn't look particularly interested anyway and I squeezed my eyes shut to avoid seeing his face, closed my ears to his foul-mouthed chatter. After him insisting it should be different with me, I still felt just like a client. I hated it.

By the time it was over I already knew that I never, ever wanted to do anything like that again. It was time to stop telling lies. It had sobered me up and I needed another drink. I said I'd get us a pint each and meet him by the bar. He wanted to sort himself out and shoot himself up I think.

When he didn't show up I felt relieved at first, but then I felt cheated and used. I'd just had unprotected sex with a male prostitute and a minor at that, and all of the implications that went with it soon dawned on me.

After The Cellar I moved on to Barney's and got slaughtered. I didn't go home all night. I was disgusted with myself. I started drinking again as soon as the pubs opened, but by the time I saw you at Barney's the next night I'd drunk myself sober once more.

I never did see Gavin again. Yes, I thought he'd made fun of me. Thought he'd used me or taught me a lesson or something. But I still fancied him. That's the part that sticks in my throat. I loathe myself but I was still attracted to him. It suited me that he was dead. I wouldn't have had to face up to any of this then. But I never did hurt him.

It's because I denied ever being there with him in the first place that I'm in this mess now. Because someone did see us there. And the police found the evidence that I'd shagged him, so I couldn't deny that any more. I'll have to have the test I suppose, but I know he was clean.

I only ever pretended to be gay, you know.

10

As if to make sure I'd heard him properly, Woodstock said it again. 'I only ever pretended to be gay.'

'Yes, Woody. I think I'm with you on that one now,' I said, for want of something — anything — more sensible to say. I was shocked and stunned. You think you really know someone when in fact you don't know them at all. There were only two things on my mind now. All of those wasted opportunities when Woody had stayed over at my place, and the things that go on in that car park.

'In the car park?' I asked, at last. I wouldn't have been bothered about being The One. 'You and Gavin?' I would have been perfectly happy with the occasional shag. 'So that was the forensic?' Spiteful bastard.

He nodded. 'I think it must be. The police hinted as much. We went out there at about nine-fifteen. Afterwards, I waited and waited. But he never showed up.'

Served him right, I was thinking. The lying toe rag. 'You thought he'd got what he wanted and then walked out on you?' Woody nodded again. 'And because of this 'evidence' you're immediately guilty?'

'Not just the evidence, no. I'm also gay — '

'You just said that you weren't. Several times in fact.' My voice was giving away the fact that I was mad at him for deceiving me.

'As far as *they* are concerned I'm gay. Bisexual doesn't count. Because I smoke dope — that automatically makes me a junkie — because I, too, don't have any family to speak of. Because I lied. Because he was a minor. Because we were seen. And I resisted arrest too, blacked a copper's eye in the process.

'Oh yes, they can certainly build up a good case against me.'

'Phew. So what's their motive then? I presume they've worked that out too?'

'A lover's tiff, I think.'

'Oh, so they do consider it accidental then?' I added dryly. 'And do they have a weapon?' I'd got the impression that they didn't.

Woodstock shrugged his shoulders. 'Dunno.'

Our escorting officer cleared his throat noisily and looked pointedly at the clock. I gave him what I hoped was one of my most dazzling smiles, and continued. It still didn't add up to me. I'd met the officers in charge of the case. They seemed pretty regular guys.

I didn't believe that they'd go for a story like this one — apart from the positive identification that someone had made. They must have had something else.

'Woody, did you tell the police that you'd, er, done it with Gavin? Once they made it clear that they knew, that is? Did you admit to it?'

'No way. He was only fifteen.'

'So?'

'He was under age.'

'But you still agreed to an intimate sample?' They had to have taken some of his blood, or a swab, or something.

'I didn't. They took a non-intimate sample instead. One of them arseholes pulled my hair.' He rubbed at his head as if feeling the sting all over again.

'And you still didn't tell them?'

'I didn't think they'd trace a puddle of spunk to a hair taken from my head,' he spat.

'Per-lease! Spare me the detail.' I cringed at the thought.

'Woodstock, you are up for a murder charge. Having sexual intercourse with an under-age male is not high on the police priority list right now. They need to find a *murderer*. And the longer you refuse to admit — to them — that you had sex with the guy, when they can prove,' I made little quote

101

signs with my fingers, 'beyond shadow of a doubt that you did, the more guilty you are going to seem.

'That, plus the ID, is probably why they charged you. They must think you have something to hide.'

Woodstock's pleading brown eyes gazed at me from hollow, shadowed sockets. 'If I tell them, do you think they'll let me out of here?'

'They probably already know. I don't know. You should have got yourself a solicitor.'

'But I'm innocent.'

'Even the innocent need solicitors, Woody.'

'Yeah, well. They made me see one of theirs didn't they? A duty solicitor or someone. Fat lot of good he did me.'

'Time up,' barked the prison officer.

I got up to leave, hesitated, and gave Woody a quick peck on the cheek. He'd lied to me — albeit quite harmlessly — and he'd led a lot of us up the garden path. He'd treated a lot of women abysmally. But some lads do that. He was still my mate, though. And he still needed to know I was there for him. I could tell him what I thought of him when he got out. And no doubt he'd learned his lesson. I just hoped he'd get the chance to prove it.

'Chin up, mate,' I said, grinning. 'They

can't keep you locked up for something you didn't do.'

He stood up too, but was firmly pressed back down into his seat by the prison officer. 'So you *will* help me?'

'I don't know what I can do.'

'You can do a damn sight more than I can stuck in this hole.'

'You'll have to help yourself too.'

'So will you help me?'

I let him wait a beat. 'I'll see.'

He let out a huge sigh of relief. 'Thanks Marce.'

I patted his arm before I was led away. I presume he was led the other way once I was safely through the door.

* * *

Back at the station I had another word with Anderson.

'What if he admits he had sex with the guy?' I asked.

'It probably won't help him now. We already know he did, and him denying it until he's already locked up only substantiates his guilt — in the eyes of the law.'

'How can you *know* he did?'

'We have the proof.'

'What kind of proof?'

'The ID for a start.'

'Oh, right. So your 'witness' watched them shagging, yeah? That's not proof and you know it.'

'Yes, well . . . we have the evidence too,' he continued.

'What kind of evidence?' I wasn't letting on how much I already knew.'

'Forensic — '

'Forensic? Already? I always thought that took *weeks*.' I never miss an episode of The Bill, thanks to my video recorder.

Anderson fidgeted. 'Yes, well . . . once he knew we had samples, he more or less admitted it.'

'He *admitted* to murdering Gavin?'

'No. He admitted that they were out there together, after first denying it.'

'Right. So you don't actually have any proof yet, and you don't have any confession? When he gets out of that place he is going to hang you out to dry.'

Anderson shifted position, a little annoyed, but then squared his body towards me. That's common throughout the animal kingdom. When you feel intimidated, make yourself look bigger and you'll be fine. 'We've got our man, Miss Craig.'

'And there's no way I can get him out of that place?'

'If you believe he's innocent — and we don't — you have to give us the real killer on a plate. Preferably with concrete proof *and* a confession. But I would have to advise you not to put yourself in any danger. You'd be wasting your time anyway.'

That made up my mind.

'But, Miss Craig,' he added, as though reading said mind, 'don't get doing anything silly. We've got our killer. Case closed.'

Arsehole.

11

Life wasn't such a gas any more. In fact, it was quite unpleasant. I needed to talk to Reefer. Until recently I only knew him vaguely, and had only just found out he was a copper. I didn't know his real name and hadn't made a note of his collar number. I didn't even know if he'd help, but as far as allies go, he was my best hope.

I had two choices. I could loiter around this place for a couple of hours, or I could wait until he showed up again at The Cellar. Though I doubted either would be fruitful, I decided on the latter. He'd already told me all the city nicks were full and when they brought us all to Acocks Green he could have been called out from any one of them.

Besides, if any of his colleagues caught us talking, his cover could be blown. Woodstock wasn't going anywhere for a while. I'd have to wait for Reefer to come to the pub.

* * *

'Hi there. This is Marcie Craig welcoming you to The Cellar — the hottest little rock spot in Brum . . . ' I played Diamond Head as usual, keeping my eyes peeled for PC Reefer. I caught sight of Roach instead and beckoned for him to come over. He probably thought his luck was in.

'Hi Marce. How's things?' He was shouting over the volume of the music so I turned it down a bit.

'Not good,' I replied.

'No?'

'I went to see Woodstock this morning.'

'Is he ill?'

'No. He's in prison.'

'Prison? Woodstock? What for?'

'God, Roach. Where have you been?' Come to think of it, I hadn't seen him since Good Friday.

'I've been working.' Roach is a long-distance lorry driver. 'So what did Woodstock ever do wrong? Was he jay walking?' He chuckled.

'You remember that kid me and Vernon found?' He looked vague. 'The night Angus and his chums invaded us?'

'Oh yes. I read about that in the paper too. You mean the stiff.'

'Roach!'

'Sorry. Go on.' He took a mouthful of lager.

'They've charged Woody with his murder.'

I waited politely for Roach to finish choking. If it wasn't for the cage, I could have patted him on his back. I needed to change records anyway, and plumped for Black Sabbath's *Paranoid*. Well, it was the way I was feeling.

'The shirt-lifter's?' he said finally, once he'd recovered. He wiped the lager from his chin with his sleeve.

'That 'shirt-lifter' happened to be a friend of Woodstock's.'

'But Woody couldn't have killed him.'

'I know. But unfortunately the police don't have our faith in him.'

'No. I mean he *couldn't* have done it.'

Sometimes I can be so dim even *I* get embarrassed. Suddenly, I clicked.

'Why couldn't he have done it?'

Roach started to look a bit shifty and uncomfortable. 'Because he was still alive after Woodstock came back into the bar.'

'You *saw* them go out to the car park?' He nodded and emptied his glass. 'Did you know what they were doing out there?'

He shrugged his shoulders and looked restlessly towards the bar. 'Same as anybody else, I suppose.'

'And you saw Woody come back?'

'He went to the bar.' He was rummaging in a pocket now for some change.

'So how do you know Gavin was still alive?'

'I went out there for a piss. Look, do you want a drink?'

'No thanks.'

'See ya later then.'

'Yeah, sure.'

Well, that was the best news yet. Roach saw Gavin *after* Woody claimed he'd left him. If I could get Roach to tell Anderson, then Woodstock would be off the hook.

I played *Life's a Gas* by T-Rex to celebrate, and went off in search of Roach.

I couldn't find him.

★   ★   ★

The next day was Saturday. By the end of the evening, with no further sign of Roach, I was ready to write off the whole weekend as a lost cause. Just in time for last orders, in walked Reefer, looking absolutely gorgeous in biker's leather and jeans. He certainly has the right bum for a pair of faded denims . . . and terrific legs. It was funny how I'd stopped noticing what Roach was wearing. Reefer waved at me as he paid for his pint and then came over.

'Hi there,' I said, thanking my lucky stars.

'Can I get you one?' he asked, holding up his glass.

109

I shook my head and said: 'Am I pleased to see you!'

'Oh yeah?' he grinned. He looked just as good in civvies as he did in uniform, so I sneaked in a quick *Denim and Leather* by Saxon as a private tribute.

'Don't get the wrong idea,' I said, once the Saxon record had started. 'I need your help.'

'Sounds serious. Let me have some of this first.' He indicated his pint — hmm, cider, a man after my own heart — then downed more than half in one go. He smacked his lips, and I could almost taste the thick, syrupy juice. 'What can I do for you?'

I told him about Woodstock, what Anderson had said, Roach's evidence. I didn't tell him about Woody's little game. That was his own secret to share with whoever he wanted to. Reefer finished his pint and shrugged his shoulders.

'How can I help?'

I put the last record on, *Paper Roses* by Marie Osmond, before answering.

'I wondered if you might be able to find out what they have on Woodstock. See if they can place anyone else at the scene.'

'Sounds pretty much conclusive to me. Besides, I don't have access to that sort of information. I'd have to tap into the system illegally and, if they find out, that's my job gone.'

'I thought they wanted you out anyway.'

'They do. And they'd kill to get something like this on me. It'll be all on computer in the incident room. They'll know I violated security, even if I don't manage to get in. I can't do it Marcie.'

'Reefer, an innocent man is locked up while the real killer is still out there somewhere. He could kill again.'

'What makes you so sure he didn't do it?'

'I don't know.' I thought about that one. The music had finished and the doormen were hurrying folk up. It was time I started to pack up too as Vernon was hovering nearby and kept on giving me and Reefer curious looks.

'I've known him a long time,' I said, but thought I just didn't *know* him as such. 'I believe he was truly fond of this lad. He was really down when he thought Gavin had dumped him.' Well, that part was true at least. 'I don't think he could have faked that. And then there's Roach.'

I looked hopefully at Reefer. Was it really fair of me to expect him to jeopardise his career? Was it fair to knowingly ignore the possibility of the real killer striking again? There was no contest in my mind. A liar he may be, but I was sure that Woodstock was no murderer.

Reefer let out a huge sigh. 'Woodstock could have lied about the time he says he last saw Gavin. But if Roach is so sure, he should make a statement. Is he here?' He looked about him at the fast emptying room.

'He hasn't been in. I haven't seen him since last night. I think he must have gone to Barney's or something. He might be there now.'

Reefer drained the dregs before handing his glass to one of the bar staff. I hoped his conscience was pricking him a little.

'I'm still not sure,' he said, frowning. But I could feel him giving in. I applied a bit more pressure.

'Doesn't anyone in the incident room owe you a favour?' I asked.

His eyes lit up as an idea struck him. 'Actually, there's this tasty little piece who's got the hots for me. She might help.'

Ouch! Where *did* that pang of jealousy come from? I brushed it away. No time for selfishness or silliness now. He was still doubtful, so I tried one last time. 'Ple-e-e-ese.'

'Okay,' he sighed, again. 'I'll see what I can do. But the first sign of trouble and I'm outta here. I do like my job, you know.' I could have kissed him — again. It's a shame about that cage really. 'Look, I'm off to Barney's myself now. Do you fancy joining me?'

That was a tough one. I didn't really want to go as I'd be working there the next day, but I didn't really want to turn him down either. He was quite nice, and he might not ask again.

'I'd rather go to CJ's, instead,' I said finally. It's quieter there. 'I'm at work at Barney's tomorrow and it doesn't really feel like a night out. I only go there when I'm desperate.' Like the other week after the murder.

He pulled a face. 'They don't have cider at CJ's,' he said. 'And I'm meeting some mates at Barney's.'

'Oh.' So he wasn't asking me for a date after all. I declined the offer, regretfully. 'How about you joining me at Barney's tomorrow while I'm working?'

'Nah. Working myself tomorrow night.'

Oh well. It was probably just as well if he was planning on chatting up some tasty tottie at work in the next day or so. Best to keep my distance — at least for now. 'I'm done in anyway,' I said, truthfully.

'Maybe some other time then,' he said. Well, that was something, I suppose.

'Okay,' I said, giving him one of my cards, in case something came up. He told me how I could get hold of him too, if I needed to.

After we said goodnight he wandered off and, for some reason, I chuckled at his name: David Plant. PC Plant. A nickname like Reefer and a surname like Plant. A real pothead.

I had a long ride ahead of me and needed to be up early the next day. Penny and Richard, my sister and new brother-in-law, were coming home from their honeymoon. They'd gone to the Middle East or some such place. Mother would never forgive me if I didn't make the welcoming committee.

After finishing packing everything away, I said goodnight to everyone and headed upstairs. No more parking the bike for me in the car park — or not for a while at least.

★ ★ ★

Penny's welcome party wasn't so bad. We were waiting for them at their nice new little house. Mother was able to quip: 'At least one of my daughters won't be living like a tinker.'

It was supposed to be one of those surprise things, the party. But I reckon the balloons along the garden path and the twenty-foot 'Welcome home Penny and Richard' banner over the front door might have given the game away.

They both looked as though they had spent

114

far too much time in the sunshine and not enough time in the honeymoon suite. Penny can take the sun quite well being dark, we both can, and she'd gone a lovely nut brown. But poor old Richard, on the other hand, was as red as a lobster. I found myself wondering if he squealed like one too . . .

Fortunately, for me in any case, I had to be at work later. So I made my excuses, avoided Mother, and left.

*   *   *

Barney's was pretty routine. It's a bit different here. In The Cellar, us DJs are on the same level as the punters and the bar staff. At Barneys there are the three floors (heavy, traditional and fashionable — I do the traditional floor). But instead of being to one side of the dance floor, or at least up on a dais or a stage, we're shut away in a tiny room. Only those who know how to find us, or are at least still sober enough to remember the way, manage to make it through to us with requests.

It gets very lonely at Barney's.

*   *   *

After a late night I was relieved to hit the sack. And when the phone woke me in the early hours *again* the following morning, I was sorely tempted to get the thing disconnected.

'Yeah!'

'Hi Marcie. It's me, Reefer.'

'Reefer?' I checked the clock. 'Reefer, it isn't even eight yet.'

'Yeah. Sorry. But I found something out.'

'You still on duty?'

'Yeah. That's why I had to call now, before someone comes in and finds me here.'

'Can you talk now?'

'Only briefly. But I'll be quick.'

I scratched around for a pen and some paper, but as it happened, I didn't really need it.

'My friend checked the file.' I tried to imagine his 'tasty little piece' falling over herself to help him. 'Your friend Palmer — Woodstock — isn't the only person they can place at the scene. He was just one of many. With all the fag ends, urine samples, and dabs on the hypodermic, they should be able to identify at least half a dozen more.'

'Go on,' I prompted, when he paused.

'They've identified one already. Someone they had in for a minor drug offence several months ago managed to get his dabs all over a poly bag filled with pills. Someone called

116

John Beadsley — '

'John Beadsley?'

'Yeah. Why? Do you know him?'

I couldn't believe it. 'Reefer, that's Roach . . . '

12

Reefer hung up on me, which suggested that someone had just walked in on him. I hoped he didn't get into any real trouble on my account.

For what seemed like an age I sat there on the kitchen floor, clinging to the telephone receiver. If I ever decided to keep the noisy thing, I'd have to get one put in by the bed. Even if I got an answering machine, I'd want to know who was calling and would still get up and listen to it.

A constant whirring buzzed away in my ear. It was therapeutic.

If Roach's fingerprints were on Gavin's pill packet either Gavin had shared them with him, or Roach had given them to Gavin . . . or flogged them to him.

'The other person has cleared the line,' said an obnoxious sounding woman suddenly, from the other end of the phone. 'The other person has cleared . . . ' It was one of those recorded messages letting me know I'd been hung up on — in case I hadn't already noticed.

I slammed the phone down, jumped up off

the floor, showered and got dressed. It was Monday morning. I got my bike out of the lock-up and headed over to Roach's place, hoping he didn't have an early haul today, and really expecting him to be already out in any case. I needed to see him and speak to him now.

Roach lives in a house in Sheldon along with three other guys, all bikers, all Lucifer Beasts. The place is a hovel. They all work, two of them in tool rooms, and one at the Rover, so it's generally filthy dirty with none of them having either the time or the inclination to clean up after their greasy selves.

Roach's mom used to come over and clean for them, but she soon jacked it in after finding a used condom blocking the waste disposal in the kitchen. Well, what did she expect from a houseful of grown, single men?

They do have other mod cons like the waste disposal — like a dishwasher and a washing machine — but they don't seem to know how to use them. I suppose they have to find them first. I used their bathroom once and discovered a bidet lurking beneath a pile of wet and dirty linen. (I was looking for the loo roll.) They were using it to soak their dirty socks.

The doorbell plays about twenty eight

different naff tunes but that, like everything else in Roach's house, wasn't working. They'd stuck a plaster over the top of the bell push to stop people pressing it, but even the plaster was hanging off. I banged on the letterbox and waited.

No sign of life. So I banged it again, making sure it rattled annoyingly. It looked like I was out of luck. The other three were probably already at work too.

I went and got back on my bike, but as I revved up ready to go home again, I spotted Roach up at one of the bedroom windows. He'd seen me too and motioned for me to come back to the door. By the time I reached it he was downstairs and poking just his head around the door.

'I thought you'd already gone out,' I said, as I removed my lid and shook out my hair. 'I was making enough noise to wake up the dead.'

'You did a good job,' he complained, rubbing the stubble that was sprouting from his chin. On a good day, Roach looks like quite the hunk, in a Ross Kemp kind of way. Right now he didn't. 'Heavy night,' he explained, swinging the door open.

He was wearing a tee shirt, a pair of black ankle socks . . . and an early morning rise . . .

'Would you like to make yourself decent

before I come in,' I asked, nodding towards his todger and trying not to look embarrassed. 'Do you greet all of your guests like that?'

'Only the ones I like,' he shot back, waving me in and closing the door behind me. I followed him into the hall where he retrieved a pair of tracky bottoms from the banister, sniffed them, and pulled them on. The house smelled faintly of stale ale, old socks, cigarette smoke and dope — a bit like The Cellar, in fact.

'I didn't see you up Barney's,' I said at last, realising he'd said something about a good night, but forgetting that the only reason I would have seen him at the club was if he'd come all the way into the 'office'.

'Nah. We stayed in. Spliff fetched some gear over last night and the five of us got stoned.' Spliff is Roach's vice president at the motorcycle club.

I looked up the stairs. 'Where's Spliff now? He's not going to greet me in the altogether too, is he?' I didn't fancy Spliff in the slightest.

'He went home last night — '

'On his bike?'

'Yeah.'

'After you'd all been smoking?'

'Sure.' It didn't seem like such a big deal to

Roach. He can be a bit of a dickhead at times.

'And where are all the others?' I asked, referring to his housemates.

'Probably gone to work. What time is it?' He scratched at his balls.

They say you have to truly love a man to love him first thing in the morning. Seeing him like this, in full slob mode, I was wondering what it was I'd always liked about him so much.

'After nine.' I didn't need to look at my watch. I plopped my helmet down on a stair and unzipped my leather, but he didn't take the hint. 'Are you going to keep me in the hall?'

'Sorry. No. Come on in to the kitchen.' He led me towards the back of the house but I already knew the layout.

'How come you're not at work?' I asked.

'I've got the week off. Do you want a cup of tea?'

I glanced at the mould growing in the bottom of a mug he was threatening to rinse — with the cold tap. 'Er . . . no thanks. I'm not stopping long.'

'You don't mind if I have one, do you?' I shook my head. He was welcome to it. Hell, there was enough penicillin lining his cup to protect him from anything else he might catch. 'Me mouth feels like the inside of a — '

'Yes, thank you, Roach,' I interrupted. 'I don't want to know.'

'Oh. Right,' he shrugged. 'So, what can I do for you at this hour on a Monday morning when you didn't think I'd be in anyway? I must say, I am honoured.' He grinned at me alarmingly, and I remembered exactly what it was about him I liked.

'I wanted to check out your story the night Gavin died.'

He flicked a switch on the kettle. 'I've already told you once.'

'Yeah. I know. I just want you to tell me again. That's all.'

'You working for the cops?'

'Just answer the question, Roach.' I settled on the edge of the kitchen table, as all three chairs were piled high with washing.

'What do you want to know?'

He was playing for time. 'Tell me again why you went out into the car park.'

While he scrubbed at the mug with a dolly mop he kept his back to me. I couldn't see his face, but I could see his neck starting to turn an angry looking red. 'I needed a piss, so I went out there.'

'Why didn't you use the gents?'

He laughed at me over his shoulder. 'Gimme a break, Marce. I can tell you've never set foot in that place. You have to swim across to the trough the floor is so flooded, and then you don't know what you're swimming through. It's not nice, I can tell you.'

It sounded just like his own bathroom to me — and the ladies at The Cellar. 'So you went for a pee and saw Gavin with Woodstock?'

'No. Woody was already on his way to the bar. I told you that.'

'Did you speak to Gavin?'

He sighed. 'No.'

'Are you sure?'

'What is this, Marcella?' he asked, spinning around to face me, grubby tea towel hanging from his hand. (That was probably over-inhabited by micro-organisms too, judging by the state of it.) His eyes were almost navy with fury. 'Am I one of your suspects?' he spat.

Uh-oh. I'd got his mad up. 'Fortunately for you,' I said calmly, 'the police already have their prime suspect, thanks, as you well know.'

'So what's the problem?'

'Only that they've got your dabs all over Gavin's drugs.'

Roach at least had the decency to let his face drop. 'Oh.'

'You may well say 'oh', John Beadsley.' I could resort to full names too. 'But our friend Woodstock — you remember him? — is rotting away in Winson Green because you haven't given him an alibi. What's the matter, Roach? You scared they might do you for using?'

'No.' He *was* looking guilty now.

'Then what?'

He hung his head in shame and picked at the hem of the tea towel.

'I'm scared they might do me for dealing.'

13

Roach — in his own words

A lot of people seem to think that driving a lorry for a living is easy money. Well, it can be a good job if you work for the right people or get a decent contract. Same as any job. But aside from paying for somewhere to live the rest of the time, we also have to pay rent for digs when we're away. You can't always sleep in the cab. Then there's insurance, road tax, petrol. It all costs money.

I'm paying for me own cab too and often have to hire a trailer. If I worked for a big haulage firm, then it wouldn't be so bad. But why do you think I have three lodgers? I have to pay the mortgage somehow, and the hire purchase on the wagon.

Most people I know think I inherited the house, and I suppose I did in a way. But me Auntie Mo went into a home. She didn't die. Her life insurance didn't cover that possibility. So I bought the house off her. The capital pays for her care. We probably won't see any of that even after she dies, me and me mom.

The four of us lads all work so there's no

time to look after the place. I can't afford a cleaner let alone a gardener. So it just falls about around our ears. You think the house is bad? The garden's a wilderness.

Anyway, I was managing, the way you do. But then I got meself involved with a bird. No one knows her down here. She lives up north, in Morecambe. I stayed at her dad's guesthouse a couple of times. Her name's Wendy and she's a stunner. But she's also a bit loopy. I don't know what's wrong with her. Maybe she's a schizo. She can get a bit nasty, like during sex, and I'm not really into that sort of thing.

So I dumped her and found meself a new guesthouse. It was more expensive but less hassle. The next thing I hear from her is that she's pregnant and telling everyone the kid's mine. I knew that was a lie so I told her to get lost. She was calling me up on the mobile phone at all hours, begging me to come back one minute, hurling obscenities at me the next. I smashed the phone up in the end and got a new one.

Then she got hold of me address. Probably from her dad's records at the bed and breakfast, but she could have got it off the client I was driving up there for, or she might have rifled me pockets months before. I'll probably never know. And after she had the little bastard, she set the Child Support Agency on to me.

If ever there was an evil organisation, it's the CSA. It's no wonder men commit suicide after they've come calling. They're above the law. It didn't matter that I wasn't the child's father. Guilty until proved innocent, that's their motto. Wendy was able to give them exact dates that coincided with me trips up north. She must have planned it all months before.

It isn't up to the CSA to prove that you are the father. It's up to you to prove that you're not. How many relationships can they have wrecked in the years they've been in existence? It didn't matter that I already had commitments, nor that I could prove the baby wasn't mine.

'They all say that, Mr Beadsley,' they said.

It didn't matter that I had a hefty mortgage. What was a single man doing with a four-bedroomed house in any case? Wasn't that a bit extravagant? Perhaps I should sell up and move into a more suitable bedsit.

I didn't declare the lads because their rent would have been classed as income. And if I lived with a bird, then her income would be taken into account an' all.

It didn't matter, either, that I had a hire purchase agreement on the wagon, because

128

child support must come before any other debt. Men have to live with their responsibilities. And if I jacked in the job to avoid paying maintenance, they'd have me arrested and thrown into jail. I couldn't win.

So I filled in this enormous form they sent me and my assessment came back at nearly £400 a month, backdated to when Wendy first made the claim, since I'd been so obstructive. And the kid wasn't even mine.

At first I refused to pay and they threatened an attachment of earnings.

'Attach away,' I said. After all, I'm self employed and that wouldn't matter.

Then they said they'd take me to court and in the meantime me outstanding payments would accrue interest. I swore the kid wasn't mine, showed them the paperwork and everything. But they said they could only accept a blood test as I hadn't been back for me sperm count after I'd had the chop. And I had to pay for the test meself. Until I got the results, the liability was still mine.

I had to pay the £400 a month, plus interest on late payments, plus the mortgage, plus the HP, plus everything else. It could have meant selling the bike to pay for everything, but that would have soon ran out. And *then* they went and walloped a couple of extra charges on top, too. I had to pay a one off calculation fee *and* an annual collection charge. Can you believe that? I had to pay *them* for the privilege.

After a lot of thought I decided to meet their outrageous demands. They were locking men up left, right and centre. I couldn't afford a poor credit rating or a county court judgement and they assured me that if I did turn out not to be the father I could have a full refund. So I coughed up and tried to arrange the blood tests.

I was finding it really difficult to find the money for everything and Wendy kept on stalling. She kept saying the kid wasn't old enough, or there was always something wrong. Before I knew it, three months had already gone by, but there was a temporary solution about to land in me lap.

The M6 is well known for hold-ups and traffic jams between Stafford and Wolverhampton, or that general area, even more so on a Friday afternoon, and worse when there are road works, which is most of the time. On one of these days, we'd been standing still for ages and I noticed something strange going on up ahead.

A foreign trucker and a van driver were discussing something through their open windows, then the van driver handed the truck driver a ten pound note. The van driver was British, the lorry driver was Belgian. The Belgian handed the Brit a package and they had a good laugh about something.

A bit later, after the traffic had moved on a bit, the Brit made a call and, once finished, made sure he came up alongside the Belgian again. He bought another two packets of . . . whatever . . . and drove off at the next opportunity with a wave.

Had I just witnessed a drugs handover? I didn't know, but I was going to find out. As soon as I could, I caught up with the Belgian and gave him a cheery wave. He'd already clocked me in his wing mirror and he crawled along until we were level.

'Hello,' he called out, and laughed. 'You like?'

'What is it?' I asked.

'Golden Virginia.'

He was flogging tobacco.

'How much?'

He held up a package the size of a house brick. 'Ten pounds only.'

I thought it looked like a good deal and bought a pack off him. Then we exchanged mobile phone numbers and separated.

I managed to shift the stuff easily enough, and at quite a profit too. And me and Georges set up a regular thing. After a few weeks he suggested something a bit stronger.

The tobacco had worked out all right, so I thought, why not? I needed the money.

Georges got me a bit of cannabis resin and a few Es. Gavin became one of me regulars. He took the pills while the lads helped me out with the resin. And there was still the tobacco. I'd got nicked once, too, during a raid on CJ's. But I'd already moved most of the stuff and they could only do me for possession. I paid me fine and carried on — just more carefully. It was easier to make ends meet and I'd soon saved up enough to cover the blood test.

The nicking made me realise I had to stop. Next time I might not be so lucky. I couldn't keep it up for much longer.

Wendy's kid must have been almost twelve months old by now, and still she was coming up with excuses. The CSA, meanwhile, had gone through a bit of a makeover, so I went back to them. I was about due for a review anyway. They agreed to scare Wendy into action by threatening to withhold her benefit if she didn't get the test done. They can do that too, apparently. And she caved.

What bit of stuff I had left, Gavin took off me and me and the lads kept the cannabis for our own use. Gavin had the last of the Es on the night he died. I went out to the car park, like I said, and bumped into Woody on his way to the bar. Gavin was getting himself ready for a fix, but I think he took one of the pills instead. I thought he was following me back into the pub, too, but he can't have been.

Those results came back last week and the baby — a boy, I only just found out — isn't mine. I took the week off work to celebrate, I've been working so hard to pay it all. The CSA are arranging the refund and I should be able to pay off the loan for the cab. The admin charges and the test fee still stand.

But do you know the craziest thing? If me and Wendy had been married, I would still have to cough up for a kid that wasn't mine. It seems in the eyes of the law, CSA-style, I'd still be considered the one financially liable. Whether it proved it wasn't mine or not.

That can't be very fair, can it?

14

Bugger It!

I'd got myself all worked up to be mad with him and now I felt sorry for him. Roach's confession certainly knocked the wind out of *my* sails. On the one hand I was a bit disappointed with him for resorting to selling drugs. But on the other, I could see his point and he *had* decided to jack it in.

'Your tea's gone cold,' I said, for want of something better to say.

He glanced at the cup, felt it with his hand, and chucked it down the sink, flicking the kettle back on again. I was surprised he'd needed to feel it. The surface had congealed and shrunk away from the sides of the cup.

'Do you want one this time?' he asked.

I shook my head. 'Roach, you have to go to the police.'

'Okay, I'll go. But I'm only going to give him an alibi. I'm not admitting to anything else.'

'You don't need to admit anything. They already know. Aside from already having your fingerprints, remember, they've already got you on record. Don't you think they would have picked you up by now if they were going to?'

'I suppose so,' he said, sulking. 'But what should I say?'

'I don't care what you say,' I hissed. 'Just get Woodstock out of that stinking hole.' I was angry with myself and with him. I slammed out of his house and kicked my bike. Why didn't he want to help Woody? Why was I being such a wimp? He was a drugs dealer, for God's sake. But, also, he could have stopped Woodstock getting banged up too.

There was no way I was riding home in this state . . . and anyway, I'd left my crash helmet on his stairs. I decided to go for a walk instead, and found myself in the park we used to go to when we were both kids.

Who knew what kind of adults we'd grow into when we were young? Not our teachers. Not our parents. And certainly not ourselves. We all just wanted to get there as quickly as we could. Maybe we all turned into disappointments no matter how well we were brought up. I sat on a swing and mulled. I was definitely disappointed with Roach.

For some strange reason I decided to go and see my mom and dad, who only live about twenty minutes' walk from the park. My parents still live in the same house they bought nearly forty years ago. Creatures of habit. I left the swing swinging on its own.

By the time I got there Penny and Richard were already visiting too.

'No work today then?' I asked.

'No,' said Penny. 'We both took an extra day off to recover from the honeymoon,' she beamed. I caught a secret little look she exchanged with her husband. Well, it wasn't very *secret*. No doubt they'd soon get the hang of it, given time.

'How about you?' asked Richard.

I was about to remind him that I didn't work during the day when Mother piped up instead.

'Marcella doesn't *work* for a living, Richard. You know that. She can't do an ordinary job like anybody else,' she sneered. 'My eldest daughter's a *disc jockey*.' She said it as though she were repeating a swear word she'd just heard for the first time.

'No. Marcella has to go gallivanting about at night so she can idle the day away in bed.'

'Yeah, like now,' I said.

Richard stifled a grin and looked pointedly at his watch. 'My, is it really ten o'clock already?'

I quite liked my new brother-in-law, I decided, who winked at me just then. Mother graciously smiled at his wit, but I don't think any of us missed the sour expression on her face as she turned to go into the kitchen.

'Tea anyone?' she called, politely.

We all agreed. Richard winked at me again, and gave his wife another one of those meaningful looks. If they kept that up, I'd need to carry a sick bucket around with me.

And so passed an otherwise pleasant morning at Mom's and Dad's. They're both retired now so I knew they'd probably be in. They never do anything on the spur of the moment, or go away unannounced. In fact, they usually give everyone ample notice if they do go away or even if they just go out for the day.

Dad was upstairs for most of the time, in his 'hobbies' room — my old room as I'd been left home the longest. He was building an *Airfix* model.

Richard is tall, slim and blond and, considering his sharp sense of humour, he does blush rather easily. He wears metal-rimmed round glasses that give him a dishy Joe-90 sort of look. He's quite fit and healthy as he hang-glides and backpacks whenever he can, for pleasure . . . for *pleasure*! Fortunately Penny likes backpacking too, and that's where they'd been for their honeymoon — in Bali, as it turned out.

They've both got good jobs. He's a chartered accountant and she works for a local management consultancy. I honestly don't know what Mother's problem is sometimes. Penny more than makes up for all of my shortcomings.

When Richard took to pacing the lounge carpet, I noticed he was playing with two of those Chinese silver ball thingies. I hadn't realised he was a stressed-out sort of person, and told him so too.

'No, I'm not,' he replied.

'Richard's too laid back to get stressed,' agreed Penny, truthfully.

'I just find them a bit soothing. It's the noise they make.' To demonstrate, he made them tinkle.

'My gaffer at The Cellar is always playing with those things,' I said. 'Well, he used to. I think he must have lost them. I haven't seen him with them for ages. Now he *is* heart attack fodder. He has such a short fuse. Maybe that's why he drinks.'

Mother tutted.

'I just find them soothing,' repeated Richard, returning the balls to his trouser pocket. Now that did look odd.

'Anyway, Marcella,' said Mom. 'To what do we owe the honour of *your* company so early this morning?'

Gee, it was nice to feel welcome. Two sarky comments in one day from two different

138

people — and it still wasn't twelve o'clock yet.

Actually, I'd almost forgotten myself. But there was no way I was going to tell her how disappointed I was with Roach. 'Not that *nice* young man you went to school with, dear?' she'd say.

'Yes, and by the way, did you know he deals in drugs?' I'd reply. And I certainly wasn't going to admit to realising what a disappointment I must be to her and Dad.

Instead, I lied.

'Oh, I was just passing.'

'And where's that nasty machine you normally ride about on?'

Oh no! I'd left it outside Roach's house. Before I could go home, I had half an hour walk ahead of me.

'Actually, Mom,' I said, jumping to my feet. 'I've left it at a friend's. I'd better go.'

I dashed to the door yelling my farewells to the others and up the stairs to my dad.

'Hmph. I might have known she wouldn't be staying very long,' I heard Mom complain to Penny and Richard.

An hour and a half I'd been at my Mom's and Dad's. The longest I'd managed in a good while. It must have been the company. I felt sorry now that I hadn't got to know Richard sooner. I suppose it was the way that

Mom raved on about him. Yes, that probably did put me off. He'd turned out to be quite an ally on the old Home Front.

And he was sexy too.

By the time I got back to Roach's house it was well past noon and I had a stitch in my side. He'd strapped my helmet to my handlebars, so I knew he must have gone out. He arrived back on his bike, though — a Honda 750–4 — just as I was climbing on to mine. I wondered, idly, if he'd been to the cops.

He had, bless him.

'How did you get on?'

'Bloody waste of time,' he shrugged, undoing his chinstrap.

'No good?'

He pulled off his helmet. 'They kept me hanging around for ages, and then said there was no one available to take me statement, and anyway, the case is closed.'

'How can it be closed? They haven't found Woodstock guilty already, have they?'

'No. But he's been charged. They suggested I get in touch with the officer in charge. Do you know who that is?'

'I presume it's DS MacGregor. Or you could try DC Anderson. Failing that, there's also a PC Plant, too, from Steelhouse Lane. Which one did you go to?'

'Steelhouse Lane.'

'Then you probably need to go to Acocks Green. I don't know. Reefer said you should give them a statement — '

'Reefer? Who's he?'

'That's PC Plant,' I said, trying to keep my voice steady. I didn't want to blow his cover.

Damn. It really was as though the police *had* got their result and weren't bothered about the truth. 'Do you know who you spoke to?'

'Nah. But by the looks of him, he was just a snotty little YTS. Do they have them in the police?'

'Dunno. They might not still have them anywhere. Didn't he say anything else?'

'Just that I might be called in to the trial by his defence as a witness. I did try, Marcie.'

I looked at him and knew he was telling the truth. 'Yeah, I know. Thanks for trying anyway.' I switched on the ignition and gave the engine a couple of revs.

'What are you gonna do now?' he asked.

'I dunno. It looks like the next thing I should be doing is finding as many witnesses as I can.'

'Like who?'

'Angus — '

'That prick?'

'He was there on the night. Don't you

141

remember? One of his mates attacked me and he came to my rescue.'

'He fancies you.'

'He does not.'

'Yes he does.'

'So what?'

Roach turned up his nose in disgust and changed tack. 'Who else?'

'Daisy.'

'What can she do?'

'I don't know . . . yet. But I'm sure she saw someone . . . or knows something.'

'Anyone else?'

'Pendle probably.'

Roach snorted. 'He won't help much.'

'Why not?'

'Well, apart from the fact that he was probably three sheets to the wind, by *opening* time, he wasn't even there.'

I thought about that one for a moment. 'Yes he was.'

'Why didn't he do something when that prospect was playing up? He wouldn't have pulled a stunt like that with you if the gaffer had been there.'

Yes. That was true. Drunk or not, that temper of his could always pack a punch, in more senses than one. And he didn't like any trouble in his pub. Ken Pendle would have had the little runt flat across the bar in a shot. Many had seen him do it to his wife in the past. Now, she'd had a gob on her. When I came to think about it, Roach was right. Pendle hadn't been there. I remembered him coming in through the door with Vernon at last orders.

'That leaves Angus and Daisy,' I said finally.

He grunted some kind of agreement. 'What're you gonna do first?'

I nodded towards his neighbour's house where one of the net curtains was twitching erratically. 'If I don't scoot soon she's going to come out here and complain about the noise.' Both of our bikes were running, and his doesn't have any baffles.

Roach looked over, stuck up his middle finger at the woman, and grinned back at me. 'Don't mind her. She's a nosy old bag.'

Charming. 'Nah. I'm off anyway. I'm going to go and get me some dinner.' We have it at lunchtime in Birmingham. 'Then I'll see if I can get hold of Daisy. She's normally up town on a Monday afternoon. Business is still okay then, apparently.' I tightened the chinstrap on my helmet — have you noticed how no one *ever* does that on the telly? — and revved the bike again, to make sure it wasn't about to cut out.

143

'Do me a favour, though,' I said, before going.

'What's that?'

'Spend some of your holiday tidying up that pig heap you live in.'

He grinned and called: 'See ya,' before bumping his bike up onto the drive.

'Tarrar.'

I rode into town and grabbed myself a baked potato with cheese and baked beans. I use this little caff at the top end of New Street — opposite where Bogart's used to be. The place has been there for years in some shape or form, but most people seem to prefer the burger bars and pizza places. It's cheaper and I can always get a seat. It's a tiny shop crammed between a newsagent and a hippy shop. I don't go in the shop that often so can't remember the name . . . come to think of it, I *do* go into the caff a lot, but I can't remember its name either.

In the old days when Mister Bill's used to be *the* place to be on a Saturday afternoon, there was still a *Woolworth's* in New Street. We all used to have a skin full of beer at the bier keller, and then meet up in the canteen on the top floor. I was always surprised when they let us in. Any other shop would have been scared, and would have thrown a load of drunken rockers and bikers out.

Woollies moved out of town a while back, though it's since returned. And those of us who still felt the urge to eat had to find somewhere else. I found this little caff and I've stayed loyal to it ever since. They really pile your plate up, for a fraction of the price at other places. And it's fresh.

After dinner I spent the afternoon trying to locate Daisy. I know a few of her haunts and loitered around in them, hoping I wouldn't get picked up. Fortunately, I know some of the other girls too, so didn't get done over for trespassing onto their patch. We even exchanged pleasantries and a few jokes.

In the end I asked one of them if she knew where Daisy was and she said, after checking her watch, that she'd probably be at The Cellar by now. I made my way over there, looking forward to a swift half — the place stays open all day for the market traders — and there was Daisy, just leaving.

'Hi Marcie,' she bawled. 'How's things?'

'Not good.'

'How's Woodstock? I didn't get to see him.'

'They've charged him with Gavin's murder, Daisy.'

'But they can't.'

'They can and they have. He's in The Green now, on remand.'

'What, *Winson* Green?'

145

'Yep.'

She looked in the general direction of the prison and then looked back at me. 'But Woodstock didn't do it,' she blurted.

'You know that. I know it. Roach knows, and so does Woody. It's a shame the police don't, really.'

'No. It's impossible. They can't have charged him.'

She sounded pretty certain. I frowned at her. 'Were you there, Daisy?' I'd always suspected she might have been. She didn't reply. 'How much did you see?'

'Woodstock and Gavin shared a joint before they . . . you know . . . then. Woody left him and Roach came out.' She gave me a sideways glance.

'I know why Roach was there, Daisy. It's all right.'

She released some of the tension in her shoulders. 'Well, anyway, they had this argument — '

'Who? Gavin and Roach?' Roach hadn't said anything about a row.

'No. It wasn't Roach.'

'Then who was it?'

She looked away from me, checked her watch, then strained to see up the road behind me.

'What's the matter?' I asked, looking over

my shoulder and back at Daisy again. 'Are you waiting for a bus?'

'No. I'm meeting a client. I'm going to be late if I don't hurry.'

She was clearly uncomfortable and appeared to be struggling with herself.

'Daisy?'

'I can't break a client's confidence.'

'You can if it gets an innocent man off the hook . . . ' She wasn't biting. 'You're not a doctor, and even they're allowed to break a confidence in a murder case.'

She took a deep breath and glanced back into the pub. 'I'm not certain he did anything, though, because I left just then. So I'll give you a clue. But you dare tell him I told you anything and I'm dead.'

'Who?' This was really annoying me now.

'Never mind that for the moment. You'll have to find that much out for yourself.' She began to totter away along the tiles, on her spindly legs. 'And remember, I'm not really sure he did anything anyway.' Her micro-mini skirt was way too tight and her yellow stilettos were way too high. 'Find out what they were arguing about . . . find out how he died — '

'*Who?*'

'And everything else will fall into place.'

I didn't understand. But she was putting

147

some distance between us now. 'Who, Daisy? When?'

'Three years ago,' she called back.

'Where?'

'At the Royal Infirmary.'

'Daisy!' I called after her and took a few steps towards her retreating back. But she either hadn't heard, or didn't want to. I watched after her thinking, never mind. It'll keep. As she disappeared around the corner I descended the steps myself to the black hole below.

I will always regret not going after her. I never saw Daisy again . . .

15

I almost collided with Ken Pendle on my way down the stairs into the pub. He was on his way up the steps with Vernon. The Cellar has always used Vernon's company for security. It was us who recommended him to the brewery and now all of his work comes from there. They don't like moonlighters much anyway and prefer all of their staff to be exclusive to them. They tried it with me, but until they could guarantee me five nights a week, I told them they could whistle.

'Sorry, boss,' I said. 'I didn't see you there in the dark.' I nodded towards the bouncer and greeted him. 'Vernon.'

'Marcie,' he replied.

'It's the wrong day for you, isn't it?' grinned Pendle. 'A bit early too, Marcie.'

Oh, I do like his little jokes. 'I fancied a swift one, boss.'

'Come on in then. You can have this one on me.' He turned around and came with me back down the steps. 'See you later, Vernon.'

'Boss,' replied the doorman, who continued on out of the pub.

'Gee, thanks,' I said to Pendle. He must

have been drunk already. That's usually the only time he ever buys a drink for anybody — which just happens to be most nights. Not that he actually 'buys' them. He just helps himself to the pumps and optics. 'But weren't you on your way out?'

'What? No. I wanted to catch Daisy before she left. For a quick word. But it looks like I wasn't quick enough. Maybe Vernon will catch up with her.'

I let Pendle 'buy' me a half a pint of sweet cider — on draught — well, I *was* driving. Otherwise I might have really took advantage and let him stand me a whole pint. Best to make the most of his generosity. You never know how long it might last . . . or not, as the case may be.

I only ever have a half when I'm driving, or riding my bike. Any more and I might forget I'm supposed to stop, and keep going. Then I'd have to get a taxi home. It's an expensive habit, drinking. I perched on a bar stool next to the bar.

Stone Age Sal, president of the Cycle Witches, wandered in bang on half past three. She empties the dustbins and rubbish bins in town for the council and always pops in when she's finished. I knew she wasn't in on the night Gavin died, but I hoped she might be able to tell me where I could find Angus. She and him have this thing going — in her dreams. She's an easy lay and Angus takes advantage of that. Nothing more.

I let her buy a drink before sliding down off my stool and sidling up to her.

'Hi Sal. How're you doing?' I tried not to let my nose turn up at the faint whiff of dirty bins.

She looked at me as though she'd just scraped me off the bottom of her shoe, or like I'd just slapped her in the face. Okay, so maybe I don't make a habit of making polite conversation with her, but there was no need for her to look at me like that. She could be so hurtful at times.

Before answering, she checked over both of her shoulders to make sure I was really talking to her.

'What do you want?'

Oh, wow! She had bad breath too. I held up my hands in mock defence and also to deflect some of her smells, and took one step backwards.

'Okay, okay. I give up. I need your help.'

'*You* need *my* help?'

'Yeah. I need to get hold of Angus, and thought you might be able to tell me where he's likely to be.'

She sneered, giving me a vicious glint of those metal teeth. Then she took a long swig of her beer. 'You fancy him or something?' she grunted at last.

'No,' I snapped, rather too quickly.

'Why? What's wrong with him? Not good enough for the likes of you?'

I was in a no win situation here, obviously. 'No, nothing. He's all right really,' for a Rider I added, to myself of course. 'And anyway. He's spoken for, isn't he?' That's it, Marce. Butter her up.

'Yeah, well. You just remember that. That's what I say.' It's what I'd just said as well, wasn't it? 'He's mine, so you can keep your robbin' hands off.'

I had no intention of laying a single finger on him, dearie. What a shame Angus didn't realise he belonged to such a delightful person.

Apart from the mean teeth, Stone Age really does have wild hair. It's a dirty blonde sort of colour. Ash, I suppose. She's about five feet nothing but quite broad shouldered. Like a man. Everyone knows she works weights, at the same gym Daisy uses. I wondered how she would look covered with baby oil and wearing a miniscule bikini . . . probably like a man in a bikini. Because she'd just come in from work, she was wearing a day-glo coat, which came down to her knees.

'So,' she was saying. 'What do you want him for?'

'I need to talk to him about the last time he came in here.'

She screwed up her plain features as though she were concentrating . . . or straining to have a fart. I hoped she didn't follow though. 'Wasn't that Good Friday?' Wow! Was she keeping tabs on him or what? 'The night that faggot got done in?' I cringed at the expression, but nodded anyway, at the same time as swigging my cider. 'Well, Angus didn't do it.'

'I know. But neither did the kid they've got locked up for it. That's why I need to talk to Angus.'

'Why? Who've they got for it, then?'

'Woodstock.'

'Woodstock?' she snorted. 'Well, he wouldn't hurt a fly.'

'Exactly.'

I got this crazy image of Sal offering to give Woody a blow job and him preferring his own hand. I would *not* let that smirk creep across my face.

Stone Age glanced up at the clock behind the bar and drained her glass, all in one movement. 'I gotta get the truck back to the depot.'

'So where will I find Angus?'

She thought again for a minute before replying. 'He'll probably be at The Den around eight tonight.'

Great. I finished my own measly half as she collected her huge rubber gloves from the bar top and stomped off up the stairs. The Den is a worse hole than this place and just happens to be the clubhouse of the Death Riders. I should have guessed he'd be there, really.

The Den — admission solely by invitation only.

★ ★ ★

At five minutes to eight I arrived outside The Den, a dirty hovel at the back of the White Lion public house, in desirable (not) Balsall Heath. I was a bit reluctant to leave my bike unattended, but the Riders had all left their bikes in the pub car park. I thought that maybe mine would be okay out here too, but then decided that any regular would spot it and realise it wasn't one of theirs. I had absolutely no desire to emerge from the Riders' clubhouse and discover my precious bike had been pinched, and I certainly didn't relish the idea of walking through this area in the dark in search of a bus stop or a taxi. Kerb crawlers might take me for a prostitute, as might the numerous Asian vigilantes who hang around on street corners in an attempt to improve the neighbourhood.

This community would report anyone to the police if they thought it would clean up their streets. What they do is make a note of the car registration numbers, get in touch with someone they know who has access to the right sort of information, find out the owner's name and address, and either write to them threatening to tell the wife, or pass the details on to the police. As far as I can tell they're doing a pretty good job too. The streets are definitely cleaner. But shit sticks and the whole area is still avoided by those who have no business there.

Anyway, I wheeled my bike right up to the clubhouse door, and stayed astride it while I waited, with the engine running. That way we'd both be safe. No one could nick my bike with me on it, and if I got the faintest hint of trouble I could burn off out of there.

Because of the number of motorbikes parked outside, I knew there were Riders inside. Angus was here already too, or at least his bike was. It's unmistakable as it has a painting of the Grim Reaper on the petrol tank.

Not knowing any funny handshakes or secret knocks, I had to wait for someone else to go in, or come out, and let Angus know I was there.

Twenty minutes later I was in luck. A tiny 125cc phutted to a standstill and the guy dismounted and walked over, taking his crash helmet off on the way. As I caught sight of the shock of bright orange hair glowing in the dim light, I realised I wasn't in luck after all.

Of all the bikers in the whole of Brum the one man I needed to rely on for a favour was a wanker. Only Ginger, the creep who tried to rip my hair out at The Cellar on the night that Gavin died.

'Hi Ginger. How're you doing?' I decided that confidence was the best thing right now.

'Well, if it isn't Marcie Craig. How're *you* doin', girlie? I think we have some unfinished business, don't you?'

'Oh sure, in your wet dreams, sunshine.' I didn't really care if I upset him or not. But he could prove useful and I did need the favour. While he struggled to come back with a smart reply, I changed tack. 'I'm surprised to see you here, actually,' I said truthfully. 'I thought Angus gave you the boot.'

'He did, thanks to you. But then you pissed him off and he gave me a second chance.' He looked me up and down with those leering, green eyes and turned his nose up. 'I don't know what it is he sees in you myself. You look just like any other split arsed cow to me.'

Ouch! Another one of my least favourite expressions. 'Has he let you in yet, then?' I meant 'in' to the gang.

'Nah. I'm still prospecting. But he will soon.'

'You sound pretty sure of yourself. How do you fancy earning a few more brownie points?'

'Like how?'

'Like, why don't you run along in there and tell Angus I'm here?'

'Run along yourself,' he mimicked. 'You're a cheeky cow. You can go on in there if you want.'

Oh yeah, like if I wanted my face broken. 'I can't stop, I'm in a hurry,' I lied. 'Angus will be dead impressed with you if you let him know I want to see him.'

Ginger thought about that one for a while as the engine on my bike purred along. I could imagine the cogs creaking into action in that thick skull of his. I reckoned he must be weighing up the pros and cons inside his head. Finally he relented.

'Okay. You wait here.'

In this dump? I wasn't going anywhere.

Now, either Angus is keener on me than I originally thought, or he was standing quite close to the door. No sooner had Ginger

157

disappeared through it than Angus appeared at it. I cut the engine, climbed off my bike and removed my helmet. With Angus here, neither me nor the bike were in any danger.

'Hallo, Marcie. What do you want?'

'Oh, I'm fine thanks, Angus. How are you?'

'Cut the crap, Marcie. The only reason you're here is probably because you want something from me.'

My, either he was pretty cute, or the jungle telegraph had beat me to it. 'Okay, Angus. It's a fair cop. I hold my hands up.' And I did.

'So?'

'Do you remember the last time you came up to The Cellar?' He didn't answer, just glared at me. 'Oh good. You do. Anyway, that was the night this lad got himself murdered.'

'So?' he asked again.

'A friend of mine, well, a friend of yours too, actually, has been charged with the kid's murder. He's on remand at Winson Green.'

'Who?'

When I told him, Angus snorted just like Stone Age Sal had. And he reacted with the same expression too. They were obviously made for each other. 'Woodstock couldn't hurt a fly.'

'Precisely. It seems that everyone in this city knows that except the cops.'

He shrugged. 'So what do you want me to

do about it? Get him out?'

'No ... well, yes.' Actually, there's a thought ... 'I wondered if you could remember anything about that night that might help get him out of the frame.'

'But if he did it ... ?'

'That's just it. He didn't. And being in The Green will probably kill him.'

'The pigs must think he had something to do with it, else they wouldn't have charged him.'

'They do think so. But you and I both know he couldn't have done it. Not Woody.'

He rubbed his stubbly chin thoughtfully. 'Why should I help him?'

'Because he's a mate. And because you might remember what it's like to have a good friend wrongly accused of murder.'

Angus winced. About ten years ago, I thought it was, a mate of his, his old vice president actually, had tried to help a taxi driver who'd been stabbed one night. When the taxi driver died, Angus's mate got put away for fifteen years. The bloke who had actually murdered the man only got a twelve month sentence — and that was suspended.

Angus continued to rub his chin as he tried to remember something. 'We were only there for a bit. We had the one drink and then we left. There was just that bit of trouble you had

159

with Twinkle Toes in there.' He cocked his head towards the clubhouse door. 'We didn't stick around after that.'

'And you're sure you don't remember anything else?'

He thought long and hard, he really did. But still he came up with nothing. 'Nah. That's all. Sorry.' Damn. 'Tell you what, though. I'll ask around, see what I can find out.'

'Cheers. Thanks for trying, anyway.' I switched the engine back on and gave the engine a bit of a rev. 'If you do think of anything . . . '

'I'll be in touch,' he finished for me.

'Cheers. I appreciate it.' I started to put my helmet back on but he caught hold of my arm.

'Hey,' he said.

'What?'

'Don't I get a kiss?'

'What for?'

'For helping.'

'You didn't.'

'I tried,' he grinned. 'And I'm going to try harder.'

'But you haven't yet.'

'Call it a down payment.' He grinned again and cocked his head to one side. Coy prick. But it was tempting . . . he might be a bit of a

160

pillock, but he *is* quite nice looking. Rugged, rough and ready.

'Listen,' he said. 'I'll make sure Woody's looked after.'

'And how can you do that when he's already inside?'

'Where do you think they've been keeping Stu for the past seven years?' Was it really only seven? I'd thought it was much longer. 'I'll get Stu to look out for him.'

'Thanks.'

'Now, about that kiss . . . '

'Okay.' I yielded and gave him a quick peck on the cheek. But that wasn't enough.

'Come on, Marcie Craig. You can do better than that.'

So I closed my eyes and thought of England . . . and, truly, it wasn't so bad. He was quite gentle, in fact. And at least he let go of my arm then.

'I guess I'll be seeing you around,' he said finally, turning and heading back in to the clubhouse.

'Sure,' I replied as he disappeared though the door, so I addressed the door instead. 'Yeah, I'll be seeing you.'

Not one of my more successful meetings. Although I did discover one thing. Angus, president of the Death Riders motorcycle club, is actually human after all . . . shame old Stone Age isn't too.

Unfortunately, I spent far too much time mulling over this latest little gem and not enough time worrying about clearing off. I should have got my sweet little ass outta there as soon as we'd finished. After another quick rev of the engine, which always makes me feel good for some unknown reason, I tried again to replace my helmet.

A faint whiff of dirty bins told me I had company.

16

I don't know where they'd come from, or where they'd parked their bikes. But I was a bit surprised to see five Cycle Witches, led by their prehistoric president.

'Sal. You never said you'd be here too.'

'I wasn't going to be. But after our little chat I thought that maybe I'd better come along after all and watch out for my interests.'

'I don't know what you mean.' And, really, I didn't.

'Angus. Remember?'

'What about him?'

'Off limits,' chimed in Gloria, a busty slag with dyed yellow hair . . . although the bottle must have claimed it to be some kind of blonde.

'I told her already. I'm not interested.'

'Didn't look like it just then,' added Sylvia. She was the skinhead of the bunch — and probably the dyke.

Shit. 'That was just a friendly gesture.'

'Friendly isn't the word I'd use,' said Stone Age, stepping intimidatingly closer.

'I was just showing my appreciation. It isn't how it must have looked.' I backed away. That

163

was a mistake. The only thing behind me was the clubhouse. I tried standing so my bike was between us. That was mistake number two.

'We could see you, you bitch,' scoffed Gloria. 'We were watching you the whole time.' Ah. And if I'd known I could have left my bike after all — under the watchful gaze of this lot.

'But it's too dark now to see anything,' I argued.

'There's no wriggling out of it now,' said Gloria, and she pointed at a lamp fastened to the building above my head.

If I had the gumption I pride myself with at times, I would have hopped on the bike, helmet over arm, and fucked off out of there before they could do me any damage. Sod the police and their stupid helmet laws.

Instead, I froze. Stupid bint.

They drew menacingly nearer. I had nowhere to run. My back was against the clubhouse door (kept locked from the inside), and my face was against five goons from a female motorcycle club.

My bike was between us. I started to mount it, but Stone Age gave me one almighty shove causing me to drop the bike and collapse beneath it. The engine was still running and I was going to get my face broken anyway. I should have taken my chances with The Riders. At least men don't fight as dirty as women do.

Pinned beneath Harley I was chicken feed. It was too heavy for me to lift, so all I could do was switch off the engine. My legs were trapped and I protected my head with my helmeted arm. That didn't last long. Someone dragged it off me and hurled it across the car park. Then five pairs of fists rained down onto my skull, alternating with ten sets of talons clawing at my face.

One blow cracked my skull into the concrete floor beneath me, causing all of my teeth to vibrate and a whistling sound in my head. Dirt or gravel ground into my bare hands. I felt a boot in my chest, knocking the wind out of me.

All of my flesh felt on fire . . . another crack on the back of my head as it hit the concrete again . . . and then it all went dark . . .

★   ★   ★

When I woke up I wasn't sure where I was. The last thing I remembered was kissing Angus outside The Den. Now why on earth was I doing that? Somewhere there was a shining light. I was lying on my back, that much I could tell. My vision was a complete and utter blur. I didn't want to open my eyes at all. Was this what having a migraine was like? I'd never had one of those before. No wonder everyone made such a fuss when that happened.

I tried to move. Someone very close to me started to groan. I waited for them to finish and when they did I tried again. But again, someone groaned. A dark shape moved into my field of vision, if you could call it that. I moved once more and my whole body felt as though it was being fed through a mincer.

'I think she's coming to, now,' said the blob into a megaphone. 'Try not to move,' it shouted at me. Try not to *move*? There was no danger of that. I felt so sore. Every muscle throbbed. Every bone ached. Had I been trampled by a herd of elephants? Or maybe I'd driven my bike under a bus.

I was curious to see if I recognised the blob. I screwed up my eyes and creaked my head to one side. Ouch! Bells pealed and cymbals crashed. My vision remained quite blurred and, for a second, I thought there were six blobs instead of one. I've heard of seeing double, but this was ridiculous.

Voices bellowed away somewhere close and the first one I recognised was that of my mother. That's it. I was in a nightmare. I groaned again, realising for the first time that it was me who had been doing it all along.

'I knew you'd come to no good riding around on that horrible motorbike,' she screamed. I wished someone would turn the amps down. 'Nothing but trouble. Well, you're not going out on it again. That's for sure.'

'Hi Mom. Thanks for coming.' Or at least that's what I was trying to say. It probably came out like the mouthful of cotton wool it felt like. I wanted to remind her that I was now thirty two years old and could basically do whatever I liked, with or without her permission. But my face hurt. My mouth hurt. My head hurt. I must have had an accident, and, to be honest, I really didn't fancy the isn't-it-time-you-acted-your-age? argument. I decided on a muffled 'Yeah Mom, I'm fine, thanks for asking,' instead.

'And there's no need for sarcasm either, my lady. I can see precisely that you are *not* fine.'

She caught that part, then.

'Where am I, anyway?' I asked.

'You're at the Midland Hospital.'

Yeah. I guessed I must be in a hospital somewhere. My vision was improving now and I caught a glimpse of her dabbing at her eyes with a hanky. Dad's friendly face appeared over her shoulder, concern written all over it. I started to smile at him, but

167

thought better of it.

'Hi Dad.'

'You take it easy, love,' he said, winking at me. I think he was relieved to see me awake. 'Don't you mind your mother,' he continued kindly, leading her away. 'She's a little upset.'

Yeah, her and me both.

The next pair to pay court were Penny and Richard, still on their honeymoon, I thought for some reason. Maybe they'd become joined at the hip. They were always together these days. I couldn't understand anything. Confused.

'How are you feeling, Marcie?' asked Penny.

'Sore, thanks. Hey, aren't you two in Bali somewhere?'

'No. We're at home, Marcie. Here, with you,' she said, gently.

'Then you must be at work. Why aren't you at work? That's it. You only had the one extra day off work. How come you're not at work? Am I hurt that bad?'

Penny and Richard exchanged a sympathetic look before she answered, and a sick bucket popped into my mind. Then, for a moment, I was sure I was seriously injured. 'Er . . . it's ten thirty,' she said. 'In the evening.'

'Oh, right. So it's Tuesday, is it? How long

have I been out of it?' I could play the wounded soldier as good as the next man.

Again they swapped looks. 'No,' said Richard. 'It's Monday.'

'Monday?' I struggled with that one for a bit. 'So I've been here for a *week*?'

They looked sadly at each other, then to me, and then Penny shook her head. I was glad she wasn't shaking mine. 'I think they brought you in about an hour ago.' She turned to her husband. 'I think she's a bit bewildered.'

'That'll be the concussion,' he agreed. 'Maybe we should let her rest.'

'Hey, I'm still here, you know.'

'Yes, of course you are,' patronised Penny, though not on purpose I was sure. 'We'll come back and see you again tomorrow night.' They smiled and wandered off.

I rolled my head back into the middle of the pillow, which felt like a rock, and closed my eyes. God, I was tired. Someone cleared his throat, making me jump back to life. I must have dozed off. I moved my eyeballs to avoid dislodging my head too much, to see two more people standing by the bed. So there *had* been six of them altogether. I hadn't realised I was so popular.

'Roach!' I exclaimed. 'Angus?' I asked. I'd been in only an hour and already they'd

169

found me. And they were together. I was honoured.

'Um . . . Angus called the ambulance,' said Roach, as though reading my mind.

'Thanks Angus,' I said, dutifully.

'Then he came looking for me so I could let your folks know.'

'Thanks again. What happened? Were you there too?' I really couldn't remember any of the accident.

'Sort of,' said Angus. 'I'd just gone back inside the club. Don't you know?'

'I can't remember. But I must have been hit by a juggernaut the way I feel right now. How's the bike? What's the damage?' I caught the two of them exchanging one of those looks Penny and Richard had. 'I guess it's that bad then, huh?'

'You . . . er . . . got beat up,' said Angus. 'Outside the clubhouse.'

'Who by? How did I do?'

'Don't you really remember?'

I hazarded a guess. 'Stone Age Sal?' She was the only person I could have possibly upset. There was a glimmer of recollection. 'The Cycle Witches. I guess I didn't do so well after all then.'

'Not really. Your mate Ginger was on his way back out and he saw them running off. He almost tripped over you. You . . . er

. . . dropped your bike.'

'Correction,' I interrupted. 'Stone Age dropped my bike.'

'Well, whatever. You were stuck underneath it and it seems he doesn't like the sight of blood much — not anybody's he knows at least.'

'He'll make an ace Rider.'

'He's doing all right. He told me about you and I made the phone call. You know the rest.'

'Thanks,' I repeated.

'You gonna press charges?' asked Roach, carefully.

'Dunno. Will I have to?'

'I don't think so. Only if you remember who it was.'

I took the hint. 'Then I probably won't.' He nodded his approval. Hey, maybe I'd get initiated into the Lucifer Beasts for that.

'Well at least you're all in one piece,' said Angus. 'Stupid bitch. Five onto one? Women don't half fight dirty at times.'

'Ahem,' I said. '*Some* women fight dirty at times.'

'We'll sort it,' said Roach.

'There's really no need — '

'He said we'll sort it,' said Angus.

I was hardly in a position to argue. 'Okay. And thanks again.'

'Any time.'

'I hope not.'

I think I must have started to doze again because the two of them started to make leaving noises. They'd both done the decent thing, and for that I was grateful. They'd even put aside their differences on my account. Two rival bikers chumming it, eh? Can't be bad. And both presidents too.

'I'll be seeing you then,' said Roach.

'Yeah, bye,' said Angus.

'Cheers.'

A nurse popped by to make sure I was comfortable (*comfortable?*), then I finally drifted back off to sleep. At least here there would be no early morning phone calls to wake me up . . . no, here they just shake you awake at six o'clock in the morning instead to make sure you're still alive, and then they tell you to go back to sleep.

I did.

*   *   *

I had always felt quite proud of the fact that I'd never spent a single night in hospital. I wasn't even born in one. I'm one of those people whose bones bend instead of break, and I never seem to get any life threatening diseases, touch wood. I even escaped having my tonsils out when I was eighteen because they, the hospital, forgot to give me enough notice. In those days they wouldn't operate on a pill patient unless she'd been off it for at least four weeks beforehand, other than in an emergency. They gave me four days. These days I believe they'd rather risk whatever the reason was than risk an unwanted pregnancy.

Hospitals have never been my most favourite of places either. I'm sure my parents both think I'm being selfish, but when my dad ended up in hospital with suspected appendicitis, and when Mom went in for her hysterectomy, I just couldn't face the prospect of going to visit them. I left all of that to Penny and waited until they were both safely back home again. I don't know why. I just never liked the idea of hospitals. Fear of the unknown, I suppose, like my fear of the dark. What a wimp.

After the nurse had kindly let me go back to sleep, and when I was allowed to re-wake-up in my own good time, I had nothing better to do than gaze around the ward they'd put me on. I didn't really get much of a chance the night before.

There were twelve beds, most of them empty. In fact, there were only four of us patients in the whole ward: two guys and another woman, all three road traffic accidents by the look of them. I wondered idly if they'd all been involved in the same pile up. It happens sometimes, especially the speed some idiots drive down our over-crowded motorways.

The blokes were sitting up and reading newspapers, one the *Daily Sport*, the other the *Independent*. Well, it takes all sorts, I suppose.

The woman remained lying down, on her back, fidgeting and mumbling every now and then. Perhaps she'd been anaesthetised. Her long blonde hair fanned out across the pillows and her face looked badly bruised. I found myself imagining how my own face must look. I couldn't see anything else of the woman because the quilt was pulled right up to her chin.

At one end of the ward there was a desk island manned by about six people, all in nurses' uniforms, some male and some female. I couldn't be sure how many there were altogether as they kept nipping in and out through one of the many doors that led from that end of the room. I'd always thought that hospital doors came in pairs, but apart from the main entrance to the ward, all of these were single. Aside from the one that was clearly the way out, or in depending on whichever side you're coming from, two led

174

to patients' toilets and one led to an office. I can only guess which the other two were for. One probably led to the operating theatre while the other must have been the recovery room.

Or the morgue.

At the opposite end of the ward there were four more doors: one double set leading to a TV lounge, and another two leading to more toilets. Four toilets. Blimey, we had one each. There was a fire exit too.

All of the woodwork was painted a peach colour while the walls, also glossed, were duck egg blue. Very 1980s. The highly polished floor tiles had peach and green flecks against a sandy background. All of the beds had quilts on them, either in duck egg for the men, or peach for the women. The empty beds had the bedding stacked up neatly at one end.

At each of the twelve windows that flanked the room, one for each bed, was a pair of curtains that didn't look as though it served any purpose. They weren't big enough to join in the middle. They were of a deep orange with a dark green stripe. Sand coloured roller blinds cut out the sunshine when required. It all looked very nicely co-ordinated. I wondered how much the interior designer had cost the health service.

The desk island was made of pale teak wood, and some modern wooden screens shielded a seated area. This was probably for visitors, or for patients waiting to be admitted or collected. This small area was carpeted in deep duck egg blue with peach and sand flecks. A satisfied, peaceful hush hung in the air, not the clinical silence I'd always imagined.

Hey, this place wasn't so bad after all. I'd expected it to be stark and white, but this was quite cosy, if a little dated. I must admit that I wasn't very impressed by the peace and quiet. But apart from that, this was all right. I was almost willing Mom or Dad to go down with something, not too nasty, so I could make amends.

'Good morning, Miss Craig,' sang a black lady nurse who had come to plump up my pillows. 'Or do you prefer Marcella?'

'Morning,' I replied. 'And it's Marcie, thanks.' I recognised her vaguely from the dawn awakening I'd received several hours earlier.

'And how are you feeling?' She spoke with a strong West Indian accent and her bonny face was broken by a dazzlingly white smile. And do you know? She looked genuinely interested.

'A bit stiff. And I ache all over.'

'I should say so. It looks like you took quite a beating.'

I grinned, painfully. 'Yeah, so I gather.' She was okay. Friendly. Not at all how I expected. I must have seen too many Carry On films.

'Do you feel like some breakfast?'

'What have you got?'

'You can have a full breakfast if you want, or we can do you some cereal. Or there's croissants.'

I ran my swollen tongue swiftly around my teeth to make sure they were all still there. They were. And no wobbles either. A choice for breakfast, eh? This was just like the Ritz. 'I didn't think you could have a fry up in hospital.'

The nurse laughed, a deep hearty chortle. 'We grill it I'm afraid, girl. Is that what you want?'

Heck, a grilled, cooked breakfast was just as good as a fried one. 'Do you grill the eggs too?'

She laughed again. 'They're poached.'

I nodded, almost with glee, definitely with pain, and she walked away.

On the wall above the doors leading to the day room there hung a clock. Nine o'clock. Was that all? Who knew how long I had to kill before a doctor came to tell me I could go home.

I thought about calling Penny to ask her to bring me some magazines. Then I remembered she was back at work today. I was a bit more with it than I had been the previous night, but I could remember feeling confused.

I thought about ringing Mom to make sure she went to feed the animals. But then I thought again. She would have remembered to do that anyway, or asked Jackie, my cleaner, to pop in, and she'd be insulted that I felt she needed reminding.

I thought about trying Roach . . . and then I remembered my bike.

17

I tried to get out of the bed but it hurt too much. I must have groaned quite loudly. Both of the men patients glanced over in my direction, and the kindly nurse dashed back to my bedside, her cardigan flapping wildly from the effort. A badge peeped out from under the navy-blue jumper telling me her name was Clarice. I hadn't noticed that before.

'What are you trying to do by getting out of the bed, child?' she scolded.

'I wanted to use the phone.'

'You see this little button here?' She picked up a contraption that had been resting on my locker, and waved it at me. 'You call me with this, but only use the red button in an emergency. I will bring you the payphone, girl. There's no need for you to be walking about the place in your condition.'

'I haven't broken anything, have I?'

'No. But you is badly bruised and you must rest.'

Duly admonished, I let her tuck me back up in bed before she scurried off to fetch me the phone trolley. I scrabbled about in the

179

locker for some change and found a pile of 10p pieces. That would have been Mother, no doubt. Maybe she wasn't such a bad old stick after all.

Roach was out. Either that or he was so fast asleep he couldn't hear the phone. I knew he wasn't due in at work as he'd told me he had the week off. The smell of cooked bacon drew me to my breakfast, which was actually quite good. I might have enjoyed it more if my mouth wasn't so sore — and if I knew where my bike was.

I thought about poor old Harley left on its side outside that hovel and had visions of it being taken apart, piece by piece, never to be seen in one whole again. First the mirrors. Then the badge. Then the handlebars. Then the wheels . . . maybe it was best not to think about it, but I dwelled on it all morning, trying Roach at various intervals.

Dinner was almost as good as breakfast: a plate of lamb chop, mashed potato and peas was brought to my bed by Clarice. She'd covered her uniform up by now with a white, plastic pinafore-type apron, but she kept her watch hung on the outside and the badge was still visible. It seemed that she had been assigned to me for the day, or at least as long as her shift. If I needed anything, I just pressed my little black button and Clarice looked after me. She even helped me to the loo and back. There was no way *I* was using a cardboard bed pan.

A couple more patients were wheeled in throughout the day, both men. The only other woman patient, who had been lying down earlier, had since come to at about half past eleven. Two of the nurses made a bit of a fuss of her, so I assumed she'd had an operation during the night.

At around two o'clock in the afternoon the doctor finally made a guest appearance with some X-rays, which, I assumed, must have been taken the previous evening when I was still unconscious. He looked to be in his early sixties, so I felt safe enough with him, supposing that he must know what he was talking about. The name on his badge was unpronounceable.

'Well, Miss Craig,' he said, jovially. 'And how are we today?'

'Feeling much better, thanks,' I replied, cheerfully. It must have been catching.

He smiled at me but didn't look as though he really meant it. Well, there was years of practice down the drain.

Clarice pulled a curtain around the bed so he could examine me in private. 'You'll be pleased to know that nothing's broken,' he said. Clarice had already told me that much. He had a feel of my abdomen. 'Has she been eating, nurse?'

Could he tell?

'Oh yes, doctor. She managed a full breakfast, and a lunch.'

'No loss of appetite then,' he mused, poking and prodding around my ribs. My trunk was stained a rainbow of shades. No wonder I ached. 'Does that hurt?' he asked, as he was digging three fingers into my diaphragm.

'No,' I replied.

'That?'

'No.'

'And that?'

'No.'

He started to stroke my body then. First my neck. Then my arms. Then my fingers. Bloody pervert. He asked if it all felt roughly the same and I agreed that it had . . . strange fellow.

'Hmm.' He clipped his stethoscope into his ears and had a little listen. 'Breathe in.' I sucked in. 'Breathe out.' I blew out. 'In . . . Out . . . In . . . Okay. Thank you.'

He hummed again as he wrote something on a chart that had been at the foot of my bed. Then he shone a little light into both of my eyes, one at a time, and had a good look at my ears.

'Any dizziness?' I shook my head. 'Nausea?' No. 'Headache?'

'Yes, I've got a cracking headache, doctor.'

'Hmm,' he repeated, snapping the light shut and putting it in his pocket. 'Only to be expected.' *So why ask?*

He examined the cuts around my face and hands and dabbed at my bruises with his fingertips. Then he nodded. 'Well, I can't see any obvious problems.' He sounded almost disappointed. 'You're very badly bruised and you lost consciousness. But you're eating all right and there's no dizziness or nausea.' He wasn't asking this time, but I agreed with him all the same.

'Is there someone to keep an eye on you at home?'

'Yes,' I lied.

'Good. Well, we shan't keep you here any longer than necessary.' No wonder all the beds were empty. 'Get yourself home and take it easy until at least next Monday. Any problems, see your GP. I'll give you some painkillers, and nurse will discharge you just as soon as I've completed my rounds.'

'Okay, doctor. Thank you.'

He pasted that smile across his face again, so I pasted one across my own too. Then he moved on to the next occupied bed.

Phew. That was a relief. I could go home. I

had to wait until he'd finished so I spent the time trying to get hold of someone — anyone — on the phone who could come and get me. They were all out. All two of them, which surprised me a little, because Mom and Dad never go anywhere without telling you first.

Maybe they were around at my place. I called my own number but nobody answered.

I checked the clock. Almost visiting time. So I waited for someone to come in and visit me.

★　★　★

At three o'clock, Roach walked in.

'Hi Marcie.'

'Hi Roach. Where's my bike?'

He roared with laughter, causing everyone else on the ward to look. 'Yes, I know it's good of me to drop by, but it's no sweat, honest. You're obviously feeling much better this afternoon.'

'I've been ringing you all day. Where's my bike? I've been worried sick.'

'It's in your lock-up. Me and Angus took it back between us, before coming up to see you last night.' He took some keys from his pocket and placed them on the locker. They were my keys. 'That prospect of theirs offered to put it in his dad's garage, but Angus didn't

184

think you'd appreciate that very much.'

'Cheers.' How perceptive of Angus.

'So, how are you feeling?'

'Doc says I can go home.'

'Great. So how come you're not dressed?' He glanced down at the white gown I was wearing, generously provided by the hospital and not at all flattering.

'I couldn't get hold of anyone to come and collect me.'

'Right. So where are your clothes?'

I shrugged. 'I dunno. In the locker I suppose.'

'Are you ready to go home?' he asked, bending down to retrieve my things from the cupboard.

'I'll say. My body's crying out for a nice, hot bath.'

He pulled a face. 'Hurting that bad, then?'

'No, not really. It just aches. All over. I just fancy a good old soak.'

'Are you up to riding behind me on the back of my bike?'

I grimaced, but agreed. 'I think so.'

He tossed my clothes onto the bed. 'You can't wear them. They're covered in blood.' I hadn't realised. 'Do you want me to go and collect you some clean stuff? Then I can come back in your Jeep and you can go home in style.'

That was a good idea. And quite

thoughtful. 'Do you mind?'

'Course not.'

An embarrassed pause followed for some reason, during which he remembered he'd brought something with him — for me.

'Here. I've brought you something to read,' he said, holding out a crumpled carrier bag. Why do men never use the handles that come with these things? They always have to twist and screw them up, and then throttle them with their fists. 'It'll give you something to do while I go over to your place and back.'

'Thanks,' I said, taking the bag from him. Inside was a hastily written card — To MARCIE, GET WELL SOON, LOVE ROACH xxx — a box of Milk Tray and about half a dozen bike and music magazines. 'Thanks,' I said again, this time with more enthusiasm. 'I could've done with this lot this morning.'

He was just about to leave me to my new-found entertainment, and start his 30 mile round trip, when in walked Angus, looking as white as a sheet. I'd heard the expression, but this was the first time I'd ever seen it in action.

'What's up with you?' I asked.

'It's Daisy,' he replied, the hand clutching a bunch of tulips hanging limply by his side.

'What about Daisy?'

'She's dead.'

18

'What do you mean, she's dead?'

'I mean, someone killed her. Last night.'

'Oh my God.' I sank back down on the bed. 'I don't believe you. Daisy? Dead?' But Angus wasn't joking. I could tell by his face. And anyway, it would have been a pretty sick joke.

'Where?' asked Roach, simply.

'At the back of The Cellar.'

'How?'

'The same as before. A blow to the side of the head.'

'It's the same person, isn't it?' I realised. 'Whoever killed Gavin also killed Daisy.' I didn't feel sick or anything. Maybe it was the shock. Maybe I was feeling kicked about enough. It just wouldn't sink in.

Just then I noticed two uniformed coppers hovering at the end of my bed. 'What the hell do you lot want now?' I snapped. A disgusted hiss escaped from Roach's lips and he gave me a filthy look. 'Well I didn't invite them.'

The younger copper raised an eyebrow, while the other cleared his throat and spoke. 'We've come to ask you a few questions about last night,' he said. They'd both removed their helmets and stood there bare headed. Both had close-cropped hair, one fair one dark. The dark one was slightly older. Aside from the lines just beginning to show on his face, his sideburns were also tinged with grey.

'What about last night?'

'We wondered if you'd like to make a statement,' said sideburns.

'I got beat up. Very foolish of me.'

'Did you recognise your attacker?' Maybe blondie didn't know how to talk. Or he'd just come along to take notes.

'No.'

Angus and Roach each pulled up a visitor's chair and sat. I remained perched on the edge of the bed. The policemen stood.

'Would you remember them again?'

'No.'

'Are you sure, Miss?'

'Look, I've just been told that one of the nicest ladies on this planet has been found dead, murdered. And you've come in here to ask about last night? I don't believe it. Don't you have a murderer to find?'

'Aside from it being routine, Miss,' continued the older one, 'we also need to find out if this event is at all connected to another . . . er . . . event, which happened shortly afterwards, we believe.'

'They already caught me on the way in here,' added Angus. 'They wanted to know where I was, between ten and twelve last night.'

'He was here, with us,' blurted Roach.

'Yeah,' I agreed, although I'd had no idea of the time.

'Can anyone vouch for you being here?' the old one asked Roach.

'He just said,' said Angus. 'We were all together.'

'Hmm,' piped up the younger one, at last. 'Very convenient.'

'Just ask the hospital staff if you don't believe us,' Angus spat.

'And what about your own attacker, Miss?' asked sideburns.

'Look, you should be out there looking for Daisy and Gavin's killer, not wasting time in here over something so petty.'

'Daisy and Gavin?' he asked.

'Yes sir.' Obviously rank went with age. 'Er . . . 'Daisy' was the . . . other event yesterday evening. And 'Gavin' was the young homosexual they found outside the fire door at the back of The Cellar on Good Friday. Sir.'

'But they've got somebody for that one, haven't they?'

'Yes,' I interjected on the young constable's behalf. 'But they made a mistake.'

'How can you be certain they were the same person, Miss?'

'Because Daisy knew who Gavin's killer was.'

'So why didn't she come to us?'

'Because she was frightened for her life,' I hissed. 'And judging by what happened to her last night, she had good reason.'

A silence descended around my hospital bed. It still wouldn't sink in. Daisy was dead. She knew her killer. Which was probably how she got herself killed.

'So, Miss,' continued the senior officer at last. 'About last night.'

'I don't know who it was, why they did it, where they came from or where they went to. And no, I probably wouldn't know them again. It was dark and I banged my head. Amnesia.' I fixed my face into a sweet smile, and still it hurt.

'But do you wish to press charges?'

'No.'

'Or make a claim?'

'No. Thank you.'

'Very well.' Blondie snapped shut his notebook. 'Then we'll wish you good day.'

'Just get out there and find Daisy's killer. Before he kills again.' They exchanged one of those looks that say the public simply don't appreciate them, and as they disappeared

190

around the wooden screen, I turned to Angus and Roach. 'They have to let Woodstock go now, don't they?'

Roach shrugged. 'Dunno.'

Angus said: 'They told me any new information couldn't be presented until the trial. So they still might keep him in until then.'

'Unless they find out who really did it,' I mused. 'With a confession.'

Now the nausea set in. I was pretty sure it had nothing to do with the bump on my head. This latest piece of news was a bummer. I felt sick to the pit of my stomach. I expect Roach and Angus did too. We were all very fond of Daisy. It was different with Gavin. I didn't know him. But Daisy was a friend. A tart maybe, but a kind hearted, affectionate tart. I dropped back onto my arms.

No wonder she had a regular base of clients. Her punters always kept on coming back for more. They couldn't get enough of her. None of us could. And none of us ever would again.

Somewhere, in what seemed like my distant memory, I remembered something Daisy had said. Was it really only yesterday? I must have had some terrific bump on the head. I still couldn't remember much from the previous day. But this came to me from out of nowhere.

'Find out how he died . . . Three years ago . . . And everything else will fall into place . . . '

I shot back up to an upright position. Did I cause Daisy's death? I hadn't repeated anything she'd said to me to anyone. So maybe the person who killed Gavin had already found out that Daisy knew.

My head hurt like hell as I racked my brains. It had only been yesterday afternoon that I'd seen her, for heaven's sake. Where was she going? To see a client. Could it have been 'him'?

I climbed off the bed before remembering the fashionable white gown, loaned to me by the hospital, gaped at the back. Fortunately I did still have my knickers on, and although Angus had the decency to smile and look away, Roach made a great show of leering with his eyes *and* tongue hanging out.

'Why don't you make yourself useful and pull the curtain around, or something?' I suggested. Visiting time must have almost been over, but Angus had not long got here, just before the police, and Roach was my lift home.

'What're you doin'?' asked Roach now.

'I'm getting out of here.'

He got up, pulled the curtain around the bed, but continued to stand just inside.

'I'd better be off,' said Angus, dragging his chair through a gap in the curtain. He was still holding the flowers. 'Here, these are for you.'

'Thanks,' I said, taking them off him and placing them on the bed next to Roach's bag. 'And thanks for coming,' I called after him. 'See you around.'

'Sure.' I presume he mooched off home. I had no idea what Angus did with his time. Then I caught sight of Roach, still loitering.

'Do you mind, Roach?'

He gave an innocent little shrug and pulled a face, but stepped outside the cubicle anyway. I found my clothes again, which were crumpled and caked with dirt and blood, but winced myself into them in any case.

'What's going on in here?' asked Nurse Clarice as she tugged open the curtain. I was just easing into my tee shirt, which meant I was decent at least, but she pulled the curtain shut again regardless. She looked me up and down while I pulled on my boots. 'You ain't leaving?'

'I sure am.'

'But the doctor said — '

'The doctor said I could go.'

'But I still have to discharge you officially, first.'

'Sorry Clarice, but you were too slow. You've had a good two hours.' I fastened my watch. 'I'm discharging myself.'

'I thought you liked it here,' she said, as though it was a hotel, and it was so nice I felt like it was. I thought I caught a sad glimmer cross her face. Shit. I didn't mean to upset her.

'Look, Clarice, you've been really great and I have enjoyed myself. You've looked after me while I've been here. In fact, next time I get into a fight, I'll just go ahead and check myself back in again. But a friend of mine got herself killed last night while I was in here and I need to find out what happened. Is there a register of deaths in here?' I remembered that Daisy had said something about a hospital.

'She won't be in there yet if she only died last night.'

'Yeah,' I laughed. 'I know. But it might help me find out who her killer was — '

'You mean she was murdered?' Her eyes grew wider with surprise and the whites gleamed against her lovely black skin.

'Er . . . yeah.'

'But what's it got to do with you, child? Surely it's a police matter?'

'Yeah,' I repeated. 'You would have thought so, wouldn't you?' I reached for my leather jacket, flinching from the pain. 'But if the police hadn't locked up the wrong man by mistake, and if they'd continued to look for the killer he got framed for, then my friend might still be alive.'

'You mean there have been *two* murders?' I nodded while dragging an afro comb painfully through my long, tangled curls, and shrugged into my leather. Clarice let out a low whistle and opened the curtains. My armpits felt sticky and my teeth wanted a brush, but I needed to find out that information. Clarice went and got some paperwork from the main desk.

'So do you keep a death register here or not?' I asked her while she checked me out and gave me a prescription for my painkillers. I gathered together my things and clutched them to my chest.

'We'll only have the deaths — and births — that happened here in this hospital. There are some archives too, from other hospitals that were swallowed up by this one. Or you could try the registry office. You'll find our deaths in a nasty little cupboard, one you can walk in.' She handed me a sick note that would take me through to next Monday.

'Okay, thanks Clarice. I hope I don't see you again soon.'

'Me too,' she grinned. 'Records are over in the other building. Good luck.'

'Cheers. Come on you,' I added to Roach, who had made himself comfy in the next, non-existent patient's easy chair. He put down the magazine he'd been reading and followed me like a lost sheep.

'What're you gonna do then, Marcie?'

'Something I should have done before steaming off to see Angus. What time is it?' I asked absently, while also looking at my watch.

'Close on half four,' he replied, unnecessarily.

'Damn.' That meant everyone would be going home soon and I might get locked in. 'I'll have to come back tomorrow.'

'Are you sure you feel up to travelling on the back of me bike?' He jangled my keys in his hand. I would have left them behind. 'I was going to get your Jeep before the bacon arrived.'

Actually, I wasn't feeling up to it after all, and after he'd waited too. 'Nah, sorry. I think I'll be better in a taxi. But thanks for hanging around.'

'Okay,' he said, handing me my keys. 'Take care of yourself and I'll come over and see you tomorrow instead.'

'I'll be coming up here for a bit in the morning,' I said.

'What for?'

'Long story. I'll fill you in tomorrow.'

'Okay then.'

'Tarrar.' He lumbered off to collect his bike and I headed off in search of a taxi rank.

Back home I ran myself a nice, hot bath and stayed in there until the water went cold. Then I let all the cold water out and filled it up again with hot. Luxury. I must have been snoozing while the hot water eased out my poor, aching muscles, when the telephone rang rudely.

'Yeah?' I said, dripping all over the kitchen floor. I'd already flooded the hall.

'Marcella!' It was Mother. 'We have come all the way over here to visit you at the hospital and you've only discharged yourself.'

Oh God.

19

The next morning, feeling stiffer than ever, though I told myself it would have been worse if I hadn't had the bath, I took the Jeep into town and parked up at the hospital. I'd managed to squeeze into an old navy blue skirt and a white blouse and, apart from my face, which was a delightful mix of pale yellow, blue and brown, I thought I looked quite the little filing clerk. I blended into the background nicely.

The Midland Hospital is a maze of corridors within a maze of buildings. I think it must have started out in life as one of those cottage hospitals, and as nearby houses became vacant they were commandeered by the National Health Service. Most of the older buildings are now empty and derelict.

What was once a good sized car park is now a building site, while the local health authority makes an attempt to house all of the services under one roof. 'Centralising' I think they call it, though anyone who lives on the opposite side of town might not necessarily agree.

At least the hospital was busy, which

helped with my own camouflage and it was well signposted too. The corridors were draughty, but I didn't come across any patients on trolleys left lying around as frequently reported in one particular Birmingham hospital — a relative of mine being one example.

The ward I'd been in, in Accident and Emergency, was in the new block, hence my pleasant surroundings the day before. Clarice had told me that the deaths register was in the next building, attached to this one via a bridge link. I got my bearings and followed the signs for MEDICAL RECORDS. No-one stopped me and any funny looks were double takes at my face. Maybe I would stand out after all.

I found the births and deaths registers together in the same little room. Clarice had called it a cupboard. I could see why. Medical Records were actually further on, but I had neither the inclination nor the authorisation to go looking through anybody's personal notes — or not yet anyway. I didn't have a name for a start. There was no security surrounding this little room and it seemed that anyone who really wanted to could go inside and have a good look around.

So I did.

The walls, three of them, were lined with

floor to ceiling shelves and piled up on every single shelf were loads of big fat ledgers, probably about fifteen by eighteen inches in size, and mostly roughly four inches thick. Each ledger had a date span, in year form, written in marker pen on the bound edge. They hadn't even bothered to keep a single year in a single ledger, just kept on filling up the book until they couldn't get any more in.

The ledgers were made up of a hard front cover and back cover, with loose leaf pages that were added in as necessary, the most recent on the top. The pages were secured by three metal posts with a plastic cap snapped onto the top. The posts went through the front cover too, which is where the caps popped into position, but they were secured on a metal bar built into the back cover. Some ledgers had lost or broken at least one cap but, generally, they were intact.

Every pile of ledgers was topped with a thick film of dust which, as I disturbed the books, went straight up my nose to settle at the back of my throat. The way it stung made me think I must have had at least one punch on the nose the other night. The ledgers were in no particular order. It seemed that whoever used them found the year they wanted and just replaced it where they could when they'd finished with it, leaving a pattern of finger prints in the grime.

Three years ago Daisy had said. I found the one I wanted. Nineteen ninety three was sandwiched between the whole of 1992 and the first part of 1994. Fortunately it wasn't on a high shelf or under a mound of others, and it wasn't quite four inches thick either, thank God. Nevertheless I guessed it would still take ages to plough through.

The entries were written in chronological order and I had no idea what time of year whoever he was had died. I nicknamed him Jasper for my own benefit. That was the name of my last cat before Sylvester. I found the beginning of 1993 and began, hoping I wouldn't slip into 1994 by mistake. This was going to take me forever.

I figured, well hoped, that as we were still in April now, maybe Daisy meant April three years ago. But, as I pored over the lists of names (phew! a lot of people must die in hospital), I didn't spot a single one I recognised. There were plenty of Smiths, Jones and Singhs, but nothing sprang to mind. I even checked the few months on either side of my year, just to make sure. Nothing.

My head was hurting, my chest was aching, and the dust was stinging my eyes now, as well as my nose and throat. I needed a drink and a wash. It was no good. I'd have to come back another time. I'd been there more than three hours already by the time I realised. Time to go home and get changed. I felt a bit daft in my sensible clothes, particularly as they were now so dirty. They weren't very me at all. I must have looked a right tramp. Jasper would have to wait for now. Well, he wasn't really going anywhere, was he?

I drove home, got washed and changed, had a late dinner, then went to Roach's for the rest of the afternoon.

'Did you find what you wanted?' he asked.

Again I'd declined his offer of refreshment. 'No chance.'

'How're you feeling?'

'Stiff and sore still. And I'm going to have a bad back an'all.'

'What is it you're looking for?'

'Someone who died three years ago.'

'What's their name?'

'Dunno.' I explained to him about my own personal name tag for him.

'So when, three years ago, did your Jasper die?'

'Dunno.'

'Do you know where he died?'

Suddenly it came back to me like a bombshell. I hadn't remembered before. Before I even said the words I realised my mistake. 'The Royal Infirmary . . . '

Roach, unfortunately, didn't know when it was a good idea to keep his mouth shut. 'So why check the records at the Midland?' he asked, somewhat unnecessarily.

I felt stupid. 'I know. I've just wasted the whole of this morning, haven't I?'

'Maybe they'll let you check the records at the Royal?'

'Hardly.' I felt my shoulders sag further. 'They closed it down last year.' Birmingham hospitals had been quite badly hit in the cuts over the past few years. Probably like most places.

'Shit,' said Roach.

We spent the next half an hour or so in companionable silence as we both brooded with our own thoughts.

Roach's living room was a mess, as usual, with empty beer cans strewn about the place and ashtrays spilling over with nub-ends of fags and joints — the joints having been smoked to within a fraction of an inch of their lives. The carpet looked like it hadn't seen a vacuum cleaner in months and may have been a rusty brown colour once. I could see it competing with what the carpet in The Cellar used to be like. One end of the room was stacked high with expensive hi-fi equipment, colour television, video recorder and cable TV box.

The brown three piece suite sagged in the middle of every cushion, and a wall mounted gas fire had one of its radiants cracked — probably the result of someone's boot. Nicotine stained curtains hung at the bay window where a piece of cardboard had been Sellotaped over a broken pane. The ceiling was also a thin beige colour and probably stained with yet more nicotine. The room smelled of stale smoke, stale dope, and stale ale.

'You live like pigs,' I said finally, unable to stop the rush of words. 'My place might be untidy but at least it's clean.'

Roach shrugged. 'It's somewhere to doss down, isn't it?' Knowing how much the house had cost him I was surprised he treated it with such little respect.

'You could at least Hoover up occasionally.' I don't generally like to wear my boots inside the house — any house — but there was no way I'd risk this place in just my socks. I wouldn't know what I was stepping in. Roach's own socks, ex-white sports socks with a little red ring around the top, were black all across the bottom. For some unknown reason I suddenly remembered Woodstock. 'Can I use your phone?'

'Sure. Help yourself.'

Roach's phone is in the hall next to the front door. It's one of those trim phones that became popular in the 1970s. I was jealous of all my friends who had the latest design when my mom and dad still had one with a bell. They still have it now and it's probably worth more than any of the new ones. Funny that. All the mod cons Roach has in his house, he couldn't be bothered to update the phone. At least it was working.

I called DS MacGregor. Luckily he was in.

'Hallo Marcie. How're you?' Wow. I'd finally graduated from *Miss Craig*.

'I'm fine thanks,' I lied. I didn't even know if he knew I'd been in hospital, and I didn't want any lectures from a copper.

'What can I do for you?' asked the Scotch baritone.

'I was wondering when Woodstock might be allowed home, so we can go and get him — if he hasn't already, that is.'

There was a very brief pause. 'Your friend Palmer won't be out for a long while yet.'

'Why not? You must know he's innocent now.'

'Why?'

'Because of Daisy. He couldn't have killed Daisy if he was locked up, could he?'

'No, but — '

'So you can't keep him locked up any more, can you?'

There was another pause. 'He still killed the boyfriend — '

'How can he have? Whoever killed Gavin also killed Daisy. And Woodstock couldn't have killed Daisy, so he can't have killed Gavin.' It made perfect sense to me.

MacGregor sighed loudly down the phone. 'What makes you think they were the same person?'

'It's obvious isn't it? Both crimes were exactly the same. A blow to the side of the head. At the back of The Cellar. At the same time of night.'

He sighed again. 'You are remarkably well informed. But just because they are similar, it doesn't make them the same. Anyone could have copied the first crime. It was well documented by the press. I'm afraid Palmer remains locked up. We've got Gavin's killer, Miss Craig.' Whoops. I'd slipped back down the ranks again. Well, I didn't care.

'But I have someone who swears Gavin was still alive when Woodstock left him.'

'Then I suggest you ask him to give his statement to DC Anderson — '

'He tried. No-one had time to talk to him.'

'Did he talk to DC Anderson?'

'No.'

'Then I suggest he tries again.'

'And then will you let him go?'

'No.' He sighed once more, clearly losing his patience with me . . . once more. 'All of the evidence will be produced at the trial. It's out of our hands now.'

'Thanks a lot,' I snapped, and banged down the receiver.

'Any joy?' asked Roach, cleaning out his fingernails with a penknife and letting the bits fall to the floor.

'No chance. Woodstock stays in jail until at least the trial. But you can still go and give your statement to DC Anderson.'

'Okay. Now will you let me cook you some tea?'

I glanced around at the hovel he lived in and remembered the worse state in the kitchen. He looked so hopeful.

'Okay,' I said. 'But you can do it round at my place.' I made a mental note to suggest he take a shower too. He wasn't cleaning his nails in my house.

20

To this day I have never known how men can spend two minutes in a bathroom and still leave it looking like a bomb site. What a mess.

I know most of my place would look like this most of the time if it weren't for Jackie, but I do like a clean and tidy bathroom. Maybe it's because this is the smallest room in the house and gets cluttered easily. Maybe I'm a cleanaholic at heart (fat chance) and have simply never noticed. But Roach didn't have any excuse. All he had to do was switch the shower on, step inside, switch it off, step outside again, and leave the room.

I'd left him having his shower while I had a lie down on my bed. The morning had been too much and I was knackered. When I heard him finish in the bathroom and switch the radio on in the kitchen, I padded into the bathroom for my turn. What a nightmare.

Roach's clothes were strewn across the floor. Boots. Grubby socks. Sweatshirt. Oily jeans. Leather jacket. Denim cut-off. He'd managed to soak three towels. There was a piece of soap lodged in the plughole, embedded with toe-nail clippings. And every single item of shower gel, talcum powder, deodorant and toothpaste had been opened up, squirted everywhere, and then abandoned.

Lids of varying sizes littered every available surface. And he'd left long, black bristles in my Ladyshave. Bastard. He would have soon complained if I'd shaved my armpits with his razor. Thank heavens he didn't need to use my hairbrush too, him having a shaved head . . . I glanced again at the Ladyshave, but shook away that unpleasant thought.

I spent a good twenty minutes tidying up before I could run myself a bath. Once submerged, however, in the fruit-scented, frothy water, I was finally able to relax and wind down. I don't know how long I lay there warming my poor aching body, but the delicious aroma of melted cheese soon dragged me back to the land of the living. I was suddenly hungry again. How come I never seem to lose my appetite?

As my belly grumbled, quite painfully in fact, I quickly washed myself and ducked my head backwards under the water, managing to get soapy stuff in my eyes. I felt around for a towel, then remembered they were all soaking wet and now in the dirty laundry basket. The nearest fresh ones were in a cupboard down the hall. I groaned. With

Roach in the house, or caravan, there was no way I was going to fetch a clean towel in the buff.

Making do with the best of a bad lot in the basket, I cleaned my eyes and wrapped my head in one very wet towel and used one that was merely quite damp to rub myself dry. I dusted on some talc and reached for my bathrobe hanging on the back of the door. It's lemon and white to match the bathroom . . . but it wasn't there. Mother must have 'tidied it up' somewhere else when she was here looking after the animals. Or maybe I'd simply forgotten to put it back before going to bed the night before.

Wrapped in the damp towel, I dashed back up the hall into my bedroom and changed into a sloppy, comfortable tracksuit I normally keep for doss days. Then I made my way to the front of the caravan.

Towards the back of the van there are the two bedrooms — a good-sized double (mine) and a tiny twin — the bathroom, an airing cupboard and the central heating boiler. There's also a small lobby, or hall, where there's an unused telephone point and another cupboard. At the front is a nice sized lounge with a bay window overlooking the park, and a separate, small dining area. All of the furniture came with the van when I bought it and is probably starting to look a bit shabby. I only had to buy the portable stuff, telly, video, stereo, stuff like that.

In the middle of the van, right at the centre of things, is an enormous fitted breakfast kitchen with all mod-cons, split level oven — rarely used — hob, microwave, washing machine. Again, everything came included so I reckon I got a good deal.

It was in the kitchen, where he was cooking, that I finally caught up with Roach, that delicious smell, and my bathrobe. He was standing barefoot, wearing one of Jackie's pinnies over the robe, which in turn he was wearing over his Motörhead tee shirt and Tasmanian Devil boxer shorts.

'Very sexy,' I said, sarcastically. 'What on earth are you doing wearing that?'

He looked down at himself, saucepan in one hand, spatula dripping cheese sauce onto the floor tiles in the other, lemon and white bathrobe straining to cover his body, apron covering what the bathrobe didn't. Then he grinned back at me.

'S'all right, innit?' he proudly asked. 'I was keeping my clothes clean.' I glanced at the grubby tee shirt and tried not to imagine the boxers. Keeping the food clean more like, I thought, 'Do you think it suits me?'

'Oh yeah. I'll be borrowing your eyeliner

pencil next.' I wandered over to the stove, avoiding the globs of sauce on the floor, redirected his hand with the spatula back over the pan, and peered into one of the other pans. There was a kind of sick-coloured lumpy goo in there, but it smelled good. 'What're you cooking?'

'Macaroni cheese. Is that okay?'

'There's a frozen one in the freezer.'

'Yeah, I know. But it's much better this way.'

He'd bought the ingredients on the way, when we stopped at the One Stop. He certainly wouldn't have found anything in my pantry.

'What time will it be ready?'

He checked the clock and sniffed one of the pans — the one with the puke in. 'Probably about ten minutes.'

At about that point Sylvester started circling my ankles. He could probably smell the cheese, which meant the mice could too. I decided to feed them, and the fish. Then I went into the living room. Roach followed me leaving tea simmering on the stove, switched on the telly and started flicking through the Cable channels.

I subscribed to Cable when a trial offer for three months came through the door, when it first came to Birmingham. After the initial three months I'd cancelled my subscription. They stopped taking their money out of my bank account but forgot to switch my Cable off, leaving the equipment in case I changed my mind. I keep it all at the moment, free of charge. One of these days I'm going to be halfway through a film and they'll suddenly realise, cutting me off at the crucial point, leaving poor old me high and dry. I just forget to remind them that I've still got it when I'm not paying for it in case they send me a whopping great bill for all the backdated airtime I've been enjoying.

Roach sprawled across the floor and I was glad of the pinnie, to protect my carpet. Spreading out on the floor was probably a luxury for him, judging by his own living room floor. If Jackie hadn't been in that day to tidy up, it being a Wednesday, there probably wouldn't have been any room for him to sprawl in anyway.

As he flicked through the channels he caught sight of a babe with her band on MTV. He couldn't tear his eyes away from the boobs almost spilling out of her leather waistcoat. Actually, her band wasn't so bad and I made a note of their name and a mental note to order their new CD, if it was out yet.

There were clues all over the place, but I still didn't realise there was something else that I'd forgotten . . .

When the babe and her band made way for Bon Jovi, Roach got bored and went to finish tea. Not exactly a man's band is Bon Jovi. Well, not that they'd admit it.

21

Tea, surprisingly, was actually quite tasty. I hadn't realised he was such a good cook. We settled down in front of the telly, but at about twenty-five to eight, the phone rang. In case it was Mother again, I got Roach to answer it.

'Yeah? Oh, hallo Ken . . . ' his chin bounced off the floor a couple of times and it only took me a second to realise which Ken he was talking to — particularly as I only know one. 'Yeah, that's right. It's Roach. No . . . er . . . didn't anyone tell you? Marcie was in an accident on Monday night. Yeah, she's doing all right.'

Shit. I'd forgotten to call the pub to let Pendle know I was on the sick for a week or so. Roach held the telephone receiver a good few inches away from his ear while Pendle ranted on. When he finally paused to draw breath, Roach continued.

'Look, I'm sure Marcie would have called you herself, only she's flat on her back in bed,' he lied. 'Me? I'm just keeping an eye on her. Yes, of course she knows I'm here.' He pulled a face. 'Yeah, I'm sure she'll be up and about again by the morning. I'll get her to call

215

you, shall I? Okay. See you . . . and sorry — '

By the look on his face Pendle had hung up on him. First my sister's wedding. Then telling Mom and Dad I was out of hospital. And now work. My memory was getting worse.

'Thanks, Roach,' I said, genuinely grateful.

He replaced the receiver in its cradle. 'Jesus, Marcie, fancy not ringing in sick. You'll lose that job if you're not careful. Have you told Barney's yet?'

'No, but I will do. Anyway, I won't lose that job at all. I've been there too long — longer than Pendle even.' Ken Pendle had only been there for about two years, while I'd been there for the whole of my career. Thirteen years. 'He'll have cooled off by the morning, and then he'll be like a pussycat,' I predicted, correctly.

I told Roach he could stay the night if he wanted, in the spare room of course. But he preferred to ride all that way home instead. He probably had some dope back there that needed smoking. I wondered idly if he really would give up the dealing.

⋆　⋆　⋆

The next day was Thursday and I slept in late, which is unusual for me despite what my

216

mom thinks. It had gone half past eleven by the time I surfaced. Those pills Clarice gave me must have been something.

My doorbell rang just as I was sinking my teeth into a bacon sarnie. I had to wipe the melted butter off my chin before answering it. It was Ken Pendle, my boss, bearing fruit and flowers. And he was sober too.

'Hallo Marcie. You're in then?' he said. I looked down at myself and then, pointedly, at my surroundings. 'What the fuck happened to your face?' he said, before I could open my mouth.

I remembered what Roach had said the night before about me losing my job and remembered my manners at pretty much the same time, putting the brakes on the sarcasm and choosing humble grovelling instead.

'I'm sorry no-one called you, Ken. Only I was out for the count.' I stepped aside and opened the door a bit wider so he could come in. 'I suppose it never occurred to anyone that you might need to know where I was.' The gabbling continued to spew forth as I ushered him into the lounge.

'Nah, don't worry about it,' he said absently as he took a good look at my kitchen on the way through. 'Roach told me last night on the phone. It's not your fault. How are you feeling anyway?'

'Sore,' I grimaced. 'But happy to be home.' The wind had blown his thick thatch of grey-blond hair all over the place. He seemed okay. I'd gone to bed in last night's tracksuit and was still wearing it, so I felt a bit scruffy, but at least I was decent. I might have been a bit smelly too and I hadn't cleaned my teeth yet. If I stayed far enough away from him, he might not notice. He stood nervously in the middle of the lounge.

'I would have come to see you at the hospital, only I didn't know.' He sounded hurt, but passed me the goodies anyway. 'Here. These are for you.'

'Thanks.' I went back into the kitchen to put the flowers in the sink and left the fruit on the side before switching on the kettle. My jaw was still a bit tender to be munching on apples, but I was sure I could manage the grapes. Pendle hovered in the doorway until I told him to sit down. I followed him into the living room and joined him on the settee. 'I wasn't in the hospital that long anyway.'

'You still look pretty rough,' he complained.

'Cheers,' I said. 'You should have seen the other guys. Actually, it looks much more gruesome than it is. Yesterday was the worst.' I lifted my chin like a brave little soldier so he could have a good look. The bruises were

218

beginning to fade to a more flattering beige by this time. 'It's much better now.'

'What happened?'

'I got beat up.'

'Who by?'

'I dunno.' I wasn't grassing Sal and her cronies to Pendle. He'd probably go all heroic and bar them from the pub, which would drop me in even deeper trouble with them.

'Did they do much damage?'

'Only what you can see. Concussion and a few cuts and bruises.'

I heard the kettle click and went to make us a drink. I know Pendle likes a cup of coffee. I'd made enough for him at the pub whenever he was on the wagon, so I knew how he liked it.

'I'm surprised they let you out so soon,' he said when I came back, taking the mug with both hands.

'Yeah well, I couldn't have stood being cooped up in that place a moment longer than necessary once I heard about Daisy — '

'You know about that already?' He reached into his trouser pocket and began fiddling with his little silver balls.

'You found them then?' I asked.

'Nah. This is a new set. I don't know what happened to the others. Who told you?'

I was puzzled. 'About your balls?'

'No. Daisy.'

'Oh, Angus came to tell me and the police confirmed it about five minutes later. They came in to ask me who beat me up on Monday.' A thought dawned on me. 'How long did they close the pub up for this time?'

'We were back open for business by Tuesday teatime. They took less than twenty-four hours.' He rolled the balls around in his palm and they tinkled merrily.

'I went to see Woodstock on Friday,' I said, changing the subject neatly, I thought.

'What for?' The clinking stopped momentarily, but he started again.

'Because he asked me to.' I took a swig of my hot, sugary tea. 'They should be letting him out now.'

'Why ever for?' He blew on his coffee before taking a mouthful, and the balls clinked in his hand.

'Because the person who killed Gavin also killed Daisy. Woodstock couldn't have done it because he was inside when Daisy got done.'

'When are they letting him out?' *Chink! Chink! Chink!*

'They're not. That's the problem. They think he did the first one and someone else copied him with the second.'

'Then he's in the right place. Serves him right.'

'But he didn't do it.'

'You're good friends with this Woodstock then?'

'I've known him a long time, yes. In fact, when he comes out — '

'*If* he comes out,' corrected Pendle.

'*When* he comes out,' I corrected right back, 'I might see if he wants to stay here with me for a bit.'

'Here?'

'Yes. I don't suppose his landlady will want him back after this. It wouldn't surprise me if she's already let his room and bagged up his belongings. It'll be nothing new to Woody. He never stays in one place longer than five minutes.

'You'd let him stay here?' He sounded horrified, looked wildly about him at his surroundings, and clinked mercilessly with the pair of balls.

'Yeah. Why not?'

'Because he's gay.'

'Ken, Woody's not gay and you know that as well as I do.' The words sounded strange coming from my mouth. They sounded strange full stop.

'But I saw him.'

'You saw him once. He was drunk. Was experimenting. He didn't know what he was doing. Whichever way you look at it. How

221

many women have you seen him with?' There was no answer. 'How many times have you seen him with a bird?' Still no answer. 'You were part of his little charade and you kept it to yourself, kept his sordid little secret. So don't try to tell me any different.' I paused for a breath and we both gulped at our drinks, more for something to do with ourselves than for thirst, I imagine. 'And anyway,' I added. 'So what if he *is* gay? What business is it of yours?'

'I worry about people.' *Clink! Clink! Clink!* 'You might catch something.'

'Like what?' Did he think Woodstock had the lurgy or something?

'Well . . . like AIDS.'

I burst out laughing. 'Rubbish!' I snorted. 'I won't be sleeping with him, Ken.' Or not in the near future at any rate. But I kept that to myself. 'You can't catch AIDS just by sharing the same space.'

'No, of course not. But he might be a drug addict. You can catch it from the needle.'

I remembered the hypodermic needle we'd found next to Gavin's body, and the poly bags filled with pills that had Roach's fingerprints all over them. I didn't really blame Ken for tarring us all with the same brush. But, as I'd recently found out for myself, you never can tell, can you?

I leaned forward towards Pendle. 'Ken, even if Woodstock is a user, or an addict, and I'm not really sure that he isn't, I can assure you that I am not. So unless he bleeds all over one of these cuts,' I indicated my face and hands, 'and he *is* a carrier, which just because he may or may not be gay doesn't mean that he is, I think you'll find that I'll be quite safe.' Well, it sounded reasonable enough to me. 'Now, are you going to drink that coffee or would you prefer something stronger?'

He laughed, good humouredly, and sank back into the settee beneath the front window. He returned his balls to his pocket with one hand and cradled his mug with the other. 'I have to lay off the booze, unfortunately. I'm driving.'

'Right.' How else would he have got here?

I suppose it was nice of Pendle to drop by, even though it felt a bit strange. I wondered if he visited all of his staff when they were off sick. I'd finished my bacon sarnie while I made the drinks but, it being close to dinner time, I could feel the beginnings of a rumble in my belly. I pondered on how long he planned on stopping. I didn't really want to have dinner with him.

'Who's looking after the pub, then?' I asked, finally.

'They can manage a session without me

every now and then.' Every now and then? He's that pissed most of the time they're managing 'without' him anyway. 'Vernon and Basil will probably open up between them. I only popped around to see how you are in any case.' Oh are. Like he was just passing, all the way from Birmingham.

'Well,' I smiled. 'As you can see I'm bearing up.'

'You don't have to come in until you're ready, you know.'

I did already know that, thanks, I said silently. The doc had signed me on to the panel for a week anyway. 'Who else will do it?' I asked.

'One of the lads probably. I'm sure they won't mind. I'll give them a call. See who can make it.'

'Who did it last night?'

'No-one. By the time we found out you weren't coming in it was too late. And neither of them was in last night.' That's right. They could have just used the house gear and my stock of CDs in the back room.

'Yeah, er . . . sorry about that, Ken.'

'Don't worry about it. I spoke to your mate . . . Roach. I didn't realise you were that friendly with him either.' God, did he think he was my dad or something? 'Has he . . . er . . . moved in with you?' He looked around as if expecting to see either Roach himself or some other evidence that he lived there.

I flashed angrily. It was none of his damned business anyway. The moment passed and I told myself he was probably genuinely interested. Some people are, aren't they? 'No, he was just looking after me.'

'And when do you think you'll be back?' he continued. 'So I can arrange the cover.'

Fortunately I didn't really need the money, unlike some people. And I'd have to ring up Barney's to cancel tonight — I do Barney's on Thursdays as well as Sundays. A couple of nights in would probably do me the world of good. The bruises, if not completely faded, should at least be cover-uppable by the weekend. It was the ego that would take longer. But I didn't need too many minutes to think about it.

'I'll come in on Saturday,' I decided out loud. So I should be able to tell Barney's I'd be in on Sunday too. 'If that's okay with you?' I added, at last remembering my manners.

'Whatever,' he replied, shrugging his shoulders. I just don't want you feeling obliged to come in, that's all.'

'Thanks all the same, Ken. But I'm freelance. I don't do it to oblige. I do it so I can eat.' Speaking of which . . .

Almost on cue, he drained his coffee and

225

smacked his lips, no doubt anticipating stronger things to come later, perhaps. 'Right, I'll see you on Saturday then.'

He jumped up and I saw him out, just as Roach was walking up the drive from the car park. He may as well move in the time he'd been spending up here just lately.

They exchanged a few words as their paths crossed, and then Ken Pendle was on his way again.

22

'What did he have to say to you?' I asked, as
Roach came up the steps into my van. He
glanced over his shoulder at Pendle who was
just disappearing around the end of the drive.

'Oh, nothing much. Just something about
the weather.'

'That's nice,' I murmured. Why didn't I
believe him?

'How about you? What did he come to see
you about? It wasn't to have a go about last
night, was it?'

'No, not really. Which reminds me, I must
call Barney's and let them know I won't be in
again until Sunday. Don't let me forget.' I was
determined not to forget that too anyway. I
didn't. I made the call later on that day. 'No,
he only came to see how I was and to tell me
not to come back until I'm ready.' I closed
the door behind us and put the kettle on
again, to make yet another cuppa.

'And when will that be?' he asked, taking
his jacket off and hanging it on a cupboard
door handle. He was really making himself at
home.

'Saturday,' I replied, moving the leather to

227

a proper coat hook that was on the wall right beside us. I was tidying up after him as though we were an old married couple. 'I told him I'll go back on Saturday.'

'But I thought the doc said — '

'He did. But there's not much point in me moping around here. I'd far rather be working. And it isn't exactly *hard* work, is it? I can always get one of the doormen to hump my gear around if I get into trouble. And besides, apart from not getting paid while I'm out of the game, somewhere out there,' I nodded towards the bay window at the front of the van, 'there's a nutter getting away with murder. Someone has to find out who it is.'

I made us our tea and we moved into the living room where Roach promptly started flicking through the cable channels again. And there was me thinking he'd come to see me.

'What's going on anyway, Marcie?' he asked, finally. 'Are you working under cover for the cops or something?'

'As far as the cops are concerned, they've got their man. Or they have for Gavin. I don't know yet what they're doing about Daisy's killer. But I think they reckon it's a different person. They're determined to keep Wood-stock behind bars and won't give up until they've got another killer with concrete evidence and preferably a confession.'

'And they expect you to give them that?'

'No. DC Anderson told me not to do anything silly. He said they believe they've got the right person and I should keep my nose out.'

He looked thoughtful as he gulped down some of his tea. 'Why don't you do as they ask?'

'Would you?'

He shrugged. 'But why are they so convinced it was Woodstock?'

'Because someone claims they saw him do it.'

'But surely it's just their word against his?'

'That's what I said.' I relayed the conversation I'd had with Woodstock back to Roach, missing out the juicy bits of course. I still determined that it should be Woody who reveals his secret to his friends, and not me.

'So they're using him as a scapegoat,' said Roach when I finished.

'It looks that way,' I agreed. 'But now someone else has been killed, someone more important than a homeless, lonely rent boy, although granted only marginally according to them. Prostitutes are also pretty way down in the pecking order. But the police are going to have to work a bit harder.'

'But you spoke to them only the other day,

from my place. If they're not connecting the two killings, they have to treat the two separately. They've got their killer for one. Why should they work harder for Daisy?'

'I reckon it's because they're embarrassed. Claiming it's a copycat killing is a cover up. They must *know* it's the same person, but they can't be seen to admit that until they *do* have someone else. They've cocked up and they have to make sure they get it right. They've got to pull their fingers out, haven't they? They may not have valued Gavin's life very much, if what Woody says is true. But now two people are dead . . . they have to give more value for two lives. Don't they?' God, I sounded pathetic.

'I'm going to see Woodstock in the morning. Do you fancy coming along for the ride?' I was getting nowhere inside my own head so I changed the subject.

Roach shrugged again. 'I can't. He hasn't sent me a visiting order.' He finished off his tea and started looking at his watch. That was a short visit. He must have been just passing too.

'Will you be down The Cellar tomorrow night, then?'

'Probably.'

'Well, I'll see you there — '

'But I thought you weren't going in until Saturday.'

'I'm not going in to work. I'm going in to have a drink, if that's still allowed.'

'In that case then, I probably will.' He stood up from the floor, took his cup through to the kitchen, and came back sticking his arms back into his leather. 'Are you gonna be all right, anyway?'

'Yeah, thanks. I'll just have a sickie today. Then I'll be back on the case tomorrow.'

'Okay. I'll leave you to it then.' I started to get up. 'I'll see myself out,' he grinned.

I knelt up on the settee and watched through the window until he disappeared around the edge of the drive, then I got up to make myself a second bacon sandwich. Comfort eating, but I was starved and that was all I had in. Then I ran myself another nice, hot bath.

★ ★ ★

'When I get outta here,' Woodstock was saying, 'I'm gonna get me a proper job.'

'What do you mean, a proper job?' I asked.

'I've been mooching around doing casual work and renting a poxy bedsit, which by the way isn't there for me any more.' I wasn't surprised. 'If I get a proper job then I can buy a place of my own.'

'Do you think it's that easy then, to get a proper job I mean?' I'm afraid I wasn't very convinced.

'It's easier when you've got eight o-levels, though, isn't it?'

'Eight?' He nodded. That did surprise me. 'It's easier if you're aged sixteen, I suppose, and straight out of school with eight GCSEs. How come you didn't get a proper job before then?'

'Dunno,' he shrugged. 'I suppose I couldn't be arsed. It was too easy with the council paying my rent for me, maybe.'

I smiled. It was good to see he still had hope. 'I am going to get you out of here, Woody.'

Big brown eyes, resigned now as opposed to sad, looked at me. 'I know you will, Marce. But I hope you make a better job of getting me out than of whatever you were doing when you got that face.'

We both laughed, then he quietly said: 'I'm really sorry about Daisy.'

'Yeah. Me too,' I agreed, and we spared her a few moments of silence, each with our own thoughts and memories.

'Why do you suppose he killed her?' he asked, after some time.

'Because she knew who he was, I think.'

'How?'

'She was out there. Doing a trick.'

The colour drained from Woodstock's face. 'Did she see me and Gavin?'

Oh dear. This could really embarrass him if he thought she'd *seen* them. 'She . . . er . . . knew you were out there. But if she did see . . . um . . . you, she didn't mention it.' How would he feel if he knew Pendle had seen them? Pendle was still alive. Daisy wasn't. I wasn't going to be the one to break it to him. I added quickly: 'But she also saw someone arguing with him after you came back in.'

Woodstock sighed. 'And that's who killed him — them?'

'I think so. And I think that Daisy thought so too.'

'Who was it?'

'I don't know. And if I did, do you think you'd still be in here? But she did tell me to find out how someone died and everything else will fall into place.'

'Who died?' I shrugged my shoulders. 'When? Where?'

'At the Royal Infirmary. Three years ago.'

'But that place closed down a while back.'

'I know.'

'And that's all she said to you?' I nodded. 'Shit. Well, you've got your work cut out for you.'

233

'Tell me about it.'

He paused and then said: 'I'm learning how to use computers while I'm in here.'

'That's good,' I said, trying to show some enthusiasm. Computers have never interested me.

We chatted for a while longer, but then it was time for me to go. Again.

* * *

As I was on the road anyway, and as I was in Birmingham on my way back along the Coventry Road, I decided to go and see Mom and Dad. After all, at least I really was 'just passing'. If I arrived at lunchtime she'd probably make me some dinner. Dad was out at the local shops getting his newspaper. He said the daily ten minute walk was his only form of exercise these days. Mom was in, though.

'Is the paper out already?' I asked when she told me where he was. Dad always reads the *Birmingham Evening Mail* but it was only just after one-thirty.

'He's gone for the lunchtime edition. We're going to be out at tea time.'

'Out?' That was a surprise. 'Going anywhere nice?'

'We just fancied a *Beefeater* for tea so your

father's gone to get the *Mail* now.'

'Oh, that's nice,' I said, still wondering why they hadn't made their usual announcement that they were going out.

'I did try to call you this morning,' she said. 'But you weren't in.' Ah, that would explain it. 'You really should get yourself one of those answering machines, the line of business you're in. You probably miss all sorts of important telephone calls.' Mother could be very logical at times, and I made a mental note to think about it. Then I made another mental note to get a notebook. My memory wasn't as reliable as it used to be and it never was very good even then.

'Out at all hours of the day, you are,' she continued, never being one to miss a dig. 'You can't be *that* ill after your accident, can you?' She couldn't let anything rest, could she? I didn't bother to answer the question in her voice. She would have been even less impressed if she knew I'd spent the morning in prison.

Mom and Dad are always complaining that, since their retirement, they weren't as well off as before. But they always managed a *Beefeater* whenever the whim took them, or a *Little Chef* or a *Toby* . . .

'All of this thinking about food is making me hungry,' I hinted heavily, checking my watch at the same time.

'What thinking about food?'

Ah. *We* weren't actually thinking about food, were we? *I* definitely was but Mom was probably wondering where I spent all of my spare time. She wasn't all bad, I reasoned with myself, as she took the bait.

'Haven't you eaten yet?'

'No,' I nodded, in agreement . . . somehow.

'I'll go and make you something then. Is cheese on toast all right?' she called over her shoulder.

'I'll say,' I said, my mouth watering already. My mom makes a mean Welsh rarebit.

Dad returned just as I was finishing my dinner. He'd read most of the paper on his way back from the shop. One of these days he'll walk into something . . . or under something.

'I see there's been another murder up at that place where you work,' he said.

I choked on a sharp crust of toast. 'Another one?'

'Don't eat with your mouth full, Marcella, there's a dear,' said Mom.

'Yes,' said Dad. 'Monday night. Didn't you know?'

Phew. For a second there I thought there had been a *third* murder. 'Oh, that one. Yes, I'm afraid so,' I agreed sadly. 'Nice lady — '

'Lady? That's not what it says here.'

'What . . . ?' Was there something else I hadn't known?

'What does it say there then, dear?' asked Mom.

'She was a known prostitute — '

Mother looked horrified. To me she said: 'You really do mix with some . . . ' she searched her narrow-minded vocabulary to find the right words, ' . . . undesirable sorts, Marcella.'

'Daisy was a very good friend and a very nice *lady*,' I said, emphasising the word for Dad's benefit. 'Everybody loved her to bits.'

'Yes,' said Mother, distantly. 'I'm sure they did.'

'Daisy?' said Dad. 'It says here that her name was Jean something or other.' He started to scan the page again but I grabbed the paper from him.

The body found on Monday night in the Hill Brook car park, at the rear of The Cellar public house, has now been identified. It is said to be that of 47 year old Miss Jean Deakin, a known prostitute in the area. Her next of kin, a daughter, has been notified. Police are treating the death as suspicious, but refuse to comment on whether or not it has been linked to a previous incident.

The article went on to discuss details of Gavin's death only three weeks ago. Was it only three weeks ago? I didn't read any more. The photograph was definitely Daisy. Forty-seven, eh? We were all convinced she was only about forty-one at the most. And a daughter.

There was still so much we didn't know about people, even if we had known them for years. Was I to keep coming back to this? Daisy. Jean Deakin. A daughter. I was sure that nobody knew about *her*. But I suppose we weren't too far off when we guessed her age. At least we got the right decade. I found myself wondering about Daisy's daughter — there was no way I could call her Jean. What was she like? How old was she? Where was she?

'Well, they'll have to put more of an effort into finding the killer now,' I said, out aloud.

'What do you mean?' asked Mom, who had given the newspaper article only a cursory glance.

'Their excuse before was that Gavin was a nobody and no one would miss him.' I was repeating Woodstock's definition again, and not DC Anderson's. 'They can't sweep Daisy under the carpet. She has family. They have to do something now.'

'I doubt it,' said Dad, reclaiming his newspaper so he could finish reading it. He was a bit cross with me. We were always brought up that Dad read the paper *first*, and then *we* could look at it. 'Apart from the two deaths being unconnected at the moment, they're not going to pull out all the plugs for a common street girl.'

As he rustled his paper back into some sort of order it dawned on me that he was probably right. The cops weren't going to go all out over a prostitute, were they? Family or not.

23

Of course, I couldn't really expect anything else, could I? Gavin was gay, a junkie, and officially homeless. Woodstock was also gay (or so everyone believed), a suspected junkie, and he had no family. He was the ideal scapegoat — apart from the fact that he was safely banged up when Daisy was killed. The police should have no alternative but to let him go. But they hadn't, claiming red tape in their defence.

Now they had a dead prostitute on their hands as well. Maybe they hoped to be able to sweep that one under the carpet too. But Daisy had a daughter. A known relative. Surely they couldn't pin this one down as just another dead prostitute, could they? I was thinking about Woodstock's theory and realised I was getting as narrow-minded as him.

I left Mom's and Dad's and decided to go straight to The Cellar, after parking the bike up in the lock-up at home. I'd be able to get some tea when I got there. Pub grub. Real food. Great. I called a taxi. I wouldn't be working and I needed a drink. It was better to be safe. It's a good job I didn't take the bike anyway as, after Daisy's body had been found on Monday night, the car park was still closed. Although I didn't relish the idea of going out there after two murders, I don't really like to park the bike upstairs either.

Even though I don't drink that much, nor that often, I do like a drink occasionally. A nice cool, sweet pint of cider. The first one went down in a dream and I took the second over to a quiet corner on one side of the door. Most of the punters tend to fill the place up from the centre, so I could observe things from a distance here without being seen too easily myself — unless, that is, someone was particularly keen to find me. It's quieter at this end too — no speakers — so I was able to think more easily.

Pendle spotted me almost straight away.

'You're early,' he said, looking up at the clock over the bar. Twenty-five-past three, a few minutes fast as usual. 'You haven't changed your mind, have you?'

'What, about working you mean?' He nodded. 'Nah. I was going to cook something but didn't have the energy.'

'So you haven't eaten then?'

'I had some cheese on toast about two hours ago.' It was too early for something else yet.

'Do you want anything else?' As I shook my head, which didn't pound so much any more when I did that, he eyed the fast disappearing cider I was chucking down my neck. 'Hmm.' Patronising hypocrite. It was okay for him to assault his liver day in and day out, but he frowned on anyone else doing it. He went off to see some of his other customers, but by the time I made it to the bottom of my third pint he was back.

'Oh, thanks,' I said, surprised at the fresh pint and a massive plate piled high with chilli con carne and big beefy chips. I stood up and reached in my pocket for some cash. Very nice of him, but it would have been much nicer to be allowed to make up my own mind.

'No, no, no,' he said, restraining my arm. 'This one's on the house.'

'Really?' He can't have been pissed already, can he? He nodded. 'Er . . . cheers.' Maybe it was an excellent choice after all.

The chilli was great. Perhaps a little dry after being reheated, but great all the same. Free food generally is, though, isn't it? There's nothing quite like having a meal cooked for you, apart from it coming free of charge, and I'd had both. I hadn't even realised how hungry I was either. That snack my mom had cooked for me earlier had filled a gap then. But another had formed since, without me even noticing. Maybe Pendle wasn't so bad after all. Then I wondered if it was me who was going soft. I'd thought that about two different people in one afternoon.

With a full belly and a pint by my side, I was able to think a whole lot better.

Whoever killed Gavin had also killed Daisy. Fact. I didn't care what the police said. Both bodies were discovered in the car park at the back of The Cellar. Fact. Both had been drinking in the pub. Fact. They had both died from a blow to the side of the head. Fact. Both murders had happened at night. Fact. The killer was still free. Fact. And he, or she, was free from police suspicion too.

The weapon used to kill Gavin hadn't been found yet. I had no idea how far they had progressed in finding Daisy's murder weapon. But I had no reason for thinking the two weapons were different — at this stage.

The chances were that the killer was probably connected with either The Cellar or any one of the other premises that backed onto the car park because both bodies were found there. As far as I knew, The Cellar was the only premises that would still be open at that time of night that also backed onto the car park. Scruffy Murphy's, just around the corner, backs onto a different car park. The Cellar had to be the connection.

Pint number four was going down a hell of a lot slower than the others had, which was just as well. I didn't want to numb my brain too much. I racked said brain trying to remember who had been in on the night Gavin had died. I'd already given a list to the police. But Daisy definitely hadn't been in that night.

I backtracked to Monday afternoon to see if I could remember who was here then. My head started to hurt again with so much effort. I knew what had happened that evening because Angus had filled me in. What I didn't actually remember was being duffed up by Cycle Witches. I also remembered Daisy giving me her clue. But who had been in here that day?

Try as I might, I could only place three people who would have been here on both occasions — and I knew that I wasn't the killer. And one was definitely spotted re-entering the pub just before closing time.

Daisy had certainly been in a hurry to see someone. A client. So I was sure she didn't say who that was or who she'd seen arguing that night with Gavin. This was so infuriating. The doc had mentioned something about concussion, but he didn't say anything about memory loss. I was pretty sure that Daisy hadn't said anything significant, apart from

244

that business about checking out that mysterious death. I wondered who Jasper could really be.

'Hallo Marcie,' said a friendly voice. I looked up to see Roach grinning down at me and bearing two pints. I smiled back and he placed the cider in front of me. Pint number five. My gut wall groaned at the prospect. 'You were miles away,' he said. 'Mind if I join you then?'

'Of course not. I asked you to, didn't I? And besides, you've come bearing gifts.'

'Evening Roach,' said Pendle, who had come to replace my empty plate with a bowl of apple pie and hot custard. I smiled gratitude up at him. 'That should help line your stomach,' he said. And he should know.

Roach sat on a stool beside me and downed half of his pint of lager in one go. 'You didn't change your mind about working then?'

'Nah. I told Pendle I'd be here on Saturday and he seemed quite happy with that.' I took a mouthful of pudding. 'Woof! This pie's hot.' It was delicious though. 'You eating?' I asked Roach, but he shook his head.

'Who's on tonight then?' he asked instead.

We both looked across at the empty cage and glanced up at the clock. 'Dunno. But it's still early yet.' Just because I like an hour or so to get ready doesn't mean that everyone does. Still, it was already half past six.

In between Pendle bringing me my dinner and Roach arriving I must have been mulling — or day dreaming — for ages. Bleeding concussion. I hoped it wouldn't always be like this. I finished off a very flat and warm pint number four — or the dregs — before starting on the fresh pint. I'd nearly had enough to drink now anyway.

Roach finished his first pint, then went and got himself two more. Buying in bulk. He didn't allow his beer to go flat or warm. And in no time at all he'd caught up with me and had another two pints in reserve on the table in front of us. Five pints is about my limit so I sipped mine slowly, wishing I hadn't drunk the first two so fast.

At half past seven Roach looked again at the empty cage. 'Whichever one it is who *is* doing it is cutting it a bit fine, isn't he?'

'Well, I'm not doing it,' I said.

'Why not? You're better than the other two put together.'

'Creep. Anyway, I'm too pissed to do it now. This is my fifth pint. I'll be slurring in a bit.' If I wasn't already.

'What do you mean in a bit?' he laughed, and I punched him on the arm,

See. 'I can't work in this state.'

Roach burst out laughing. 'It'll probably be an improvement.'

I elbowed him sharply in the ribs . . . well, into the padding of his denim cut-off, his leather jacket, chunky sweater, and at least two tee shirts. 'That don't say much for the other two then, does it?' I asked, referring to his previous comment.

Conversation with Roach is so easy, even if it is about nothing in particular. We ended up yakking for the next half hour, I can't remember what about. By eight o'clock it was obvious that my replacement wasn't replacing me, or not on time at any rate. In the end, Pendle staggered over, pissed as a newt now, proverbial cap in hand.

'Can you help me out, Marcie?' he slurred. 'It looks like Mac has let me down.'

'I'm sorry, Ken. I've had too much to drink. I can't do it.'

'Oh well,' he spat, 'thanks for nothing,' before stumbling away and making me feel instantly guilty after all the kindness he'd shown me over the last couple of days.

Roach started to rise after him, but I still had enough faculties to stop him.

'Leave it, Roach.'

'There was no need for that.'

'It's okay, Roach.'

'But — '

'It isn't worth it. You'll only get yourself barred and I'll probably get the sack.'

'I don't care if I do get barred.'

'Well I do, and I care about losing my job, believe it or not. Leave it, Roach. Please.'

Roach sat back down, reluctantly, just as Dave, the other DJ, staggered in beneath a box of CDs. I jumped up to help him and my head immediately wished that I hadn't.

'What're you doing here?' I asked, opening the flap in the corner for him.

'I might ask you the same thing. Ken called me at about four o'clock this afternoon saying that you were on the sick.'

'Four o'clock? But he knew on Wednesday night that I wasn't very well, and he came to see me yesterday bearing fruit and flowers. He told me to take the week off if I needed to. But he reckons he called Mac and that Mac let him down. He's in a foul mood.'

'This is the quickest I could make it at such short notice. I told him that.' Dave paused and cocked his head towards the room at the back of the bar. 'Has he been drinking?'

'Is the sky blue? Don't ask stupid questions.'

'What's the matter with you anyway? You look fine to me ... well, apart from the face ... '

I tilted my face towards the light and

swung my hair behind me to show him the full Monty. He winced. 'Don't ask stupid questions,' I grinned.

I returned to Roach. 'Looks like Pendle really ballsed it up this time, doesn't it? He didn't call Mac at all and Dave told him he couldn't make it any earlier. Pendle only called him after I'd already been here half an hour this afternoon.' I took a sip from my sixth pint . . . or was it my seventh? Now where did that come from?

Roach took another great swig of his lager. The look in his eyes meant he wasn't going to waste any more valuable drinking time worrying about Ken Pendle.

On several of his many trips to and fro, usually fro minus a load, Dave dropped by to get the low down on my injuries. By now the many pints of strong alcohol had numbed any remaining aches, pains or grumbles I might have, though I knew that by morning I'd have a stinking (literally) gut rot and a thumping head, neither anything to do with my Monday night pasting.

I thoroughly enjoyed my evening out and if it didn't unravel any of the mystery, I certainly felt a lot more relaxed about everything. Maybe it was the company. Okay, so he looked like a slob first thing in the morning, but didn't we all? Right now he was back in Ross Kemp mode, and didn't he look sexy. I have to admit, again, that I really do like Roach, even taking his other sins into account — and especially when I'm pissed.

The music was great and the cider slipped down a treat. I could feel a stupid, happy grin evolving on my face. Dave even played a couple of tracks for me, 'To cheer you up.' Hell, I wasn't even down. And Ken Pendle didn't come my way again, not even to apologise. In fact, he must have really been knocking the stuff back somewhere, because he didn't appear again for the rest of that evening.

In my wisdom, what was left of it, I decided that I'd had enough to drink and, in fact, I certainly had. So I'd already started to make leaving noises when Roach offered to take me home.

'But you've had just as much to drink as I have,' I said. 'More, in fact.'

'I mean in a taxi, stupid,' he said. 'I've left the bike behind Murphy's.'

'Good thinking, Batman,' I said, standing up, but falling back down again on the seat. Even in this befuddled state I knew what would happen tonight, once we got back to my place. We'd had a good evening with plenty to drink, leaving no inhibitions whatsoever. We were both grown ups, and we both fancied each other. I was finally going to end up in the sack with Roach. And, to be honest, the thought didn't put me off at all. In fact, I got quite excited at the prospect. It really must have been the booze.

I tried standing again but could feel myself swaying, so I perched my backside on the edge of the table. Roach caught his pint glass before it toppled over and chose then to finish his drink. He finally smacked his lips and slammed the empty glass back down on the table.

'Come on then,' he said, as if he'd been waiting for me all along. He wiped his mouth on the sleeve of his jacket. 'Let's go.'

Like an eager child on my way to the zoo, or something close, I jumped up off the table excitedly. On our way through the door we bumped into DS MacGregor and DC Anderson on their way in.

'Going somewhere, are we?' asked the Scotsman.

'Yesh. Roach ish taking me home.'

'I hope not, in his condition.' Neither of us could be bothered to explain. 'Actually, it was . . . ' MacGregor cleared his throat. 'It was Mister Beadsley we were after.'

'Oh yeah?' said Roach.

'Yes,' replied Anderson. 'Do you remember coming in to the station to try and talk to someone?'

'Yeah. I went to Steelhouse Lane.'

'Well, we'd like you to accompany us there now . . . oh, Acocks Green though.'

'Hang on,' I cried, seeing my plans for the night dissolving into thin air. 'Why aren't you out there looking for Daisy's killer?'

'That's exactly what we are doing, Miss Craig,' replied Anderson.

24

Naturally they wouldn't let me go with Roach to the police station, not in their nice warm car anyway. I had to make my own way there. Fortunately there are plenty of buses to Acocks Green. Well, one every twenty minutes at least at that time of night. I caught a number 37 at ten o'clock and was at the station by twenty-past, due to the walk up from the main Warwick Road. They'd had a good twenty-five minutes head start on me, which in a car meant they would have got there before ten, while I was still waiting in the cold for a bus.

Why couldn't they have taken him to Steelhouse Lane? It was only around the corner from The Cellar. By the time they'd negotiated the complicated one way network in the city centre, I would have beaten them to it on foot. Obviously the place was still full of drug barons and warlords . . . and obviously they were keeping an open mind about whether they'd need to keep him in.

After my long walk up Dudley Park Road — all up hill — I was knackered. I needed a drink of pop and a seat. Already I was starting to feel dehydrated, but at least I had a clear head by now. This time the plastic seats in reception were empty. It wasn't chucking out time in the pubs yet so it wasn't going to be busy, was it?

'Can I help you?' asked the desk sergeant.

'Yeah. Thanks.' I got back up off my seat and moved closer. 'I'm looking for my friend Roach . . . er . . . John Beadsley. DS MacGregor and DC Anderson would have bought him in about twenty-five minutes ago.'

He subconsciously glanced to his left to the room where I had been questioned on Good Friday. Oh good. That meant he hadn't been charged with anything . . . yet. 'I'm afraid you'll have to wait while they question him.'

'Can I have a drink then, please? I've just raced here from Birmingham and I'm done in.'

He sniffed, no doubt smelling the alcohol on my breath. 'Raced?'

'Yeah. Don't worry. I came by bus and on foot. I've just run up here from the Warwick Road.'

'I'll . . . er . . . fetch you a glass of water.'

Gee, thanks. At least MacGregor had got me a can of pop before.

I'm not sure if he was supposed to leave his post, but I took advantage of the situation anyway, and poked my head around the door to one side of the counter. The three of them were in there all right.

'You can't come in here, Miss Craig,' said Anderson.

'Why not? I've been in here before.'

'We're questioning your friend. You can't come in.' He remained seated on their side of the little table while MacGregor let out an impatient sigh.

'She could always get herself arrested,' muttered the Scot.

'You haven't arrested him,' I said, cocking my head towards Roach, who was sitting on my side of the room. He had his back to the door and needed to swivel in his seat to see me.

'Leave it, Marce,' said Roach. 'You'll only make things worse.'

'Mister Beadsley is helping us with our enquiries, Miss Craig,' continued the younger detective. 'You are quite right. We haven't arrested him.' Then he added: 'But it can always be arranged . . .'

'Marcie,' pleaded Roach.

'Why can't I sit in with him?'

'Because it doesn't work like that. He is nether a minor — and if he was, you're not his mother — nor is he under arrest. He is not entitled to company. And even if he were,

255

that wouldn't mean you. Now please leave, Miss Craig, before we have you escorted off the premises.'

'Yeah, you'd like that, wouldn't you? A bit of physical — '

'Marcella!' hissed Roach. 'Will you shut your mouth.'

Charming.

Ignoring my ungracious behaviour, MacGregor stood up and gently guided me back through the door. 'I suggest you either go home, or make yourself comfortable in reception.'

The door swung to behind us and a rather bewildered desk sergeant blinked at us from behind the counter. MacGregor said: 'I see the police constable has brought you a glass of water.' He turned to the policeman. 'You couldn't get her a tin of Coke or something from upstairs, could you?'

'Sure, Sir,' he replied, and disappeared again through the door on his side of the counter.

'Now, Marcella. I promise you your friend is not under arrest. He is merely helping us with our enquiries.' Did he just call me Marcella? 'You want us to find your other friend's killer, don't you?' I nodded, sipping the water the desk sergeant had left behind. I hadn't drunk *that* much cider but it was still enough to dehydrate me. 'Well then, wait here. The sooner we are allowed to talk to Mister Beadsley the sooner he will be allowed to go.' The police officer returned with a cold can of pop and MacGregor opened the door to the room again.

Roach was standing beside the door waiting for him. 'I'll be all right,' he said to me. 'You go on home.'

'I can't go home and you know it.'

'Why not?'

'No buses, remember?'

'Shit. Well, wait there quietly then. I'm sure we won't be long.'

I stuck my tongue out at him, the patronising git. But he'd already gone back inside the room. Nice of him to give me some change out of his pocket for a taxi.

It would have been so much easier to get home from town. Taxis for a start. Steelhouse Lane is a massive police station opposite what used to be the General Hospital. It occupies the whole corner of the main road. Outside there are always cars parked and quite often police vehicles are double-parked too, leaving only enough room for a single vehicle to pass at a time.

The place looks like home to dozens of cells and, as it backs onto the law courts, is in the ideal place really. I couldn't believe it was still full, and Digbeth too. Acocks Green is tiny in comparison. They probably have four or five cells here, at the most. I didn't want to find out exactly how many.

The can of Coke was too cold. Opposite the station is a chip shop, but it was already closed for the night. There's a McDonald's up the road though — well, about fifteen minutes walk away. I pulled my leather around me and began the walk. They sold me a cup of tea in a polystyrene cup, which kept it warm enough while I walked back. By the time I reached the station again, it was just the right temperature to drink. That was better. I smacked my lips.

I checked with the chap on the desk, who said Roach was still there, and I made myself as comfortable as you can on one of those police waiting room plastic seats, designed, naturally, to be quite the opposite. And I settled in for the night.

It's amazing how quickly you can sober up under certain circumstances. I sat and I waited and soon I felt so good I could have taken the last bus back into town and taken Roach's bike home myself. Unfortunately my driving licence is just too precious for me to lose and, anyway, I didn't have the key. I'm also too nosy to give up so easily.

An ageing hippy, who looked vaguely familiar, slouched in and had a quiet word with the desk sergeant. Then he sat down opposite me and sucked on an unlit cigarette, the glazed expression and sweet, clinging smell belying the joint he'd already finished off outside.

Two slaggy looking girls followed him in, tits and bums hanging out, and plonked themselves down two chairs away. The one with burgundy hair blew shocking pink bubbles with her gum and let it burst in a dirty mess all over her face.

A thin-faced, sad looking chap loitered in the doorway, in two minds whether or not to come in, whereas another, clearly a tramp, had no qualms about wandering in and settling himself across four chairs before dropping off to sleep almost instantly. Good for him. They might not notice him for ages before chucking him out.

There was already an old man leaning against the leaflet rack that had been my roost on that first visit. He'd been there for a while now, but came to life to ogle the two whores.

Such a popular place.

On the other side of the desk a phone rang incessantly, and when that one gave up, another started. I could hardly believe there was only a single police officer on his own, left to look after all of these people and with so many phones.

A door burst open behind the desk sergeant and Anderson appeared. He didn't even acknowledge me as he collected a wad of papers and made to retreat again. I jumped up and coughed, then called out to him. As he turned he spotted me. Recognition followed by annoyance flitted across his face, but as the desk sergeant opened his mouth — I presume to tell me to sit down — Anderson put out an arm.

'It's okay, Dick,' said Anderson, tossing the papers onto a table. He walked towards me and Dick sat himself back down.

'Are you still here, Miss Craig?' he asked, good natured.

'No. I left an hour ago.' His face dropped into a frown, so I changed tack. 'Sorry,' I said, truthfully. It was sufficient. I made a note to remember that one. 'I'm tired, that's all. I was only wondering how Roach was getting along.'

He towered over me from his side of the desk. 'I've already told you once. Mister Beadsley is helping us with our enquiries. There really isn't anything more you can do. He may be here for a while. Why don't you go on home?'

'Because you've banged up my lift.'

Anderson took a deep breath. 'First of all, he isn't 'banged up'. And secondly, he's had quite a lot to drink. I sincerely hope he wasn't thinking of riding his bike.' He paused a beat. 'But more than that, I hope you weren't planning on hopping up behind him.'

'No, he wasn't and nor was I. We were going to get a taxi.'

'So go and catch your taxi.'

'I can't. Roach was paying.' He didn't need to know I had enough money to pay for my own fare and, actually, had I called my dad he would have come out to me like a shot. But I wasn't going to tell Anderson any of that, and I'd left home years ago. Anyway, he was getting quietly mad.

'You do realise,' he said, his voice dropped to barely a whisper, 'that if I was half the dickhead you seem to think I am I could arrest you for being out on the streets without enough money to get home? Technically, that's vagrancy.'

'I would have had enough money to get home, but it's all in Roach's pockets.' How could this be the same bloke who'd made such a great roadie at my sister's wedding? 'It's not my fault. I had my ride home arranged, until you lot came barging in with your hob-nailed boots. And because you wouldn't give me a lift, I had to fork out on bus fare and a hot drink — '

'Nobody asked you to come.'

He had a point. 'Touché,' I murmured.

Anderson sighed, brushed a hand through his hair, and fished in his pockets. He offered me a crisp ten pound note. 'Will this do?'

'Are you supposed to do that?'

'No, not really. But if it gets you off my back I'm all for it.'

'Thanks — '

'It's a loan.' Awe, the man was all heart. 'Now get out of here before I change my mind.'

'But Roach — '

'I'll get him to call you, shall I? Once we've finished with him.'

'But his bike — '

'Sorted. Go home, Miss Craig.'

I guessed I was beaten, so I left. I made my way to the nearest taxi rank, which is on a traffic island in the Green itself, and went home. It felt quite comforting to see Ivy's curtains twitch next door.

★ ★ ★

The phone rang at six o'clock the next morning.

'Hi, Marce. It's Roach.'

'They let you go?'

'Of course they did. I'm off home now.'

'Is that all you called me for?'

262

'Yeah. I thought you'd like to know.' His voice faltered. 'That copper thought you'd like to know.'

'I did. But couldn't it have waited? Like until you've had a couple of hours' kip? I thought they'd charged you with something, ringing me up at this hour.'

'Cheers, Marcie,' he snapped. He put the phone down and I went back to bed.

25

I'd hurt Roach's feelings. Four hours later I pulled up outside his house clutching my olive branch — a four pack of his favourite special brew. Either Roach was the only one in, or the one designated to open the front door today — last in, first up perhaps. His hair is very short but he still managed to look dishevelled.

And sexy.

Unshaven and half-undressed — again — he leaned against the door post. He wasn't going to let me in.

'I'm sorry, mate,' I said, holding out the beer tins.

'Thanks,' he grunted, taking them from me.

We both stood there for about half a minute, each waiting for the other to say something. I was the first to give in.

'I was half asleep. I didn't mean it.'

'No?'

'No.' Crikey, it was like trying to get conversation out of a mute. 'So?'

'So?'

'Are you going to invite me in?'

He stepped to one side and pushed the

door further open. 'Come in.'

Wow — two words. I stepped inside the hall so he could close the door behind me, and straight away I noticed something was different. He was wearing boxers for a start, and they were clean, even if they did have a picture of the Blackpool Tower on the front. But the place smelled differently. No sweaty feet or dirty trainers. No layer of dust on every surface. Even the carpet had been vacuumed.

Roach pushed past me to the kitchen where I heard him put the four pack in the fridge.

'Did I wake you?' I called out after him.

'Nah. I got my head down for a bit but couldn't go off.'

'How did you get on in the end?' I asked, when he came back.

He shrugged. 'They let me go.' He still kept me standing in the hall, but at least he was stringing a few more words together.

'Why'd they let you go?'

'Because I didn't do anything.'

'Nor did Woodstock. They've still got him, *and* they locked him up.'

I made a move towards the front room and was relieved when Roach followed me, chilling out a little. And now I was really surprised. Where were all the empty cans we normally had to pick our way through? What had happened to all the half empty, mouldy

265

mugs? Ashtrays had been emptied and . . . washed? A diminished pile of magazines had been tidied onto a magazine rack I hadn't even noticed was there on my last visit. I could smell apple flavoured air freshener and didn't need to clear a space on the settee. When I sat down, he joined me.

'You've tidied up,' I said.

He glanced at me. 'I was expecting company.'

'Oh? What time?' I started to get up again.

'You were early.'

I opened my mouth to speak, but nothing came out, so I pretended I was taking a deep breath.

He smiled, but said: 'They were more interested in my drugs dealing. But I told 'em I'd given it up.'

'And have you?'

'I dunno yet. I haven't done any in a while. Not since that Gavin business, in fact.'

'How come?' My stomach lurched. Maybe it was because of me . . . ? Not a chance.

'I haven't been to Europe for a run in ages, so I've got no stock.'

'Oh.' Life's a bitch sometimes. 'What did they have to say? They kept you there long enough.'

'They just kept on asking where I was when Gavin and then Daisy died — '

'Daisy?' I could feel the dawning cross my face. 'Aha — so they don't believe they have got the right man for this murder then after all.'

'Looks that way.'

'The bastards. Why don't they let Woodstock go?' He shrugged. 'And where were you then, when they died?'

'Like you said, they already had my dabs all over Gavin's drugs, but I gave Woodstock his alibi. I think that helped.'

'And Daisy? Where were you when Daisy died?'

'You know the answer to that one already. I was with you and Angus at the hospital. They don't even need to check that with Angus because the hospital staff will have information like that on file, probably. It was me what gave 'em your personal details.'

'But they didn't think you had anything to do with Daisy's death, did they? Not really.'

He fidgeted next to me on the settee. 'I'm afraid they did.'

'On what grounds?'

He paused before replying. 'Evidence.'

All I could think of was Woodstock's 'evidence' at the scene of Gavin's death. I thought I was going to be sick, but I needed to put the question on my mind into words. He had already stiffened beside me.

'What kind of evidence?' I asked, not looking him in the eye. 'Were you sleeping with Daisy?'

Roach threw back his head and roared with laughter. 'Marcie Craig, I do believe you're jealous.'

'Am not,' I replied — too quickly. I could feel my face start to burn. 'It's just with her being, well, you know.'

'Yeah,' he smirked. 'I know.' And he chuckled some more.

I couldn't stand it. I needed the truth. For whatever reason. 'Well?'

'Well what?'

'Were you?'

'What?'

'Sleeping with Daisy?'

'No.'

'What evidence did they find then?'

'My fingerprints.'

'Again?' He nodded. 'What on?'

'A little box she keeps.'

'What kind of box?'

'You know. A kind of trinket box.'

'Okay,' I continued, patiently. Deep breaths. 'What was inside this box?'

'Two or three ounces of cannabis resin — '

'Daisy smoked pot?'

'No, she smoked tea leaves. Of course she smoked it. What else do you think she did with it? It's harmless enough.'

'It's also illegal.'

'Oh, and everything else she did wasn't? Get a grip, Marcie. You'll find out that plenty of people around here smoke the stuff. I bet Pendle's even had a crafty drag.'

'Huh. Bet he hasn't.'

'No, maybe not.'

'You just said you hadn't done any dealing since Gavin died, yet Daisy had some fresh blow?'

'Who said it was fresh? And what makes you think I'm the only supplier in the city?'

'So why were your dabs all over her box?'

'You don't do blow do you, Marce?'

'I don't do anything.'

'Yeah well, it's a communal thing. Something that's best done in company. For me anyway. Social smoking. We all share.'

'Oh.' That sounded feasible. 'And then they let you go?'

'Uh-huh.'

I did a quick calculation in my head. 'Okay, why did they take more than seven hours?'

'I dunno. They just kept on asking me the same questions, over and over again. Then they'd let me sweat for a bit, or give me a fag or a cup of tea. Then they'd start with the questions again.'

'You were a suspect after all.'

'Probably. But not any more.'

Roach eventually remembered his manners and put a kettle on to boil while he dressed upstairs. I was also honoured to see he'd shaved before coming back down, too. To prove his falling out with me was forgotten, he offered me a bowl of Sugar Puffs, but his sterilised milk was only just palatable in a cup of tea. I declined. As the smell of tea brewing didn't cause the others to surface, I decided they all couldn't be at home.

'How're you feeling anyway?' he asked, handing me a (clean) mug of steaming tea.

I mentally checked out my body. 'Still a bit stiff and sore, still a bit hung over from last night. But it feels much better now. Especially my head.' Apart from the hangover.

All the coolness had finally disappeared and we chatted amiably again. Before long we were in each other's arms and I remembered where we'd got to the night before when he'd been whisked away from me.

'Do you always do housework in your undies?' I asked, between kisses.

'I don't often do housework.'

'How far did you get?'

'I changed the bed.'

'Good.'

26

In no time at all things got back to normal
— apart from Woodstock still being locked
up, and Daisy being dead . . . oh, and me and
Roach. But apart from all of that, it felt like
normality, or as close as I would get at the
moment.

Once or twice I'd thought about getting it
together with Roach. We'd never actually
managed it for one reason or another. He was
working away or I really couldn't be doing
with his big boys' games or his big boys'
gang. I'd rather be in Gary Glitter's gang to
be honest, with no disrespect. I happen to like
Gary Glitter. It was a long time coming, I
suppose. But I suppose it was really only a
matter of time. And he had made such an
effort.

It felt very odd, though.

I settled back into a work pattern, starting
on Saturday at The Cellar. Pendle welcomed
me back with open arms, and a four pack of
cider to take home with me, bless him.

The next week was Daisy's inquest at the
coroner's court in Birmingham. A load of us
trooped across town to hear it, including

people like Angus and Roach, who took time off work to be there. We hadn't bothered for Gavin's hearing, probably because no-one really knew him like we knew Daisy. I suppose Woodstock might have gone along to Gavin's, but he was the only person missing at Daisy's that I would have expected to see.

A gang of us waited on the pavement outside, spilling into Newton Street, until it was time to go in: me, Roach, Angus, Ken Pendle, Vernon and Tommy the doormen from The Cellar, Basil and Norma representing the bar staff, a handful of street girls, and loads of others I thought I knew from Barney's and the various bike chapters, and many I didn't. We didn't say much. It didn't seem right. Stone Age Sal was there too. It was the first time I'd seen her since she'd organised my beating. We didn't speak, just glared at each other and kept a wide berth.

What a motley crew we must have looked. We should have been moved along for causing an obstruction. There was also a delegation from West Midlands Police. How many were in an official capacity was anyone's guess. I wondered if the murderer had turned up.

We piled into the court and squeezed between three narrow benches at the back. At least we *all* had upholstery to sit on this time, instead of the wooden planks at the magistrate's court.

Light coloured timber panels reached about three quarters of the way up the walls and the high ceilings were smartly coved. Four massive sets of three lights, looking like Chinese coolie hats, burned down on us. At least the windows were open to let in some air.

A middle aged dolly bird asked us all to stand and once the coroner himself had settled in (his name's Dick Whittington you know — no really), and after the preliminary identification of the deceased, the first witness was called.

The inquest streamed along in what I can only assume to be the normal fashion. Having never been to one before in my life I had no idea what was usual. I presumed the coroner knew what he was doing, though, even if no-one else did.

The police gave their evidence (discovered in the underground car park behind The Cellar public house — no valuables taken). The medical examiner gave his (death caused by a blow to the head with a smooth object — no weapon found — by an assailant unknown — no other signs present). But perhaps the most exciting part, and the real reason around sixty percent of us were probably there, was when Daisy's unknown daughter took the stand to answer questions about her mother.

Veronica Deakin, Ms, was beautiful. She could have been a model with her long straight nut brown hair and her lofty streamlined body. A greyhound. She was as sleek as a greyhound. Her mouth was, perhaps, a little too wide, but her hazel eyes were large and round, and a complexion to die for — well, I would. The clothes looked like *Jaeger* or *Country Casuals*, and she spoke in clipped, Queen's English.

Perhaps aged about twenty-five, she'd clearly had a good education and possibly held down an equally good job. She oozed affluence. Her chiselled face, though quite pale with trauma and sorrow, was composed. Who'd have thought it, eh? Daisy's daughter. I made a mental note to try and speak to the girl — at a later date, of course. She had far too much on her mind right now to be bothered with me.

Ms Deakin was denied permission to cremate or bury her mother at this stage. Everything that needed to be taken had been, but because criminal proceedings were underway, the body wasn't released even though the police had no further use of her.

Ms Deakin appealed so she could bury her

mother before having to leave the country again. Some discussions were held and the body released, pending a second post mortem.

And that was that. A lovely woman's entire life had been swept away in less than an hour. We all trailed back to wherever it was we'd come from and life resumed. It dawned on me briefly that Gavin's body hadn't been buried yet either. Or had it? I didn't know, but didn't dwell on it.

★ ★ ★

Diamond Head were already well into the second chorus of *Am I Evil?* on the following Saturday evening when Vernon called me to the phone. He was making himself a cup of tea, which was why he was in the kitchen in the first place. I cut that record short and changed it to *Child in Time* by Deep Purple. It was a live version so would give me a good ten minutes or more.

'Hello?' I said into the receiver.

'I've got to see you.' It was Woodstock calling from Winson Green.

'Why?'

'I need to speak to you.'

'You're speaking to me now.'

'No, I have to see you face to face. It's too

dangerous over the phone.'

'What do you mean, dangerous?'

'Too many ears. And remember *Squidgy Gate*.'

'Woody, that was on a mobile. And it was royalty. Anyway, you have to send me a visiting order and I haven't had one from you in over a week.'

'I'll see if I can get you one in the post on Monday. You should get it by Tuesday morning and you can come over then.'

'Right. So what do we need to discuss?'

There was a pause before he replied: 'I think I know who killed Gavin and Daisy.'

'Who killed them? How?' Suddenly I was interested, but I could hear my record moving on.

'I just remembered. It was something Gavin mentioned. I'll tell you when I see you.'

'What did he tell you? How did you remember now? Have you told anyone else? Daisy's inquest was only last week.'

'Nah. I wanted to run it by you first, see what you think. I have a lot of thinking time at the moment, a lot of remembering time. I might still be wrong, but I don't think so.'

Child in Time would soon be finishing and I had to get back behind the cage. 'Look, Woody. I gotta go. I'll see you Tuesday, yeah?'

'Sure. See you. And don't say anything to anyone,' he added.

I didn't have time for niceties. I hung up, pushed past Vernon, dashed through the bar, and back to my post. Too late.

'Sorry about that, folks,' I said into the mic as those who'd noticed jeered happily. 'Minor technical hitch.' Fortunately Skunk Anansie was already lying on top of the CD player, ready to go. 'Here's *Weak*. Well, we're all human.' The mocking jeers died away again as everyone got back to their beers. I stacked a few CDs on top of the player in advance of any other 'minor technical hitches', and thought about what Woodstock had said.

This Saturday was now going to be one of the longest of my career. And I still had Sunday and Monday to wait through too. I could hardly wait to hear what Woody had to say. What had he found out? *How* had he found out? Did he really remember something Gavin had said? Did someone — or something — prompt that memory? What?

Ken Pendle eyed me suspiciously from the doorway to the kitchen. I didn't even know he was there. He didn't like us taking personal calls usually, or making them. He must have heard me name Woody as I finished the call and he'd already made it perfectly clear before what he thought of my relationship with Woodstock, not that it was any of his business. He wasn't happy, needless to say, but soon gave up his vigil and retreated into his bottle.

Aside from having this new information to think about, I didn't have a particularly good evening. One silly little girl must have been up about five times reminding me to play the same record she'd asked for the first time. I get other requests too and try to bunch them together, style-wise. Some must think that theirs are the only requests I ever get and expect me to play them straight away. Sometimes I do, to get rid of them. I wonder if other DJs find the same thing, or are they taking advantage of my sweet nature?

I kept telling her I hadn't forgotten and soon felt inclined not to play the bloody thing at all. She was a regular, though, and would be in again next week, nagging. Best to play it for her, I thought. *Love Ain't No Stranger* by Whitesnake.

Another silly mare was up then, wasn't she? Asking for the whole of Whitesnake's back catalogue. There was no time to play them all, I said, reminding her that she'd been in for a couple of hours already and if she'd asked me earlier, then I might have managed a few more. Some punters are too shy to ask until they've had a drink or two. I did agree to play one more, *Slide it In*, and because I felt like it, I added *Burn* by Deep Purple, circa David Coverdale.

That started them all off. I had the Ian Gillan brigade, anti-David Coverdale, wanting some 'real' Deep Purple. I pointed out that they had already had *Child in Time*, but that wasn't good enough. They wanted three in a row too, and none of this was in a polite one-to-one fashion with them taking it in turns to come up to my cage. No, this was them bawling over the noise from where they stood, mouthing the words carefully, and me responding over the mic.

In the end I sandwiched another Deep Purple Coverdale track between two Ian Gillans. This in turn led to some Rainbow fans crawling out of the woodwork, which in turn led to Black Sabbath . . . somehow.

After about six or seven records down this line I finished it and played some Twisted Sister instead. Now *I* was accused of being a dinosaur when it had been *them* asking for all of the old stuff in the first place. I told them to watch while Twisted Sister reformed, but they didn't believe me. Didn't I have any Metallica? Or Corrosion of Conformity? Or the Manic Street Preachers? Or Pulp? (Pulp? I ask you. This is supposed to be a *rock* pub.)

Nevertheless, after having a bit of a

self-indulgent pogo to Twisted Sister's *I Am, I'm Me*, I played them all (there's that sweet nature again), and still had time to throw in something that I liked too. It took my mind off Woodstock's impending news for a bit. I was pleased, however, to see the friendly face of my new boyfriend.

'You having a scrap?' laughed Roach.

I wasn't really in the mood for funnies, but he was a welcome relief. 'You wouldn't think it was possible, would you? So, what do you want?'

'You.'

'Crawler.'

'It's not going well, then?'

'No, it's crap.' I told him about the petty wrangling of the evening. He'd come in at the tail end of it and had missed most of the action. 'And now some silly cow,' I tossed my hand towards the mezzanine, 'she's given me a *list*. She's even written it out herself.'

Roach laughed again and took a swig from his beer. 'You gonna play 'em?'

I checked my watch against the clock over the bar. God, it was dragging tonight, despite all the fun and games. 'Probably, unless I get some better requests.'

'Let's have a look then.' He took the list from me, read it to himself, and added a few suggestions of his own using a stubby pencil he'd dug from the depths of a pocket. I have to admit that when he handed it back to me, I actually preferred his selection.

As we were clearly having a requests night, I wasn't surprised to see one of my regular requesters appear at the cage. He comes in every Saturday and generally his choice tends to agree with my own taste in music, usually many tracks I would have asked for myself. When he showed up I was neither surprised nor discouraged when he asked for a track I didn't know off a little played CD that I did have. I played it almost immediately, quite looking forward to listening to some decent new music . . .

It was the biggest load of crap that I have ever heard. It wouldn't even make it into my shit box. I was well pissed off by now, and thus ended all further requests for this particular night.

'Sorry, no time, folks.'

Instead I played some of my own favourites and some of the ones Roach had asked for. A man after my own heart, at least I could trust his judgement. Something I'd never do with that other guy again — well, not so implicitly at least.

I filled Roach in on what Woodstock had said on the phone earlier, between records.

'What do you reckon?' he asked.

'I don't know. He was quite excited.'

'Why didn't you make him tell you there and then?'

'He was too scared to say anything over the phone. He thought someone might be listening in. I didn't have that much time anyway and Pendle would have hated the call coming through in the first place. I was surprised to hear from him really.'

'And he's not told anyone else either?' I shook my head.

Roach changed pint glasses while I changed records, then he came back and said: 'What was he scared about anyway? No-one's going to get at him in there, are they? Don't they get more privileges, more security?'

'He's probably in the safest place,' I agreed. 'And anyway, Angus has an old chum inside who he's asked to look out for him.'

Noticing the time, he downed his pint. 'Right, I'm off for a piss.' He headed towards the fire escape door that led to the car park, open again now, and I finally played the last proper record of the night.

'Here's *Night Crawler* by Judas Priest.'

Again I heard someone mutter loudly about the DJ living in the dark ages, but Judas Priest weren't all that long ago and they did come from around here. I told them to watch while Judas Priest reformed, but they didn't believe me . . . I didn't care. It was my show and I play what I like.

To teach them a lesson I finished with *MacNamara's Band*. If they wanted old, I could show them old.

★ ★ ★

Woodstock's visiting order never arrived on Tuesday morning. It had been a bank holiday the day before so there probably hadn't been a postal collection at the prison. I called Winson Green to see if one had been sent in the first place and whether I'd be able to come in without it.

'Hold the line, please,' said the telephonist. She left me hanging on for ages. After around eight or nine minutes, and just as I was about to hang up, she came back to me.

'Who did you say was calling?' she asked, carefully.

'Marcie Craig,' I repeated.

'Are you a relative?'

Alarm bells started to ring and my heart plummeted into my boots. 'No, I'm his best friend.'

'I'm afraid I'm only allowed to talk to relatives over the phone — '

'He doesn't have any,' I snapped. 'In fact, I'm probably all he does have right now.'

She went away again but when she came back this time said: 'Perhaps you'd be able to come in this morning?'

'That's what I'm calling for. I *want* to come in this morning. He was supposed to send me a visiting order.'

'I'm afraid that's not what I mean.' I really didn't like the tone in her voice. 'Mister Palmer had, erm, a bit of an accident on Saturday night. He's very ill — '

'He can't be that ill. I only spoke with him on Saturday night. What happened?'

'It's best if you come in, Ms Craig.' I hate Ms even more than I hate Miss.

I got there as soon as I could, and was directed to the prison doctor.

'What happened?' I asked again.

'You're too late, Miss Craig,' said the doctor.

'What?' I thought I was going to faint, and leaned against a wall.

'You've just missed him. He's been transferred to the Midland Hospital, intensive care . . . '

Oh, thank God for that. He was still alive.

27

Woodstock lay completely still in the big hospital bed. They might have transferred him to a normal hospital but he was still under twenty-four-hour guard — as if he was going to escape in his condition. He'd been moved because the prison hospital wasn't adequately equipped for circumstances such as this one. He was unconscious.

His lovely olive skin looked grey now, transparent and colourless, apart from the nasty purple bruising around his left eye, temple and cheek bone. The gash itself was respectfully dressed, but a bright red spot of blood had soaked through the bandage. His shoulders were well strapped but the rest of him was hidden beneath the covers. One arm lay on top of the quilt, lifelessly at his side. At least he wasn't handcuffed.

There were tubes everywhere. Some were Sellotaped to just beneath his nose, others ran into his arm. He was linked to a monitor, which let us all know his heart was still beating. He was breathing for himself, even though he was completely out of it.

The only reason I was allowed anywhere

near him was because I was the closest person to him, as far as the prison knew. They had me down as his only visitor. Even then I was only allowed to spend a few minutes with him. They said I could hold his hand and talk to him so I could see he was all right. He could probably hear me, whether he responded or would remember or not, and he was going to recover. His brain was doing all the right things. They just didn't know how long it would take. He'd already been out for two days.

I didn't know what to say to him.

A couple of hours after Woodstock had called me it appeared that he either got himself beaten up by some of the other inmates or he'd had a nasty fall. Although it was obvious he'd taken a pasting, none of his room-mates could confirm that he had. They'd said they didn't know why anyone would want to beat him up because he was such a nice bloke, but the official said they might have found out he was gay or someone may have 'arranged' it. That's what they said anyway. Unlikely but the best they could offer until he woke up.

To me it was too much of a coincidence. Woodstock had realised who Gavin's and Daisy's killer was. He called me at The Cellar to tell me that he knew. Less than two hours later this 'such a nice bloke' had been beaten senseless. Whoever the killer was, he had contacts on the inside. There was only one person I'd told of my conversation with Woody.

Roach.

Keeping my eyes on Woodstock's stony face I picked up his hand. It felt soft and warm, not at all how I expected it to be. His brown eyes gazed beyond me through half closed lids, seeing nothing.

'Come on, Woody,' I said to him at last. 'You're gonna be all right. Don't forget you have to tell me who did this to you. We're gonna catch the bastard, don't you worry.'

At the same time I was worried. Did Roach have something to do with this lot? I was sure he didn't. Daisy and Woodstock were both friends of his and besides, I knew him. He couldn't have done this to Woody, he was with me for most of Saturday . . . *most* of Saturday. He could easily have used a phone.

A couple of nurses came in to fuss about Woody while the security guard sat just a few feet from his bed. We were in a side room off the main ward. I looked up and recognised one of the women.

'Clarice,' I yelled. 'How you doing?'

As soon as she saw who I was her face beamed with recognition. 'Marcie Craig?

Don't you look different without your bruises.'

I brushed my face with the tips of my fingers. 'They've almost gone now. And I'm back at work.'

'Did you find what you wanted the other week?'

Blimey, what a memory. 'Nah. It's like looking for a needle in a haystack. Turned out to be the wrong hospital anyway.'

'Oh, that's too bad.' She glanced across at the other nurse who checked one of Woodstock's vitals then noted something down on a chart. 'Is this the friend who got framed?' She flicked her eyes over the security guard while I nodded. 'They didn't let him out, then?'

'No. But if they had . . . ' I glanced down at Woodstock's still form.

'Now don't you go thinking things like that. It doesn't help you and it won't help him.' Clarice looked at his face. 'What happened to him anyway?'

'I really don't know,' I shrugged. 'He called me from the prison on Saturday night to tell me he knew who the killer was. Then, when I wanted to visit him this morning he was already in here.'

'And did they get whoever it was who did this to him?'

'They can't be sure that anyone did.' I pulled a face of disbelief. 'Nobody saw anything.' Clarice's face followed suit. 'Is he really going to be all right, or are they just saying he will?'

She gave me a sympathetic smile. 'You were like this yourself only a few weeks ago — '

'Yeah,' I interrupted. 'But not for so long.'

'Long enough.' She checked her fob watch. 'How long have you been in here?'

'About fifteen minutes.'

'Go and get yourself a nice hot cup of tea, child. The Women's Institute have a booth out in the waiting area. Give yourself a break for five minutes.'

'Will you let me know if there's any change?'

'Sure I will. I'll see what I can find out about his injuries too. I've only just come on to this shift. When Doctor does her rounds, I'll be able to look at her notes. She'll be here soon. Are you his only visitor?'

I nodded before taking myself off, then for fifteen minutes or more I fidgeted on a hard plastic seat. This ward was in the old part of the hospital and not nearly so nice as the one I'd been in. The tea wasn't bad, though, so I had another. Then Clarice joined me. She carried a cardboard folder, green with a red

289

sticker on the spine. In the top right hand corner was a seven digit number beneath which neat hand written black lettering read: PALMER, M. Clarice had a grave expression on her sweet face.

'Your friend has a fractured skull; two small fractures to his right shoulder, where we believe he fell; further fractures to his left arm; and three broken fingers. It's as though he were hit with a rounders bat or a club. His arm was probably damaged while trying to protect his head.' I'd never noticed Wood-stock was left handed. 'The gash on his temple is quite deep and we don't know what might have caused that. Possibly something the size of a golf ball, perhaps a little bigger.

'However, he has the constitution of an elephant. He's come to a few times over the past couple of days but drifted straight back off again. That's probably the medication he's on more than anything. I can't really tell you any more than that at the moment — oh, but you're his nominated next of kin. They were able to take that from his prison notes.'

That meant they should have contacted me as soon as it happened. Maybe they had. I was, after all, out on Saturday night when it happened. Had they called back at the pub?

'So he's been in and out of consciousness?' Clarice nodded. 'Is that good.'

'It isn't bad. And for the time being at least it means he'll be kept here.'

Suddenly my stomach growled quite unexpectedly in its usual fashion. My brain must have thought the nurse had reassured me enough for normal services to resume. She chortled with glee. 'I'm pleased to hear your appetite has been unaffected by all of this.'

I grinned back at her. 'That'll be the day when it is. Is there somewhere around here I can get a bacon sarnie from?' I already knew the WI booth didn't stretch that far.

She screwed her face up in thought. 'There's a canteen in this block. Downstairs.' We were on the third floor.

'Is he likely to wake up in the next half hour or so?'

'It's possible. But he may not stay that way for long.'

'If he wakes up and you're there, will you let him know I'm here?'

'Sure. He probably already knows anyway.'

'The hearing is the last to go,' we said together.

'Now you go and get something to eat before your belly disturbs my patients,' she said, before chortling to herself.

I went back into the room to see Woody. No change. He still lay on the high, narrow

291

bed, still gazed unseeingly. I muttered a few more encouraging words, not knowing if he really could hear me but hoping that he could. After my bacon sarnie it'd be back to the waiting game.

'I'm just going to grab something to eat, Woody,' I said, rubbing his injured hand again. 'Then I'll be back. Don't move.' As if he was likely to.

I'd probably been hanging around for about an hour and I had come out without any breakfast. It was well past the middle of the morning by the time I got here after first going to the prison. Yep, I definitely needed food. I headed off towards what I thought might be the canteen . . . and got lost.

This part of the hospital was one of those old Victorian things set in one of the old houses I'd seen on my last visit. Many were closed and boarded up. Some were already derelict or being knocked down. One or two, however, were still in use as the various departments gradually relocated to the new blocks as and when they became complete. Here there were still lots of high-ceilinged tall corridors everywhere, painted with dirty yellow or mushy pea green paint. Archaic radiators, six inches thick, stuck out from the walls, also painted with gloss to match the walls. Camouflage. The network of corridors reminded me of an ants' nest we once kept at school.

In one corner there was a huge cage-like lift where you had to close both metal doors before the thing would budge. Although it was too much like hard work, I decided to stick to the stairs.

Everywhere there were nurses and porters hurrying about their work. Not one of them could sense that I'd lost my way. Maybe they were too busy. Even the signs didn't help, which were in the process of being dismantled. There was either two of everything or nothing at all.

I decided to head back to either the main entrance or Woody's ward and floor and try again. Surely I'd be able to smell the food cooking at some stage, or maybe it would come looking for me, like in the *Bisto* advert on telly.

It was the main entrance I found first. This had been overbuilt at some time, probably during the 1960s judging by the architecture. It was now, compared to the rest of the building, a modern, square-shaped area with plenty of opening windows and more slimline central heating radiators. A plain staircase led up to a selection of wards, and there was a single lift, of the more familiar type, next to that. A corridor led to the left and right behind the reception desk, and on the wall facing me was a large sign.

The sign told me that the canteen — sorry, 'restaurant' — was indeed in this block, on this floor — ground — and at the opposite end to where Accident and Emergency used to be. I had been in A&E over in one of the new blocks. This sign had masking tape over the wording, which several people had idly picked at over the preceding weeks. Beneath it a handwritten note apologised for any inconvenience caused during refurbishment of the hospital.

Intensive care was still upstairs, but I knew that already because Woody was in there. The sign also told me that I could still find Medical Records downstairs in the basement. Now that did confuse me because I knew that Medical Records was in another block. I'd been there myself only two weeks ago. I examined the sign more closely, but there was no trace of any masking tape being picked off this part of the board.

An image came to me in a flash. The notes Clarice had been holding, Woody's notes, had something else on the front cover apart from his name and number. Something that hadn't registered. In the centre someone had rubber-stamped them:

PROPERTY OF
THE ROYAL INFIRMARY
BIRMINGHAM

This was the *Midland* Hospital. The Royal
Infirmary had already closed, several months
ago.

I strode up those stairs two at a time and
ran to find Clarice still on Woodstock's ward.
By the time I reached her I was out of puff.

'Clarice . . . those notes . . .'

'Hush, child,' she scolded, steering me
away from the patient I'd waited for her to
stop dealing with. She shoved me into an
empty side room and lowered her voice.
'D'you want to get me into trouble? I
shouldn't even have had those notes.'

'I know, and I'm sorry.' I caught my breath
again. 'But they had 'The Royal Infirmary'
stamped on the front of them.'

'Yes.' She didn't sound at all surprised.
'Mark had been a patient there before.'

It was always strange to hear people refer to
his real name. 'But where did you get them
from? The Royal's been closed for months.'

'All the records for the Royal were moved
here when it closed. It's quite normal.'

'Why didn't you tell me that the other week
when I was looking for the deaths register?'

'Because you didn't say he died at the

Royal Infirmary. I could've told you they'd moved their records into this building. When the new block's finished they'll both be moved into there and merged properly.'

'But they're downstairs now?' She nodded. 'Clarice, you're an angel.'

I dashed off before she had time to answer and hurried down the stairs to Medical Records. I don't know why I was rushing. They weren't going anywhere.

Another notice informed me that I would also find the mortuary in the basement, but that couldn't be helped. My belly pulled me up by growling loudly. I ummed and ahhed but decided that the bacon sarnie could wait a bit longer. I was hot now and was going to find Medical Records — again.

I finally found a narrow flight of stone steps leading to the basement. The corridors down there were also narrow and there were no radiators. I shivered and tried to forget that the morgue wasn't far away. I thanked God it wasn't the middle of winter, although it may as well have been.

At a T-junction yet another sign told me that the mortuary was on the left and Medical Records was on the right. No contest — I went right. There were no windows down there, just a single line of fluorescent strip lights burning away. I felt my eyes contract at the false, flickering brightness and empathised with those poor sods that had to work there.

The basement walls were painted a cream colour, gloss again, with funny little bumps beneath the surface, like woodchip wallpaper, but not. A sparkly red substance covered the floor and travelled up the wall for about eighteen inches. Every so often an electric socket, one-gang, metal case, no switch, jutted out and was connected to the next by about fifteen feet of what looked like lead pipework.

Bubblegum pink glossed doors led from the corridor, but they were mostly closed or opening the wrong way for me to see in. Each one had a six inch by one inch wooden plaque screwed into it at eye level: ladies' toilet; store room; gents' toilet; Medical Records Officer (that door was open but there was no-one in sight); fire hydrant; and so on. I made my way to the end of the corridor, which opened out into a huge room, and which probably spread out beneath half of the hospital.

There were loads of floor to ceiling metal shelf systems with big, round winding handles to move the shelves along a track in the floor. Each handle had a notice above it:

WARNING:
PLEASE ENSURE NO-ONE IS INSIDE
BEFORE MOVING

Ouch, what a way to go. Well, that seemed fair enough.

Each cabinet was packed with A4 cardboard folders like the one Clarice had held. Some were fatter than others and seemed to be in every colour possible. Those that looked the newest were all the same colour. Maybe they chose a different colour per year of registration. Patients' notes. Hundreds of them, probably thousands. Between the stacks several young girls and middle aged women wearing pale blue dresses and sensible shoes pulled or re-filed piles of notes.

At one end of the room, my end, was a wall length bank of drawers. Some were open and revealed small six inch by four inch white record cards with names and addresses on. Some had a single word stamped across them in red ink: DECEASED. They all had a seven digit number on them. No doubt those would all be computerised once the move was over and done with.

On a desk next to the drawers, and beside three telephones, hummed a computer, which was drawing all sorts of wonderful, colourful geometric shapes on an otherwise blank screen. A screen saver. I tapped the space bar and the images froze while a box popped up asking for a password. Spoilsport. I wouldn't be going anywhere on there.

Perched on a shelf above the computer were three wire post baskets with labels mostly written in black marker pen. One was clearly labelled 'Post Out'. A second had 'EBH' crossed out and 'Heartlands' — the name East Birmingham Hospital had already been known by for several years now — scribbled on in biro. The third said 'A2B', the name of a courier service, in big writing, with the names of several doctors' surgeries printed in smaller writing. There was a good mix of notes in each of the baskets, including deceased.

It was very quiet. Everyone was busy in the filing area. I walked back to the shelves and watched those I could see.

'Can I help you?' barked a voice from behind — female, I presumed ... I leapt out of my leather jacket, then turned to face the most ferocious looking battleaxe I had ever seen. She was all of four feet high, with a long, bloodhound type of face, a short, curly grey perm, and pince-nez on the end of her nose. I couldn't tell what colour her eyes were due to the folds of skin that fell over them.

'Ah . . . I was looking for the canteen,' I said.

'Does this look like a canteen?' she snapped. Then, before I had time to reply, 'right area, wrong floor. *This*,' she hissed, 'is Medical Records.'

'Oh?' Innocent. 'I do beg your pardon.' She wore a badge on the jacket of her heather coloured tweed suit that told me she was the Medical Records Officer. I started to sidle away, keeping my back to the walls.

'I'll come with you,' she declared. 'In case you get lost again.'

Great. 'Er, thanks,' I said, and followed her. Because of the direction we were now walking in, I could see inside some of those rooms I couldn't see in before. One had a pile of registers in it, stacked up on a table, just like the one I'd ploughed through in the other building. We reached the ladies' loos when a phone started to ring in the MRO office.

'It's okay,' I said, when she hesitated. 'I should be fine now. I could do with the toilet anyway.' To substantiate my claim, I did a little jig, as one who is dying for a wee, and leaned a hand on the toilet door, ready to push.

'Very well,' she replied, returning to her office. I watched her close the door and heard her bark into the phone. I dived into the other room and closed the door behind me.

28

The room was small, dusty, dark and musty, though not quite so bad as the one I'd been in two weeks before. This one had only recently been disturbed, when the Royal's records had been transferred and added. The dust, however, had been transferred with it and was ingrained into every single surface.

Old wooden slatted shelves lined three of the walls. A huge table monopolised the centre of the room. It had grey, metal legs and a chipped, pale blue Formica top. It looked like it might be a canteen refugee. A thick film of grey-brown dust covered everything, but fresh finger marks showed that someone had recently had a rummage.

The fat registers I had seen from the corridor were all births. They'd had quite a big maternity unit at the Royal. I had a quick look. There was no order to them. It looked like they had been dumped in a packing crate at one end, then dumped on the table at this end. Perhaps one of the filing clerks had been nosy. If I'd been born at that hospital I daresay I would have had a quick peek at my own birth date to make sure it had happened.

But I was born in Solihull so I wouldn't be recorded here.

I tried to remember again what Daisy had said on that last afternoon. I was sure she hadn't said anything to pinpoint the date exactly. I found and hauled out the deaths register for 1993. It was on the top shelf beneath a pile of another three. Either the Royal had been a much bigger hospital than this one, or you didn't stand much chance of getting out alive.

Each individual year had at least its own ledger, while some had almost two. Those must have been the times we had something like a flu epidemic. Closer inspection revealed that there had already been one merger with another hospital in the past. There were two lots of information in one ledger.

Patiently, for me, I began reading. Have you ever tried reading a telephone directory, or even a dictionary? Ploughing slowly through a long list of deaths must be much like that.

As I picked through the massive, yellowed pages, tiny clouds of dust puffed outwards and upwards. After a good half an hour, my eyes were once more feeling tight and gritty, and my throat dry. There was nowhere to sit so my back and shoulder ached and grew stiff. Perched on the edge of the table I constantly fidgeted and shifted position.

An hour passed. Because I was taking my time, reading every line twice for fear of missing something significant, I was only in June. Unable to put my finger on anything, I had a little stretch, walked around the table twice one way and then the other. Then I carried on looking.

By the time I reached Christmas I hadn't got any closer and my belly was rumbling even louder. I caught a waft of chips — it came from under the door — and remembered the bacon sarnie I hadn't had. Dreams of bacon sandwiches were swiftly forgotten and replaced, instead, by dreams of chips. Fresh, fat, crispy chips, piled high on a plate and smothered in salt and vinegar. Steak and kidney pie too. My mouth was slavering now so I quickly finished the job in hand.

Nothing had really caught my eye or made my brain go ping, but I did make a note of one 'Steven Pendle', and his registration number, who had died in the hospital during the summer. I had no reason to suspect Ken Pendle really. He hadn't even been there when Gavin had died. But it wasn't a common name and it was the only one I recognised. I wondered if they were related and was thankful I hadn't found a Beadsley. There were no Craigs that year either.

I left everything exactly as I had found it, except for a few extra finger marks, paid a quick visit to the ladies' loo to wash my grubby hands, and sneaked back up the staircase without the dragon spotting me. Following the whiff, I sought out the hospital canteen and food, and heartily ate.

★ ★ ★

Contented, and with a full stomach, I popped in to see Woodstock. Still no change. I gave him a few more words of encouragement, waved at Clarice and went home. As I let myself in the phone started to ring.

It was Roach, and my hackles went up. I'd been unable to link him further to the crime, and he had been with me on the night Daisy died. He'd been with me the night Woody got done over too. But there was still the phone. I tried not to let my suspicions show in my voice. If I was going to confront him, I wanted to see the reaction on his face.

'It's Daisy's funeral tomorrow,' he said.

'So soon?'

'Maybe that mystery daughter of hers just wants to get it over and done with.'

'Maybe. I can't say I blame her, poor kid, can you? Where is it? Do you know?'

'Over at the Central Crematorium and

Cemetery. Ten o'clock.'

'Right.' I made a note so I could send flowers. 'Are you going?'

'Yeah. I'll be paying my last respects and all that. I've got a job in on Thursday.' He must have heard me suck in my breath, or he could feel my bad vibes coming down the line, because he continued: 'Don't worry, it's a driving job. Nothing illegal. I have to take a haul up to Scotland. I won't be back until Friday night — at the earliest.'

I sighed with relief. Perhaps he was trying to clean up his act after all. 'I've swapped with Dave tonight, because of that Friday he stood in for me. Will you be coming in?'

'I don't know yet. It's not so much fun when you're working. I might go to Barney's instead. Or the Rock Café. But I'll probably drop in for a quick one on the way.'

We hung up. I still had a couple of hours to kill before I needed to get ready for work. After ordering the flowers for Daisy I dozed in the bath to get rid of the dirt and grime from Medical Records. I had a think, too, about everything I'd learned over the past few weeks. I really hoped Roach was on the level. It would be a great disappointment if he were behind all of this. And if he wasn't . . . ? If I couldn't trust that he wasn't, then maybe the only future for us could be as friends.

After the recent dry spell the rain poured down with a vengeance on Wednesday. Typical for bank holiday week. A huge crowd turned out to see Daisy off. Veronica Deakin looked just as composed and elegant as before. I really wanted to speak to her but wasn't sure if it was the right thing to do. She was busy greeting the mourners and no doubt had a lot on her mind.

I'd dressed for the occasion in a long, black hippy skirt that had tassels along the bottom, with a plain black tee shirt and knee-length black boots. I only own two coats, my biker's leather and a donkey jacket I wear over it in the winter. For Daisy's funeral I just wore the leather. It went quite well with the skirt. Roach had made an effort too. He was wearing black cords with his leather. I'd driven over in the Jeep. He'd biked over on his Honda.

When I told him what had happened to Woodstock he looked genuinely surprised and visibly disturbed. He didn't believe me at first, so I had to assume he knew nothing about it.

As funeral services go it was okay, but it was obvious the vicar hadn't known Daisy personally, which was probably just as well.

306

He kept on calling her Jean and I was sure the only person there who had ever known her as Jean was her daughter. As I supposed she was the only truly important person there, then that was probably just as well too. And anyway, Daisy wasn't listening.

Outside we waded through the mud to an open grave, freshly dug. Here the service continued until we were thoroughly drenched, and finished with Veronica throwing a handful of dirt down on to the coffin. As people started to drift away to their cars, bikes and buses, I was able to catch Veronica gently by the arm.

'Miss Deakin?'

'Yes?' She stopped and blinked at me, struggling to remember where she'd seen me before.

'I'm really sorry about your mother,' I said.

'You were at the inquest, weren't you?' she asked, finally placing me. 'Did you know my mother well?'

'She was a good friend. We all loved her very much.'

Veronica held a large umbrella in one hand and moved so that it protected the two of us. Rain streamed over it, splashing not far from our feet, but it was slowing down. She chewed at her bottom lip and looked down at her other hand, in which she clutched a tightly balled white handkerchief.

'Did you . . . ' she stammered, for the first time showing any emotion. 'Did you know she was a . . . prostitute?' She whispered the final word.

It was my turn to look away. 'Er, yes. We all knew.'

'I didn't. I didn't even know my own mother. She always sent me away. First to boarding school, then to university, and finally to a foreign job. I had no idea . . . I didn't know her.'

She was wrestling with herself to keep control. She'd had two nasty shocks, one on top of the other. I said: 'There was nothing dirty or sordid about Dai . . . er, your mother. She was very happy and she enjoyed life.' I had a brainwave and dug deep in one of the pockets in my leather jacket. I fished out a business card. 'Listen, I know you're busy right now, and a bit upset. But when you're feeling up to it, and if you have time before you leave us again, perhaps we could have a chat? About your mom.'

She looked at me through red-rimmed eyes, but she still wasn't crying yet.

'Your mother was a lovely lady. Perhaps it would help to talk.' I pressed the card into her hand and she rushed away, taking the umbrella with her.

'Do you think she will?' asked Roach, who had been standing at a respectful distance and trying to shelter from the rain, which was now stopping.

'I hope so.'

We started to straggle behind the others when Roach swivelled his head and then stopped me. 'Hey, look at that.'

I turned to see the forlorn figure of Ken Pendle, coat collar pulled up against the weather, gazing down at a small headstone, several yards away, in a diagonal direction from where we'd just come.

'I didn't see him at the funeral,' I said. 'Did you?'

Roach shook his head and grabbed my wrist to look at my watch. 'It's not like him to miss opening time, is it?'

'Trust you to think of that. He did the other week when I was off.'

We stepped between the graves to join him and both looked down at the stone:

STEVEN PENDLE
BELOVED SON OF
KENNETH AND VALERIE
DIED SUDDENLY AT THE
AGE OF TWENTY-ONE
SADLY MISSED

'He was your son?' I blurted out, making Ken jump.

'I didn't see you there.' He was sober too. 'Did you know him?' he said to me. When I opened my mouth to speak, nothing came out, and so he added: 'You sounded surprised, as if you knew him.'

'Ah. Er. No. Only, um, it says Kenneth and Valerie. I, er, meant is that you?

I held my breath but he turned his eyes back to the memorial. 'Yes. He died three years ago.'

'How?' asked Roach, sensitive as ever. I elbowed him sharply in the ribs and he glared at me and mouthed the word 'what'.

Pendle struggled to stop himself from shaking, then spat: 'Someone killed him.'

'Oh,' I said, shocked. There was a lot of that going on around here. I changed the subject, neatly I thought. 'I didn't see you at Daisy's funeral.'

'No. I was a bit late. It was difficult, you see.' He nodded towards the carefully tended mound of earth covering his son's body. 'I managed to get here towards the end, when they started to bury her. I waited at the back, you know.'

'Did she live close to you?' I wondered why his son was buried in the same graveyard, not

310

that there were that many left for internments in Birmingham.

'She lived in the same block as my wife.'

I had only ever seen Pendle by himself at the pub, but I knew the stories of how he'd apparently thrown his wife across the bar in a drunken rage once. 'What happened to Valerie? Is she your wife?'

'She threw me out. It was the strain. The brewery lets me use one of their manager flats, for pubs without accommodation like mine.' He reached in a pocket, drew out those silver balls of his, and began clinking.

'Where *do* you get those things from?' I asked, indicating the balls. I couldn't recall seeing any for sale in Woolworths.

'Vernon gave them to me.'

'Our Vernon, the doorman?'

Pendle nodded. I think he gets them from the market. He said they'd do me good.'

'And do they?' asked Roach.

'I don't think so. They just give me something to do with my hands. Like smoking.'

Yeah, I thought. Like drinking too.

He returned his attention to the mound of earth. 'The bastard who did this to Steven,' he nodded down at the grave again, 'he ruined my life.' *Clink! Clink! Clink!*

Roach tactfully changed the subject once

more. 'Who's opening up?'

This question jolted Pendle back from wherever it was he'd drifted off to. He checked his watch. 'Basil, I think. Maybe I'd better get a move on. See you.'

We watched him walk away up the path, replacing the balls in his pocket, and then we pulled a face at each other. I looked down at Steven's grave and heard Daisy's voice: ' . . . find out how he died . . . everything else will fall into place.' How could I find out how he died?

I had an idea.

'Look, Roach. I'm not going to the wake after all.' Veronica had arranged a small do around by where Daisy lived. 'I'm going to get home, dry off. I want to make some phone calls.'

'Oh, right. Okay. I'm not going either. I'll nip into The Cellar for a drink instead.'

I gave him a hug and a quick kiss. 'Have a good trip tomorrow.'

'Yeah, okay. See ya Friday.' And he followed Pendle up the path.

I was going to ring the hospital.

29

As soon as I got home I hauled out the telephone directory. Well, it's not as fat as it used to be since British Telecom cut it down to size, but I hauled it out anyway.

It took me ages to find a number for the Midland Hospital, but I located a general enquiry number for them and called it. A friendly voice answered so I said I needed to speak to my sister urgently in Medical Records, but had left my diary with the direct number in it at home. You know how people gush a load of unnecessary guff when they're making a personal call on company time? I even told her my sister hadn't been working there long, so her name probably wouldn't be in the hospital directory yet.

She was very nice and asked me to repeat which office my sister worked in. I told her and she put me through. I hoped that whoever picked up the call didn't realise it had come through the switchboard instead of via the direct number. I understand from Penny that the phone makes a different kind of ringing sound if it comes from outside and having never worked in that kind of environment myself, I have only her word to go by. I dearly hoped the old dragon didn't pick up. She didn't.

In fact the girl who did answer the call didn't sound much older than about fifteen-and-a-half — a bit like some of the kids we get at The Cellar. I supposed she must have been a YTS or someone like that in training.

'Good afternoon,' she sang in her best telephone voice. 'Medical Records.'

'Um, I'd like a set of notes, please.'

'Yes, who's calling?' She didn't sound in the least bit suspicious — at this stage.

'Er, it's Clarice. From Heartlands.' Heartlands, remember, used to be East Birmingham Hospital. Clarice was the first name that sprang into my head. Now the girl did hesitate, so I continued quickly. 'It's my first day and this is the first call they've let me make on my own.'

'Oh, right,' she replied, suddenly sympathetic. She was very chirpy. 'I still remember my first day.' It couldn't have been *that* long ago. 'What's the number?'

'Pardon?' Oh, God. She wanted the phone number.

'The patient's registration number?'

'Oh yes, right.' I reeled off the seven digit

314

number I'd made a note of. 'The name's Steven Pendle.'

'When do you want them for?'

I crossed my fingers. 'We're sending a bike over.'

If she suspected anything yet she still didn't hint at it. 'Are you sure they're here? Have you checked the computer?'

'They haven't been used for three years,' I said, crossing my toes. 'They should be there.'

'Okay, I'll go and pull them for you now. What time will the bike be here?'

I checked my watch. 'In about forty minutes.' Well, I did have to get through town and I didn't know what the traffic would be like.

'Okay,' she said once more. 'I'll be talking to you again, then?'

I crossed my eyes. 'Yeah, hope so. What did you say your name was? For next time?' Who knew when I might need her help again?

'Janice. Bye then, Clarice.'

'Yeah, tarrar Janice. And thanks.'

The phone line went dead. Well, that was easy. So much for hospital security. I changed out of the hippy skirt and into some jeans, and swapped the Jeep for the bike. Maybe at last I was going to make some sense out of this whole bloody mess.

* * *

For a Wednesday lunchtime the Birmingham traffic was quite bad. I'd expect it to
be busy in the rush hour, but not in the
middle of the day. It was also raining again
by now and I could feel tiny rivulets of
rainwater creeping down my neck, inside
my collar — one of the disadvantages of
riding a motorbike.

It took me about an hour altogether by the
time I crossed town. On a good run it
generally takes just over half that time. I
parked up outside the hospital in the Goods
Inwards bay. I guessed that as I was posing as
trade this was the best place for me.

I thought it best to keep my helmet on,
even though it had MARCIE printed across
the front in gold letters. If the old dragon
spotted me the game would be up. She
looked like the kind of woman who only
needed to see you once and your face would
be etched on her memory *ad infinitum*. It
took me a while to find my bearings with me
coming in at a different angle, but I got there
in the end.

Another person I really didn't want to
bump into was Janice. She'd been so sweet on
the phone and very helpful and all that, but
after speaking to her so recently I'd not be

able to look her in the eye. It's much easier to lie over the phone. Of course I had no idea of knowing which of the filing clerks was Janice because I'd never seen her before. She was probably one of the younger ones, judging by the sound of her voice.

'Can I help you?' barked a familiar voice.

'Yes,' I cried, relieved. It was the old dragon but she didn't seem to recognise my face beneath my lid, or remember the voice now muffled by the helmet's padding. 'Er, White Flag Courier Service,' I announced. I'd been thinking that one up all the way here. 'I've come to collect a set of notes.'

'Name?' she snapped.

'Oh, um, Marcie,' I began, rather unnecessarily pointing at the gold letters across the front of my mouth. Then I switched, and held my gloved hand out for her to shake.

'Not yours, dimwit. I can see that. I meant the name of the patient.' I wondered if she spoke to her staff like that.

'Oh, sorry.' I fumbled in one of my money pockets and pulled out a slip of paper. 'Pendle. Steven Pendle.'

The dragon glanced at a cluttered desk and swooped on a deep-blue cardboard folder straight away. There were so many files littering the table top that I wouldn't have found the file so quickly. She matched the file to a pre-written large buff-coloured stiff-backed envelope that had printed on the front:

ATTN. CLARICE, MEDICAL RECORDS, HEARTLANDS.

The seven digit number had been written in the top left-hand corner in black felt-tipped pen. How did she find it so fast?

She passed the envelope to me and took in my appearance in one sweep. I must have looked like a Martian, clad all in black and wearing a full-faced helmet. But even Martians must be afraid of dragons.

'Is it raining?' she asked finally.

'Only a bit of drizzle now, I think.' I would have looked out of a window to check, but there wasn't one.

'Will those be all right?' She indicated the envelope, which was now in my hand. 'We don't want the ink running.'

'Sure they will. I've got panniers on my bike,' I lied. I wouldn't be seen dead with panniers on my bike, but she wasn't to know that.

'Good.' She nodded and walked away. I guessed I had just been dismissed so took my cue and left.

Once clear of the hospital building I stuffed

the envelope inside my leather, and zipped the jacket right up to my neck. I didn't want the ink to run either.

Having skipped dinner I started to look ahead to an early tea. It was closer to tea time now anyway and the weather was getting worse. I flicked my visor down against the rain but couldn't help the wet seeping through to my fingers and thighs. As a result, I rode slower. By the time I reached my little caravan the rain had soaked right through my jeans and gloves. Aside from denim, padded leather is one of the worst materials for the wet. I do have a full set of waterproofs, but I wouldn't be seen dead in those either. They look really naff and make me feel like Andy Pandy at a funeral. Wandering around town dressed in those things, and in daylight too? My street cred would go right down the pan.

The envelope was damp too, apart from a triangular shape where my storm flap had been. Fortunately it was made of strong, brown paper and Steven Pendle's notes had escaped most of it. I tossed the file onto the coffee table and ran myself a bath. I wouldn't have time to bathe, cook, eat and get to work, so I compromised. I ordered a pizza on a half-hour delivery and sank into the hot, scented water.

All I wanted to do now was lounge about

the place in my tracky bottoms eating my pizza and reading the file. Bliss. Unfortunately I had work to do. The file would have to wait.

When I got home from The Cellar well after midnight, I did get changed and settled down in front of the fire to read, with a mug of hot steaming toffee-flavoured chocolate. Delicious.

* * *

Steven Pendle's notes hadn't been disturbed for a while so they smelled musty. A couple of dead but perfectly preserved insects fell out, to the delight of my cat, who pounced on them and played with them for a while. However, once he realised they weren't going to put up a fight, he abandoned them and went to peer at the mice instead.

The guy's medical history was pretty routine for much of his short life, and the file wasn't really very fat. Then, for about the last three months of his life came problem after problem, ailment on top of ailment.

Then came the interesting bit. Steven Pendle had AIDS.

30

It was late by the time I finished reading the notes. Very late. And all of a sudden I felt exhausted. Of course, that could have been the hot chocolate making me drowsy. I saw to the animals and the fish and crawled into bed.

That night I had the best night's kip since I'd been smacked up, concussed and drugged — and no-one called me or woke me in the early hours of the following morning, so I was treated to a wonderful undisturbed lie in. By the time I finally surfaced, it was gone eleven.

Too late for breakfast and too early for dinner, I settled on elevenses or brunch. Bacon, sausage, eggs, mushrooms and toast. At the end of that lot I knew I'd survive until tea time. As I thought of tea my heart sank. Mother was expecting me this week. Oh well, you can't have everything.

I dressed in jeans, tee shirt and sweatshirt, and pulled on ankle boots over *Jungle Book* socks. It was still raining out there and the air was a bit chilly. Not at all like May. Well, all right then, exactly like May in this country. I made myself a cup of tea, re-read about

Steven Pendle's last few days, and phoned Roach.

He wasn't there. Even as one of his cronies started to tell me I remembered that Roach had a job on today. A proper job in Scotland. He'd told me yesterday at the funeral. He wouldn't be back until tomorrow night.

I checked through the notes again and jotted a few things of my own on a pad. Something was missing.

The fact that Steven Pendle was HIV Positive was about all I could make out of the technobabble. Traditionally his GP had the worst writing on the planet, which made it all the more difficult to understand. It put things into perspective, though, and perhaps explained at least some of Ken Pendle's homophobia.

I'd read through the notes several times and picked up a bit more each time, but nowhere could I find any evidence that Steven Pendle was gay. I thought that somewhere there might be some indication of how he'd contracted the disease, and wondered if, indeed, that would even be noted.

What I did determine, though, was how he died. He'd had pneumonia that had started out as just a cough and he didn't respond to any of the antibiotics. He died peacefully in the Royal Infirmary.

I needed to find out how he caught it and was sure it was in there somewhere. I couldn't see the word 'homosexual' anywhere, nor could I see 'drug user'. He'd not had a blood transfusion, as far as I could tell. So how did he get it?

The day was drawing on and I needed someone with a medical mind to help me out.

Clarice.

★ ★ ★

I called the ward at the hospital and found out when Clarice was next on duty. Fortunately she was on days so seeing her wouldn't clash with work. It took a short while, but when I met up with her in the hospital canteen a few days later, she was very cross with me. And it was Monday too.

'Marcella, where did you get these notes? *How* did you get these notes?'

Did she just call me Marcella? I figured she didn't really need to know, but she insisted and refused to help until I told her.

'You used *my name?*'

Perhaps I shouldn't have told her that part.

'Only the Clarice bit — '

'*Only* the Clarice bit? And how many Clarices do you suppose work for the

National Health Service in Birmingham? It's not exactly Jane or Tracey, is it? In fact, why didn't you use one of those names?'

'Because they're so common, I suppose. I don't know. I'm sorry. I didn't think.'

'Obviously.'

'And it was the first name that popped into my head.'

Fortunately for me Clarice is a naturally forgiving soul and she didn't stay mad at me for long. Well, not very mad. Nor for very long.

She sighed. 'How can I help?' she asked, eventually.

'Steven Pendle died of AIDS — '

'He died of an AIDS-related condition,' she corrected. 'People don't die of AIDS.'

'Okay, whatever.' I mentally regrouped. 'I can't see anywhere in his notes how he caught it. Should it be there?'

'If his notes are complete it should be.'

'I can't see it. I need someone who can dissect all of the medical terminology.'

'Okay, but on one condition.'

'Go on.'

'I send these notes back to Medical Records as soon as I've finished with them.'

Ooh, that hurt. I felt a bit possessive and resented giving them back. I was quite proud of how I'd got them and felt a bit attached to them.

'They can't possibly be of any more use to you,' she said, seeing my indecision. 'I can't let you take them away again once I have them. They don't belong to you. They have to go back.'

'Okay,' I mumbled.

We exchanged phone numbers, Clarice went back to work — clutching *my* medical notes — and I went back home feeling bereft.

* * *

'He got it off his girlfriend,' Clarice said down the phone only a few hours later.

'So he wasn't gay?'

'Not according to his notes.'

'And he wasn't using drugs?'

'Not hypodermically.'

'How did she get it?'

'An infected blood transfusion following a road traffic accident when she was younger. I cross-referenced the patients and pulled her notes too.'

'Can I see — '

'No.'

'Is the girlfriend still alive?'

'No. She died less than twelve months after he did.'

I let the information sink in. I wouldn't be able to trace her or speak to her now.

'Are you sure I can't have — '

'No, I'm not giving you any of her details. You're not stealing her notes.'

'Spoilsport.'

Clarice's terrific laugh thundered down the phone. 'Do you need me for anything else?'

I thought for a moment. 'Other than the girl's name, last known address, hospital registration number, vital statistics, oh yes, and her notes? No, I don't think so.'

'Good. Well, Steven Pendle's going back to the deaths cupboard and I'm going back to my shift.'

'Thanks for your help, Clarice.'

'You're welcome. Call me next time.'

31

So, Steven Pendle wasn't gay and he wasn't using drugs — or not to anyone's knowledge. Why, then, did Ken Pendle hate junkies and gays so much? Could it just be the whole AIDS thing? And what was the connection between Steven Pendle's death three years ago, and Gavin's death just a month ago? Daisy was so convinced the two things were related. Did she think that Ken Pendle was somehow responsible for Gavin's death? But Daisy and Ken were friends. I really didn't understand the connection.

Of course the one person who could shed light would have been Steven's girlfriend. But she'd died by now too. I wondered if Ken had gone to her funeral. I wondered if she had gone to Steven's. And what of Steven's mother? Where was she? Would she be able to help? Would she want to? I could also just ask Ken, but he was my boss — and a very temperamental one at that. He'd come to see me after I'd got home from hospital, though. Bearing goodies. I couldn't see him as a killer.

I knew that I had to find Gavin's real killer in order to help Woodstock get out. What if it turned out to be another friend of mine? Did I want to save one and lock up another?

Whatever, I needed to get to the bottom of all of this just to sort it out in my own head. Whoever had killed Gavin, it wasn't Woodstock. So he shouldn't be rotting in jail, or hospital at the moment, for something he didn't do.

Before handing my precious hospital notes over to Clarice, I'd made quite a few notes of my own, and one of those notes was the last address listed for Steven Pendle. I checked the telephone directory and found that there was still a Pendle living there. A Mrs V J Pendle. The area sounds quite lovely when you say it quickly — Lea Village. But there was no way I was taking the bike or the Jeep to Lea Village. They were throwing a lot of cash at the place to make it look nice now, but I still didn't trust the locals. This time I was on the bus. If I was going.

I dialled the number in the telephone book, and then did a really terrible thing. I lied again. Through my teeth. I really was quite shocked at how easy I was finding this lying lark. It was becoming something of a habit.

'Hello?' said a female voice, and she recited the telephone number back to me, the way people of a certain age do. Mother does it too.

'Mrs Pendle?'

'That's right.'

'Um, my name's Penny Fellowes,' I said, stealing my sister's new name. 'Er, I'm a friend of Stevie's and wondered if I might pop over?'

Silence.

'Mrs Pendle?'

'Steven died,' she said at last, with a heavy sigh.

'Yes, I know. I'm sorry. But I've been out of the country,' I said, thanking my lucky stars for Veronica Deakin, Daisy's daughter. 'And when I got back and found out . . . I was so upset.'

'Were you close?'

'Not really. Well, we weren't going out with each other or anything. He was seeing someone else — I can't remember her name.' I paused, but she didn't help. 'But I did like him. It was such a shock.'

'How can I help?'

'I just wondered if I could come on over and, maybe, have a chat? I don't know. Something.'

There was another pause. 'I'm not sure if I'm ready for that or not,' she said quietly. 'It was a shock for us too.'

'Yes, of course. Look, I'm really sorry to have troubled you. It just would have been nice. Closure, I suppose.'

She paused again, then said: 'Let me have your phone number. I'll have a think and call you back. Let you know one way or the other.'

'Okay.' I gave her the number and she promised to call me back. I didn't think it would be straight away, wasn't even certain she'd call at all. But my hand was still on the receiver when the phone rang. It was her.

'Look,' she said, nervously. 'If you were a friend of Steven's then maybe it would help me too, to have a chat. Might do me some good. No-one ever talks about him anymore. It's as though he never existed. They say that talking about things eases the pain a little.'

I squirmed. How low can anyone get? As low as a worm, perhaps? Suddenly I felt guilty. This was people's feelings I was messing with.

'No,' I decided. 'It's not a problem. Maybe I can call you again some other time. I don't want to open up any old wounds.' But it was too late.

'It's all right, really. And I do think it might help. When did you want to come over?'

I was in. And now I wasn't sure if I should pull out again after all. I'd already raised the poor woman's hopes.

'If you're sure?' She made an agreeing noise down the phone. 'Will you be in tomorrow afternoon?' She wouldn't.

'I will if I know you're coming.' Oh.

I mentally calculated how long it would probably take me to get there by bus. I could bike over to Mom's and Dad's and catch a bus from their place. I doubled my estimate. She was happy with that so we confirmed the address, she told me to call her Val, and I put the phone down.

Slime ball.

★   ★   ★

All of this mental arithmetic was making my head hurt.

Steven Pendle was twenty-one when he died, three years ago. In real life that would have made me twenty-nine. But if I was my sister then I would have been twenty-five. If I knocked off another couple of years, that was more realistic.

At least now I knew roughly which era I was supposed to have come from and I started to run through all the rock music that would have been out around the time I'd have known Steven Pendle. It reminded me of what else might have been happening in the world at the same time. The only problem now was I didn't know the first thing about Steven Pendle.

⋆　⋆　⋆

Val Pendle was a small woman with mousey hair and big watery blue eyes. Her hair was streaked with grey and her face etched with sorrow. But the skin on her neck and hands was still smooth. I placed her in her early forties, and tried to imagine her being thrown across a bar by her drunken husband.

The council flat was painted with pastel shades of gloss on the woodwork and the walls were covered with plain white woodchip. Odd sticks of furniture that didn't really go with each other cluttered the place up and every table top was covered with ornaments, trinkets, family photographs and dried flower arrangements in muted tones. Very eighties.

I was grateful for the many pictures and pounced on one, a school photo. In it, Steven Pendle was wearing a distinctive school tie that I recognised — there's only one orange, red, gold and pink school tie in this area, and it was a Catholic school. Useful. He was probably about fifteen when the picture was taken. There were others, taken before and after this one, some with his mom and dad, others with his friends. He did seem to be an only child, though.

'He looked like his dad, didn't he?' I asked, absent minded.

Valerie glanced down at the picture, her dead son's features frozen in time. Ageless. 'He did, yes. But that one isn't Steven.' Shit. 'It's his cousin, David. They did look alike when they were younger. Just like their dads.' Phew.

She picked up another photo. This was of the two boys together at a fair. 'This one's Steven, though you probably didn't know him at school, did you?'

'No, I didn't.' At least that was truthful.

I looked at the photograph and could see the difference between the two boys straight away. The only thing they had in common was their colouring. They were both fair haired with brown eyes, like Pendle.

Valerie had made us both a cup of tea while we looked over the photos.

'Did you meet his dad?' she asked.

'No. I guessed — from the other photos.'

She peered at me carefully. 'Did you ever come here?'

'No, never.'

One of the later photographs showed one of the young men just reaching maturity. He didn't have his father's bushy facial hair, or if he did he kept it well-shaved. Not like Ken at

333

all who has both a beard and a moustache bordering on the ZZ Top. The younger Pendle did have an incredibly thick mop of ash-blond hair sprouting wildly from his head. Brown eyes crinkled at the corners as he grinned at the camera, and I guessed that's how his father must have looked when he was that age, before he was ravaged by time, alcohol and emotional pain.

In a later picture, Steven was posing meaningfully in a go-cart. 'He loved that go-cart,' said Valerie, wistfully.

'Yes,' I said, finally hoping I could latch onto something at last. 'He was very good.' The photo had been sat next to a trophy for go-carting.

One of Valerie's eyebrows shot up. 'So, is that where you knew him from? Were you a member of the club?'

'Um, yes. That's right.' I hoped I wasn't digging myself in any deeper than necessary. 'Er, well they were considering my membership, actually. I usually went along as a friend.' There, that was better.

'Oh? Then you'll remember Andy too?' Her tone of voice had changed and a prickle of worry niggled at the back of my neck.

'Andy?'

She dashed from the room and came back almost immediately clutching a square photo album. After flicking through the pages she came to what she was looking for. A photo of a young lad about the same age as Steven, with spiky bleached blond hair and a gold stud in his nose.

He was wearing a black vest that showed off muscular, sun-bronzed arms, and he smiled meltingly at the camera. He was at a club of sorts. I could see a couple of doormen in the background and most of the people there were men. He reminded me of someone.

'Oh, Andy. Yes, of course. I remember him. Now he was nice looking.' I wasn't lying. He was a dream.

'Yes, such a waste.'

'A waste?'

'Well, yes. They'd been through school and college together, even shared some of the same girls.' I wondered why there weren't any photographs of Steven with him if they were that close. There were pictures of him with everyone else. 'Then it turned out he was a homosexual — '

'He was gay?' I looked at the handsome chappy grinning back at me from the page with his startling blue eyes. She was right. It was a waste, and I realised who he reminded me of. 'Well, who'd have guessed it?'

'I know. They kept it more or less to

themselves and, as you know, they were still the best of friends. But Ken wouldn't let him near the place once he found out.'

'Ken?' Well, I had to keep up the pretence.

'Steven's dad. He said it was unnatural. He hasn't even seen this photograph. It was taken at a gay club in town.' That explained all of the men.

'You were still together then?' It had slipped out, but she didn't seem to notice.

'Oh yes, right up until when he died. Steven, that is. Then Ken discovered alcohol. I'd lost my baby and all he could do was drink.'

'Maybe that was his way of dealing with it,' I suggested. He'd lost his baby too.

'Well, whatever. It's in the past now. Where it should be. It should never have escalated like it did, though — the alcoholism.'

No, maybe not. But I could see why it had. Valerie Pendle had lost her baby, the son she'd given birth too. It was clear she couldn't see Ken's grief too. Maybe she was of the old school that didn't believe men could feel a child's loss like a mother.

'How did he die, then? Steven, I mean.' I knew exactly how he died. I just wondered if she would tell me the truth — especially as I was potentially an ex-girlfriend.

Instead, she whisked away the photo

album, cleared away the tea things, and re-arranged the photographs we'd disturbed.

'You did say you weren't a girlfriend of his?'

'That's right.' Maybe she did have scruples after all.

'He died from pneumonia,' she said at last. What I didn't need to know she wasn't going to tell me.

'And what happened to Andy? Is he okay?'

She shrugged. 'I don't know. Ken had already warned him off so he stayed away. He came to the funeral, but I never saw him again.'

It was clear by now that I'd already taken up enough of her time, and that I'd definitely opened up old wounds — not just with Steven but with Ken too. After a few more minutes of idle chit-chat, about what a nice boy Steven had been and how sad for him to die so young, I took my leave.

I also took the next bus right back to the police station. Andy was the dead spit of Gavin and as far as Pendle was concerned, Andy had killed his little boy and never stuck around to take the consequences.

32

Somewhere in the depths of my poor and lately overworked brain, everything was finally dropping into place.

Ken Pendle's only child had died from AIDS. Valerie Pendle and Clarice could call it what they wanted. It was still AIDS. Steven's best mate all through school and college was gay, although according to his notes, he'd caught it from a girlfriend. Ken Pendle wasn't to know that, though. However, Steven and Andy had shared some of their girlfriends. Gavin was also gay and a heroin user. In Pendle's booze-blurred eyes both or either would make him an automatic carrier of the disease. And Gavin was the spitting image of Steven Pendle's best mate, Andy.

There were two things I needed to know. The first was, whose statement had stated that they'd seen Woodstock attack Gavin? There was only one person who could tell me the answer to that, and he'd already told me the best way to get hold of him.

'I've come to see PC Plant,' I said to the pretty desk sergeant, or policewoman, or whatever we're supposed to call them.

'And your name is?'

'Marcie Craig.'

'Please take a seat.'

I sat down on one of the hard, plastic seats in the tiny reception area while she placed a call to elsewhere in the building.

'There's a Ms Craig in reception for you,' I heard her announce into the receiver and winced again at the 'Ms'. Obviously I couldn't hear Reefer's response, but she replaced the handset.

In no time at all Reefer's face appeared around the door. 'Hi Marcie.' And he led me through the back into another, cramped little room, somewhere in the middle of the station. 'How're you doing?' he asked, as I sat in a brown easy chair and he perched on a plastic one.

'Oh, you know. They buried Daisy last week.'

'Yeah, I'm sorry about that. Truly.'

'Yeah, well. If your DC Anderson hadn't arrested the wrong bloke, then the real murderer might have been behind bars by now.'

'They're not certain that we do have the wrong bloke.'

'Did you know that Woodstock ended up in hospital?'

'No, what happened?'

'Someone got to him. Inside. He's been in intensive care.'

'Oh no. Why? Is he all right?'

'No, he's been in intensive care,' I repeated. 'And they won't let him out for ages yet. Of course he isn't all right. He knew who the real killer was, that's why. And Daisy knew and I know. What I can't understand is why your lot don't know.'

'So who do you reckon did it, then?'

'Ken Pendle.'

Reefer threw back his head and laughed. 'That's a strong accusation,' he said. 'I hope you have some evidence. He wasn't even there.'

'That's where you're going to help,' I cut in. 'I think he was there and you can prove it.' I filled him in on the Andy story I'd already learned.

Now he was off his guard. 'What do you want me to do?'

'We need to know who it was who said they saw Woodstock kill Gavin.'

'Why? We already have forensic evidence that places him at the scene. And he denied being there.'

Now it was my turn to laugh. 'Oh come on, Reefer. You know, better than I do, that that evidence was not enough to convict him. You said yourself that you could place several people at the scene, but none of them were arrested. Hell, he'd already admitted to having sex with the guy — '

'Eventually,' he corrected.

'Eventually,' I conceded. 'You find out who pointed the finger, and tell me that it wasn't Pendle.'

'We don't even have any evidence that he was there — '

'You must have, for Chrissakes. He owns the bloody pub. His dabs and hairs — and he certainly has enough of those — must be all over the place. It's where he stores the barrels.'

Reefer chewed on his top lip for a while as he thought about this, and the implications it could bring. 'You know I don't have access to that sort of information.'

'Yes. But I also know that you *do* have access to a certain pretty little clerk in the incident room.'

He chewed again. 'If this gets out, Marcie, I'll be down the steps.'

'Yes, and I appreciate the risk that you're taking. But Woodstock has already been down those steps. Once he recovers he'll be back inside. An innocent man will be locked away while that murdering bastard is still on the streets.'

'Possibly.'

'Definitely.'

'Look, I might not be able to see my friend before your stint starts tomorrow night.'

'So?' I was touched that Reefer remembered I had a shift on a Wednesday.

'So promise me you won't get doing anything daft before I've had a chance to call you.' I ummed a bit. 'Promise me, Marcie. Or I won't do it. If you're right, he's a dangerous man. If you don't promise me, then I won't promise to get the information you need.' I paused again and he grabbed my wrist in his strong hand. 'Just give me a couple of days. Then he's all yours.'

'Okay,' I relented. He released my arm and I felt the blood rush back into my hand. I could feel my mouth pout as I rubbed the stinging red mark his fingers had left. 'Ouch, that hurt.'

'Sorry,' he grinned. 'But that monster could hurt you even more.'

Reefer escorted me out again, promising to call me before I headed out to work the next night. I went to have tea with my mom and dad, and collected my bike. When I got home I called the hospital to see how Woodstock was. I'd not touched base with them for a few days, although they'd told me when he was moved from intensive care. He was sleeping normally by now, but with the threat to his

342

life lifted, he was no longer allowed visitors. All being well, he'd be back at the prison hospital by the end of the week.

All being well, he'd be off the hook by then.

★ ★ ★

The second thing I needed to know was how he did it. If it was Pendle, he must have left the car park through the vehicle entrance and walked the long way around to the pub, thus walking in through the main door at last orders and giving us all the impression he'd been somewhere else.

33

I didn't have any work to do that Tuesday night, but I didn't feel like sitting around the caravan. I found myself thinking of Steven Pendle's mate, Andy, and the gay bar he'd been photographed in. There weren't that many gay bars in Birmingham now, let alone three years ago. Or if there were, they were very underground. The one I thought had been there the longest was actually a club called the Pink Flamingo. Woodstock had mentioned the Pink Flamingo but the chances of it being the same place Andy was photographed at were very slim. There was the Windmill too, which was a pub where gays could hang out. And there were all those bars the bands like Duran Duran used to go to in the eighties.

I tried to conjure up in my mind's eye the photograph again. There was still something about it, but I had no idea where it had been taken. No point going down that route now.

I didn't hear from Reefer at all the following day so, as agreed, I went to work as usual. I'd be quite safe. Pendle had no idea I suspected him.

It was still pissing down outside, but I absolutely refuse to go to work dressed in my Andy Pandy suit. Instead I wore my old 'originals' over the top of my good jeans, and took a change of clean, dry clothes in a plastic bag, strapped to my carrier.

At that time of day the traffic is always solid all the way from Camp Hill to St Martin's Circus. The council did a really great thing one of the years, for a change, and painted in a bus lane. So, for buses and people like me on bikes, who really don't like weaving in and out of cars basically on our feet and carrying the weight of our machines, we can whiz up the inside instead.

My stint starts at half past seven, but I do like to be in well ahead of time. As I don't have a day job, like the other two, this is quite easy. So, at around half six, my usual time, I pulled into the underground car park just beneath Argos. I'd got over my phobia about parking down here, and cruised to a standstill right by the fire exit door leading from The Cellar.

Unfortunately out here there's nothing to chain the bike to. They don't have much call for lamp posts in underground car parks. I usually thread the chain through the back wheel and over the seat. Of course, if two or three big burly men come along with a nice,

345

big burly transit van, then they're going to take my bike anyway. All they'd have to do is simply lift it into the back of the van and drive off, and tackle the chain in the comfort of their own home.

But at least the heavy chain hopefully deters the opportunist who's just passing.

Anyway, I'd removed the chain from around my body but hadn't even begun to use it when I realised I had company. I was greeted by my ever-friendly boss, and my blood ran cold.

'Oh, er, hello Ken.'

'Marcie.' He stepped out through the fire exit and closed the door behind him. Then he placed himself between me and it. Have you ever seen one of those cartoons when the main character suddenly finds himself in jeopardy and gulps?

'Gulp,' I said.

Ken's beard smiled at me but the rest of his face stayed still. 'I had a chat with my wife today,' he said finally. 'She was a bit upset.'

'Your wife?' I squeaked. 'But I thought you were divorced.'

'Yes, you gave her that impression. Actually, we're only separated. She'd have me back tomorrow if it wasn't for the booze. You see, we do still speak to each other, you know.'

'Oh yes?'

'Yes. And she had a visitor yesterday. Someone who claimed she knew our son, but who never really knew him at all.'

'Really?' My dry mouth could have murdered a nice sensible pint of cider right then.

'She didn't click at first, she was so distracted. It was only after you'd gone. I didn't recognise the name, but I recognised the description. Sadly, for you, there *is* only one Marcie Craig.' I gulped again. 'Steven couldn't go-cart to save his life. But he would have loved to. The trophy with the photo was Val's. And she didn't remember you at all from the club.'

'Oh.'

'Yes, and everyone who knew him knew his poncey mate. They were inseparable. And all of their friends knew he was gay too. He came out when they were still at college. They kept it from me and Steven's mother though.'

'Ah.'

'So do you mind telling me what you were doing upsetting my wife?' He was very close now and the smell of stale ale and nicotine on his breath were making me feel queasy. Or was it fear?

'Erm, I was just interested. That's all.' Oh God. Why hadn't I called in sick again tonight and waited for Reefer to call? Then I heard a familiar tinkling sound. He was playing with his balls again, careful to keep his hands off me. Would that be because of fingerprints?

'My business is none of yours,' he hissed.

'It is if you killed a friend of mine,' I blurted out. Well, if I was going to die anyway . . .

'I didn't kill him,' he said. 'I just warned him off. You didn't even know him.' *Clink! Clink! Clink!* 'But I knew him.' *Clink! Clink!* 'He ruined my son's life. Killed him, in fact.' The balls clinked again, and I realised what the murder weapon must have been.

'Gavin didn't even know your son.' I stepped backwards, bumping into my bike.

'Rubbish!' he snorted. 'I recognised him straight away. Fucking murderer.' I pressed myself against the bike but he followed me. *Clink! Clink! Clink!*

'Ken, when Steven died, Gavin wasn't even 12.'

'They were the same age.'

'No, *Andy* was the same age as Steven. *Andy*. Gavin was only 15 when you . . . when he died.'

Pendle paused. Confusion spread across his face. 'But I recognised him. I told him to keep away from my son.' His face contorted with agony. 'He said he didn't even know my

348

son. Then he laughed. He was fucking stoned. I won't have junkies or poofs in my pub.'

'We all thought Woodstock was a 'poof'.'

'I know. I didn't realise he actually was though. But I know now, don't I? I saw them together.' *Clink! Clink! Clink!*

'Is that why you had him done over then? In prison?'

'I didn't have him done over. He'd already been locked up. That was enough for me. They should lock 'em all up. Castrate the lot of 'em.'

Well, if it wasn't Pendle . . . 'Who had him beaten up, then?'

'How the fuck should I know? Maybe it was the others. They can't stand poofs, can they, in nick? They know how to deal with 'em inside. They probably found out about him.'

'So that's why you killed Gavin?'

'I told you once. I didn't kill him. I just told him to piss off out of here and leave us alone. I wouldn't have minded killing him, though.' *Clink! Clink! Clink!* Then he stopped playing. 'Is that why you were snooping around? Did you really think I did it?'

'Well . . . ' What could I say? If he had done it, I wouldn't be here now. 'Daisy said — '

'Daisy didn't say anything. She saw us arguing, that's all. She'd already promised that she wouldn't mention it. Hang on a minute, you think I killed Daisy too? You're mad.'

Now I was confused. Daisy convinced me that she knew who killed Gavin, and I was convinced that was why she had to die too. But if I was convinced, maybe someone else was too.

'I'm really sorry, Ken.' Well, it was clear to me that I'd definitely got *everything* wrong. Served me right for poking my nose into police business.

'Yes, so am I.' He sadly replaced the balls in his trouser pocket, calmer now. 'But if you could honestly think that about me — not the poof, but Daisy.' He shook his head. 'Maybe it would be better if you went on home now.'

'But — '

He turned and was making his way back to the pub. 'Goodnight, Marcie.'

'But, Ken.'

He paused in the doorway and looked over his shoulder. 'Maybe I'll give you a call in the morning.' Then he was gone, and the door clicked behind him.

Stupid bitch. I'd totally cocked it all up, hadn't I? But I'd felt so *close*. What was it I was missing? Who else had been around on those days when Gavin and Daisy had died? When Woodstock had called?

It dawned on me then, and so did something DS MacGregor had said right at the very start. 'You were the first person to see him dead . . . you may also have been the last person to see him alive . . . the whole sequence could have been contrived.'

The more I thought about it, the more it made sense. He found the body with me. He was there when Daisy told me about the killer. He was also in the kitchen the whole time I was on the phone to Woody.

But why? Nothing added up.

I was still standing by my bike as the revelations hit me one by one, and the door to the pub slowly opened again.

34

'Are you still here, Marcie?'

Fear rooted me to the spot while I croaked a reply. 'Vernon.' Then something else struck me as he stood there outlined in the doorway. *One of the doormen at the gay club in the picture Valerie had shown me was him.* I licked my dry lips and stepped closer to my bike. 'Vernon . . . ' I repeated. He was far bigger than me, bigger than Pendle even. Only Vernon was also sober.

He closed the door behind him and moved closer to me, the happy welcoming expression now completely gone.

'You stupid bitch. You know, don't you?'

'I, er, no.' I felt my bowels loosen and the palms of my hands started to sweat.

'Well, she knew too. That Daisy,' he spat.

'What about Daisy, Vernon?' I said, finally finding my voice at last. 'What did she ever do to you?'

'She was going to tell. Fucking stupid split-arsed cow. The whore was going to tell.'

'Tell what? Who?'

'She saw me. She was going to tell the cops.'

'Daisy wasn't going to tell anyone,' I argued. 'She didn't even know it was you. She thought it was someone else.'

'She told you she knew who it wasn't, so she must have seen who it was. I had to kill her. I had to shut her up. I had to shut that stupid Gavin up too. He'd seen me. He was going to tell Pendle, I would've lost my whole business if he'd told the gaffer.'

'What do you mean he saw you? At that gay club you mean? Aren't you allowed to work the clubs? Does Pendle dictate where you work?'

'Yes, he does, actually. You know the brewery likes to lock us into golden cufflink deals. But I wasn't working, you stupid cow. I've been a regular at that club for years.'

'You mean you're gay too? But you have a wife — '

'Marcie, I never had you down as a dumbass. You. Don't. Have. To. Be. Single. To. Be. Gay.'

'Did you have Woodstock done over in prison?'

'There's another one couldn't keep his mouth shut. I wouldn't have hurt Woody for the world. But he knew too. I thought telling the cops he'd had a row with Gavin would keep him out of my way and I wouldn't have to touch him. But he was going to tell you. I

353

had to shut him up before you got to him.' I couldn't believe the change in the man. 'I expect you're going to tell now, too.'

'I already have, Vernon,' I said, hoping he'd realise they already knew and he was going to get done for it anyway. I hoped it would cool him down. I failed.

In a mad rage he lurched towards me, reaching into his pocket. He had some of those stupid balls too, and I remembered it was Vernon who had got hold of them for Ken. 'It looks like I'll have to kill you too, then,' he said, raising his right arm.

It was him or me and I didn't have time to ask any more questions.

I raised my right leg and kneed him sharply in the balls. I still had my chain. He wasn't going to kill me too. My reflexes were quick. As he doubled up, clutching his crotch, I swung at him and the heavy padlock crashed into the side of his head, knocking him sideways.

The blow knocked him off balance, but didn't knock him out. Instead the concrete floor did that for me, as his skull connected. A crimson pool of blood spread out beneath his right eye, and two silver balls thudded to the ground and rolled off in two different directions.

Epilogue

I almost killed a man two nights ago. Unfortunately, I only managed to seriously damage his skull. Fortunately for me, Vernon's only other injury was severe concussion. I didn't really have the strength to do much more harm, and I only reckon I did that well because he wasn't expecting me to fight back.

It seems that Vernon didn't work at that gay club at all, He was simply a patron there. Gavin had seen him there and threatened to tell Pendle unless Vernon handed over some cash — probably for drugs.

We all knew that Ken Pendle had always hated gays, and Vernon would have lost the security contract. The Cellar was one of his best customers and kept most of his men busy. The brewery itself looked after all of his men. It wasn't only that, though. Vernon was, as I'd pointed out, married and couldn't afford for his wife to find out that he was gay either.

Vernon also had a friend inside Winson Green, and he admitted to having Woodstock done over to keep him quiet. It was him who'd told the cops he'd seen Woody and Gavin fighting. He reckoned no-one would believe him and that Woody would get off with a slapped wrist.

Most of my evening was spent down at the station giving a full statement. I was cautioned, however, for carrying and using an offensive weapon. It didn't matter that it had saved my life. They just said that I shouldn't have been there and told me not to be surprised if Vernon sued *me* for GBH. So there's British justice for you — although I don't think it would get past a jury.

The police got their confession — from a hospital bed — and Woodstock got his pardon. I'm going to see him tomorrow at the hospital now he's up to receiving visitors, and he'll be coming home with me when they let him out. Maybe he'll be able to tell me what he remembered.

I'm having tea with Daisy's daughter next week before she goes back to South Africa. I hope we'll become good friends.

Oh, and by the way, Pendle didn't give me the sack. He reckons he's going to give up the boozing in the hope that Valerie comes back to him. They have a lot of time to make up and still some grieving to do together.

★　★　★

'Hi there. This is Marcie Craig welcoming you to The Cellar — the hottest little rock spot in Brum. For one night only I'd like to change our regular track, and dedicate this next record to our former bouncer. Here's Judas Priest's *Night Crawler* . . . '

We do hope that you have enjoyed reading this large print book.

Did you know that all of our titles are available for purchase?

We publish a wide range of high quality large print books including:
Romances, Mysteries, Classics
General Fiction
Non Fiction and Westerns

Special interest titles available in large print are:
The Little Oxford Dictionary
Music Book
Song Book
Hymn Book
Service Book

Also available from us courtesy of Oxford University Press:
Young Readers' Dictionary
(large print edition)
Young Readers' Thesaurus
(large print edition)

For further information or a free brochure, please contact us at:
Ulverscroft Large Print Books Ltd.,
The Green, Bradgate Road, Anstey,
Leicester, LE7 7FU, England.
Tel: (00 44) 0116 236 4325
Fax: (00 44) 0116 234 0205

Other titles published by
The House of Ulverscroft:

SHERLOCK HOLMES AND THE QUEEN OF DIAMONDS

Steve Hayes and David Whitehead

When Thomas Howard of Missouri had come out of nowhere, one foggy night, and rescued Countess Elaina Montague from rape and robbery, he was apparently in England to find his brother who had disappeared. The Countess offered to enlist Sherlock Holmes to help Montague in his search, though he was already investigating a rash of audacious jewel-thefts. However, the Great Detective, suspecting that there was more to Mr Howard than met the eye, accepted the case. This led to their involvement in a vicious blood feud, a spectacular — death-defying — daylight robbery and a thrilling climax below the brooding River Thames.

A NARROW RETURN

Faith Martin

Ex-Detective Inspector Hillary Greene returns to Thames Valley to work on cold cases. No longer a professional, she must cope with being a civilian — and she also has a stalker. Her superior Superintendent Steven Crayle, uncertain that she should be on his team, hands her a twenty-year old murder file that's as cold as a blizzard. Who would want to slaughter a housewife and mother of three in her own home? The original team couldn't make a case, what chance of justice now? Greene, with something to prove — to herself and her new boss — knuckles down to catch a killer . . .